PRACTICING
PARTNERS

PRACTICING PARTNERS

A MAIDEN'S BAY

ROMANCE

MARY SHOTWELL

RADIANCE

RADIANCE

An Imprint of Roan & Weatherford Publishing Associates, LLC
Bentonville, Arkansas
www.roanweatherford.com

Library of Congress Cataloging-in-Publication Data
Names: Shotwell, Mary, author.
Title: Practicing Partners | Maiden's Bay #2
Description: First Edition | Bentonville: Radiance, 2024.
Identifiers: LCCN: 2024943240 | ISBN: 978-1-63373-973-4 (hardcover) |
ISBN: 978-1-63373-974-1 (trade paperback) | ISBN: 978-1-63373-975-8 (eBook)
Subjects: | BISAC: FICTION/Romance/Contemporary |
FICTION/Romance/Medical | FICTION/Romance/Clean & Wholesome
LC record available at: https://lccn.loc.gov.2024943240

Radiance trade paperback edition April, 2025

Cover & Interior Design by Casey W. Cowan
Editing by Staci Troilo, Lisa Lindsey & Amy Cowan

To DB

ACKNOWLEDGMENTS

THANK YOU TO my publishing team at Roan & Weatherford, especially Staci Troilo, Lisa Lindsey, Amy Cowan, and Casey W. Cowan. It has been exciting to continue my writing journey with Maiden's Bay.

As always, success as an author depends on my readers. Thank you all for loving Maiden's Bay as much as I do, and having a hunger for more characters and stories that the town has to offer.

Deepest gratitude to Matt, Luke, Evan, and Avery, who have to put up with me not paying attention because I'm thinking about plot or characters, and giving me ideas even when they'd prefer I write video game stories.

ONE

Saturday, September 15

NO MATTER HOW annoying bangs could be when blowing in the breeze, Aubrie Turnbridge welcomed the disarray. Driving her five-year-old Hyundai Accent, windows down, she crested the final hill leading to Maiden's Bay.

The three-day drive from Dallas had gotten her as far as Portland last night. There was really no point in trying to make it all the way to the Washington coast when Dr. Jackson wasn't expecting her for another day. Plus, she hated driving in the dark, especially when she was exhausted.

But today—today was different. As the gray sedan tipped downward toward the earth, making its descent to town, the sea breeze clung to Aubrie's Texas-tanned skin. It was a cool damp, not the wet furnace of Galveston's beaches she had visited annually growing up.

Her cell phone jolted her out of the sea air euphoria. She rolled up the windows and hit the green talk button.

"I'm not even there yet, Mom."

"Just checking in. I knew you were supposed to arrive today."

Aubrie switched the dashboard screen back to the map. It was difficult enough to deal with Mom's worrying, let alone adding navigation in a new town on top of it.

"I promise you, I'll call when I can. It's not like I have any new information for you since I left." She gazed briefly at the sun-speckled water, the town forming a crescent around it. "I can tell you from what I've seen so far, it's beautiful out here."

Her mom's response took a little too long for comfort. *"I hope this helps you find what you need. That you're not running away from—"*

Aubrie held back a sigh. "We talked about this. I'm *not* running."

"If you say so."

"I needed something different, that's all. Dallas General was—"

"We both know this isn't about the hospital."

Aubrie wanted to close her eyes were it not for driving, anticipating one of her mother's psychological assessments. Not that Linda Turnbridge had psychology expertise. She'd say being a mom gave her enough knowledge.

"Mom, don't—"

"You were—are—so great with the kids. Any parent was lucky to have you looking out for their child. Why, if I had a child with cancer, and you were an option, I'd jump at the chance."

It was both a compliment and an attempt to stab Aubrie with guilt. The thing was, Aubrie was already so filled with guilt there was no room left for more.

"I'd better go." It was all she could muster without snowballing the discussion into a full-blown fight. Mom meant well but also had her way of overstepping. Frequently.

"Okay, then." Mom sighed, defeated. *"Promise you'll call me later?"*

"I promise."

Aubrie crept along H Street, taking in the backward C of the town in front of her. Houses adorned the cliffside like a stack of dominoes that would topple into the sea if pushed at the top of the hill. She turned right onto Pearl Avenue and started the arc through town. The GPS said her destination was half a mile away, at the southern end of downtown Maiden's Bay.

She parked in a spot along the street, letters painted on the window in front of her. *Family Practice of Dr. Bernard Jackson, MD.*

Family practice. Something Aubrie hadn't seen herself in at any point in her education.

Yet here she was. Grateful for the change.

Before walking inside, she ran her hand over her tight ponytail and ruffled her bangs back into shape. She tugged on the thin sweater over a tank top—not too cool for the September air and not too warm in case she got flustered. Meeting new people could do that to her. Somehow new patients didn't trigger the response. Mainly superiors who assumed she didn't know enough in the medical field, and strangers everywhere else who assumed she knew every facet of science.

The door set off a chime, and the receptionist at the front desk looked up from her reading. A woman waited with a teenager scrolling on a phone in chairs along the wall, next to a plant.

"Hello, there. Can I help you?" The receptionist, somewhere around sixty years old, tipped her head down to see over her eyeglasses.

"You must be Edith? I'm Aubrie Turnbridge." She offered up a hand over the desk.

"Oh, yes!" Edith stood and shook Aubrie's hand with both of hers. "So nice to meet you."

"You as well."

A yelp emanated from behind the wall that closed off the waiting room to what Aubrie assumed were examining rooms. Or maybe one room. The sign into town had said just under two thousand residents, and the building was small. Maybe they only needed one room.

"Should I come back at another time to meet Doctor Jackson?"

"No, no. Now is fine. I'll take you back."

"Are you sure?"

Edith nodded and led the way from her desk, holding the door open for Aubrie. Straight ahead was an open doorway to a room with windows in the back. Judging by the desk and stacks of books, it was Dr. Jackson's office. The women turned right, down a short hallway of white walls and generic hospital tile. Two wooden doors were closed, red and black exam room flags hanging near the top corner of each. Edith knocked on the one with the black flag turned out.

"Doc Bernie? Doctor Turnbridge has arrived."

"Please, Aubrie."

"Okay, then." Edith nodded with a smile and turned back to the door. "Would you like her to wait up front?"

The door opened forcefully, and a balding man who had to be in his seventies, if not eighties, stuck his head out. "Doctor Turnbridge?" He eyed her with a soft smile. There was a handsome man beneath the wrinkles and thinning hair. Aubrie guessed he must've been a heartbreaker as a young man.

"Hi, you can call me Aubrie." She reached out a hand, and he opened the door wide. A patient sat on the examining table hunched over, clutching his abdomen.

"Come on in."

Aubrie met eyes with Edith, who shrugged.

"I'm not sure if that's—"

"The patient agreed. Right, Hal?" Dr. Jackson turned to the patient, who nodded amidst his wincing. "See. Come on, I'll introduce you."

Aubrie took a breath and stepped inside the examining room. She set down her purse on a chair situated by a small desk with a computer.

"Aubrie, this is Hal. Hal, Aubrie."

Aubrie smiled with a nod. Although she had driven for three and a half days to start this very job in this very office, it didn't seem right to start the job like this. Surely there was more paperwork to sign, or training for office procedures. She turned to the sink and quickly washed her hands, the bare minimum of something to feel a little better about the intrusion.

"I have his chart right here." Dr. Jackson handed her a clipboard with a half-filled-out form.

Aubrie scanned it quickly. "Forty-eight, considered pre-diabetic. Blood pressure looks a bit high today." She lowered the chart.

Hal moaned, his eyes closed with the pain.

"How long have you been having pain, Hal?" She approached him. "May I?"

He nodded, and she lifted his shirt. She felt his abdomen on the left side to be sure, then lightly pushed on the swollen right.

He let out a howl of pain.

"He needs to go to the ER."

Dr. Jackson gave one nod. "Diagnosis already?"

"I think it's pretty obvious. No offense." Who knew how often Dr. Jackson saw this condition, but with a family practice for decades, he should've seen it at least a few times. "He has appendicitis. At this point, most likely acute appendicitis. He needs to get to a hospital."

Dr. Jackson stepped forward. "You hear that, Hal? That makes two of us telling you the same thing."

"I came here so I wouldn't have to go to the hospital."

Dr. Jackson patted Hal's knee. "I know, I know."

Aubrie wanted to scream. Hal's condition was nothing to take lightly, or slowly. They had to get this man emergency care, or he could die right here on the table.

Dr. Jackson turned to her, a slight grin on his face. "Don't worry, Aubrie. I called an ambulance before your arrival."

The sirens sounded, and a commotion ensued on the other side of the hallway wall. Edith appeared through the doorway with two EMTs rolling a stretcher. "Back here."

"I promise they'll take good care of you, and I'll come visit you in White Bend after the surgery."

Hal looked to want to argue, but as if on cue, he scrunched again in pain, letting out a wail.

The EMTs transferred him to the gurney and headed out.

Dr. Jackson took Hal's chart back. "How about you head on over to my office, and I'll meet you there in a second?"

Aubrie washed her hands again before leaving the examining room and headed into the office. Although Dr. Jackson had two metal bookshelves, they were mostly filled with cardboard file boxes. His books, as she had seen first walking by, lay in stacks on his desk, on the floor, and on both chairs situated in front of his desk. She lifted a pile off one chair and haphazardly placed it atop the other chair's pile before taking a seat.

The longer she waited, the more she worried about Hal's condition. She searched on her phone how close White Bend Hospital was to here—a twenty-seven minute drive in current traffic. But the ambulance may cut that down to twenty minutes or so. Depended on the number of traffic lights and intersections, and as she learned in driving here—winding roads along hills and valleys.

"Well, that was quite an introduction." Dr. Jackson dried his hands, discarding the paper towel in a trash bin behind his desk.

"To Hal, or to you?"

He chuckled. "I guess both when you think about it." He situated himself in his desk chair, scooting it closer to reach over the desk. This time, they shook hands. "Bernard Jackson. But people call me Doc Bernie." Their hands parted. "Sorry to put you on the spot like that. It was more about having a distraction for Hal while waiting for the ambulance than a test for you. Although you did splendidly. And no offense taken. It was, how did you put it? Pretty obvious it was appendicitis."

"I hope he makes it to the hospital."

"I think he'll be fine. It wouldn't be the first time two EMTs had to cut open a patient." He must've seen Aubrie's jaw drop for a split second. "I know you're coming from a big city. Houston?"

"Dallas."

He nodded. "One of the first things to know about this position, about taking over the role of primary care physician in Maiden's Bay, is that resources are limited. That can mean supplies, talent, helping hands. It's the main reason why I've required a grace period with this job."

"A grace period?" What did that mean? She could be let go if she didn't pass his testing? "I thought I was hired to work with you?"

Doc Bernie let out a cough. "Do you know what tonight is?"

Aubrie was getting whiplash with every sentence coming out of the man's mouth. She shook her head. "I don't think it's any kind of holiday, is it?"

"It's my birthday, and you're—well, I'd say obligated, but that's not very friendly, is it? I'd love it if you would come to my party. It's there that I am announcing to everyone my retirement."

"You're retiring now?" What the heck was going on? It was as if she had stepped out of reality into a situational comedy. An unfunny, poorly-written one that affected her life. "You hired me and are leaving at the same time?"

He wagged a finger. "See, that's the grace period. I promise not to leave until whoever is taking over the practice is fully trained and prepared to do so."

Switching from pediatric oncology to PCP was a big enough change. Moving to Maiden's Bay—enormous change. But running a practice? "I'm sorry, I was under the impression that I was hired to work as another doctor in the practice. There wasn't anything about taking it over in the job announcement."

He leaned over his desk on his elbows, and his face turned serious. "The town could use someone like you. With your expertise. You're young and eager to change your lifestyle. At least, that's what you indicated in your application."

"A change, yes."

"Good. Now, I know you didn't come here thinking about running this place, so I'm giving you time to not only learn the ropes but think hard about this being something long term for you. I won't force you to do anything, okay?"

This was crazy. She hadn't even been in Maiden's Bay for a day. Or an afternoon. This was not what she came for. But she had given up her apartment. Sold her furniture. What little belongings she had were in her car. What was she to do? Drive back and ask for her job back? The one she couldn't manage a day without a panic attack?

Going back simply wasn't an option. She'd have to roll with whatever the heck this situation was, for better or worse.

"Okay." She couldn't believe the word came out. She took a breath, composing herself to think straight. Well, straighter. "I apologize if I seemed shocked, but I have to admit I'm a bit surprised."

"I completely understand. The thing is, Maiden's Bay, and this practice, is not exactly the dream scenario for the best talent out there. So, when your application rolled in, I didn't want to take the chance of scaring you off before you had a chance to see the place. To understand the situation. You will forgive me, perhaps in time?"

Despite her surprise, she sympathized with this man. He probably wasn't wrong. "As long as you're honest with me from here on out."

Doc Bernie clapped his hands. "Good. Now, with that, there's one last thing, and then Edith will get you sorted with your lodgings."

Lodgings sounded good. A hot shower. Perhaps a catnap before this birthday party thrown upon her.

"At the party tonight, you'll meet my grandson. He'll also be working with you during this transition phase."

"Oh. Is he a nurse, or—?"

"Trauma surgeon. From Seattle University Hospital."

"Oh." Aubrie thought it over. "In what capacity will he be working with me, then?"

Doc Bernie checked his watch and leapt out of his seat. He took the jacket off the back of his chair and slipped it on. "He's also a possibility for taking over the practice."

Aubrie began to nod until the words sunk in. "Wait, what?"

Doc Bernie remained standing but leaned on the desk. "Look. While I would love to pass the practice down through my family, I can't say that I have one hundred percent confidence in him." He stood straight. "Don't get me wrong, brilliant surgeon. But when it comes to managing a practice in this town? Heck, managing just about anything in his life?" He sighed, shaking his head. "That's why I hired you. Not only because of your qualifications. But my grandson needs to see that I'm serious about leaving this to the best person. The right person. And if you find you truly want this, I believe you're going to be the right person."

It was a lot to take in. First, Doc Bernie leaving out clarifications about his retirement and the position. On top of that, she wasn't guaranteed the position. At any moment, his grandson could take over. This job could be over before it started. Well, before it started after Appendicitis Hal.

"Edith will give you the keys to the apartment upstairs, and the address for tonight's party. See you there." Doc Bernie left the office with a smile.

Aubrie sat in disbelief over the last half hour's happenings. Her phone buzzed, and she checked the ID.

Mom.

If there was anything worse than the situation she found herself in, it would be telling it all to her mother.

TWO

THE THROWING OF keys on the table jolted Bran Jackson awake. Such a grating sound, the metallic jingle. One that didn't go well with the remnants of his hangover, despite having slept most of it off during the day.

"You're still here." The woman with long blonde hair smiled, hand on hip. Sarah was it? No, Samantha? The name would come to him as the fog lifted in his alertness.

He clicked his fingers. "Sharon."

"Yes?" Sharon, the nurse who had been giving him the sexy glances weeks ago during his shifts, waited for his answer. In what must be her apartment.

That's right. It was coming back. The bar last night. Followed by closing out the club. Then, her place.

"I'm sorry. I didn't mean to stay so long." It's not like he had work to attend to. Ever since the probation on his residency took effect, his days turned into nights and nights into days. "We had a great time last night, didn't we?" He waited with bated breath. The last thing he needed was another coworker with a grudge against him.

She let out an exasperated sigh, as if he was such a difficult guy to deal with. If anything, he made relationships easy. No commitment, no complications. Two consensual adults having fun. Nothing serious. Unless she wanted more. Wanting more brought about the difficulties.

"Well, I just finished my shift. I could use something to eat."

Bran flashed his knee-weakening smile. Oh, he knew it all too well how handsome he was. At least, that's how the ladies made him feel. Maybe it was all about his confidence. Was that all a man needed?

He checked his phone for messages, of which there were none. At the moment, he only cared about hearing from Dr. Oliver Fredericks, the Head of Trauma Surgery at Seattle University Hospital. He hadn't given Bran an update since the probation took effect.

What did get his heart racing was the time. A quarter past two.

He threw off the covers and jumped out of bed. He slipped on his jeans over his boxers. As he wrestled with his sweater and popped his head through the collar, Sharon furled her eyebrows in confusion.

"You in a rush to eat?"

The underlying skepticism didn't escape Bran. "I'm so sorry. I'm supposed to be at my grandfather's birthday party tonight."

"Tonight? Then, you have some time."

"It's in Maiden's Bay. A three hour drive. And I wanted to speak with him before the party."

He rushed to the bathroom and threw water on his face. His clothes clung to the smell of cigarette smoke and spilled beer. What was worse, showing up like this or arriving too late to speak in private with his grandfather?

He fled the bathroom as quickly as he had entered it and stopped in front of Sharon. "I should be back in a day. Two, tops. Maybe do dinner then?"

"I guess—"

Bran kissed Sharon on the cheek and dashed out of the apartment.

That uneasiness in the pit of his stomach returned. He knew the feeling. The one that hit him when he spewed niceties to make people feel better. There was always that hint of sincere intention behind everything—that he intended to do the right thing. Intended to see her again. Intended to keep his word. That maybe this time would be different. His track record said otherwise. The follow-through was the problem. As in, it never occurred.

But right now, he had to focus on cleaning up.

It took Bran twenty minutes of running to reach his apartment, in a nicer part of town just north of downtown Seattle. He didn't mind it made him sweaty amid the pre-autumn air. In fact, it helped burn off the hangover quicker than anything else.

He quickly showered, put on clean clothes—slacks, sweater, a look between dressed up and casual—and hurried to his car in the parking garage. The black Audi A6 was a recent purchase, a good deal on a barely-used car. It wasn't the Porsche he had dreamed of owning since he was a kid, but that came with time, as did the career as a trauma surgeon. He still had half of his residency left, which may or may not happen with the recent events.

He shook off the thought and pulled out onto the street, maneuvering through downtown as little as possible. Luckily, he had missed the start of rush hour traffic—which really should've been called rush three-hour traffic with its ever-increasing time window—by the time he passed Tacoma. The rest of the drive was fairly easy going, hooking west then southwest to the area known as The Crescent Coast.

It really was a surprise more people didn't head that direction. Urban sprawl was definitely a real phenomenon, but Maiden's Bay didn't have a "mother" city. It was on its own, albeit with the other Crescent Coast communities dotting a strip of the western shore of Washington.

Approaching from the north placed him on Pearl Avenue, one of the last of the spokes in the alphabetical streets converging on downtown. The difference was that Pearl also acted as the main north-south street in Maiden's Bay.

He headed south toward Doc Bernie's office. It was after five, but there was a chance he'd still be at his practice. Hopefully, Bran's practice soon. It was the perfect solution to the ordeal he found himself in—a way to benefit Seattle University Hospital and end his probation. All he needed was Doc Bernie to sign it over.

As he drove by searching for the first open spot, he caught the darkness of the office. The hanging sign on the glass door was turned around to *Closed.* Despite having the hours listed on the door, the assistant Edith insisted on having the sign, as if Doc operated a hardware store or bistro. To her credit, Doc tended to work beyond the stated hours.

Not today, though. He'd have to intercept Doc Bernie at his house.

The name of his grandfather hadn't struck him as unusual growing up. His grandfather was a doctor, and his name was Bernie. It wasn't until fellow high schoolers laughed at him that he got the sense it was unusual for him and his brother to call their grandfather something other than a form of Grandpa.

Bran's thoughts flashed to his younger brother, Nathaniel, and for a second he got excited. Nathaniel attended a community college, but it was only forty-five minutes away—short enough to make the trip for holidays and events, long enough to choose when to stay away. Bran hadn't seen Nathaniel since residency began three years ago. Way too long. But he'd be there tonight.

His car eased up the mountainside, L Street not as steep as the latter alphabetic streets, but still a jaunt. Doc Bernie had lived in the same house since Bran could remember, a split ranch with a walkout basement on a quiet cross street in south Maiden's Bay. He parked on the street in front of the deep brown house with cream shutters.

The screen door was closed, with the front door open behind it. Bran rang the doorbell.

"Doc Bernie? It's Bran." He peered through the screen, a glimpse of the kitchen visible down the hallway. "Hello?"

He contemplated going in but then heard the old man's voice.

"Out back! Come around."

Bran walked the sidewalk that led to stepping stones along the side of the house. They were arranged like a staircase to aid in going down the hill, but a few had cracked or shifted, making for a dangerous descent if not careful. The walkout basement led to a deck spanning the entire backside of the house, where he found Doc Bernie sipping on a drink.

"Hey, Bran! I expected you at the party but didn't know you'd swing by here." He outstretched his arms, and Bran accepted the brisk hug, hand slapping on his shoulder.

"You don't walk those stones down to here, do you?" He pictured Doc Bernie tripping, or worse, hurting himself in a fall with no one around to help him.

"Those old things? Only for visitors. I come out here from inside."

Bran winced beneath a smile. He made a mental note to have someone out here to replace them.

"So, what is it you want?" Doc Bernie's lips curled into a sly smile.

"I haven't been back here in three years. Can't I want some quality time with my grandfather?"

"Oh, we'll get in quality time soon enough." He walked over to a tray on wheels, housing an ice bucket and a bottle of Scotch. "Drink?"

"Maybe a small one."

Doc Bernie filled a glass with ice and poured two fingers worth. He handed it to Bran, the ice rattling in the glass with his shaky hand. Was Doc nervous about something? Bran hadn't known his grandfather to ever get flustered.

Bran accepted the glass and clinked it with Doc's.

"Discovered your dad's out of town?"

Bran raised his eyebrows. "Actually, no, I came straight here. What do you mean he's out of town? He's not going to your birthday party?"

"Had some business to take care of in Florida."

Bran had no idea what business a property manager from Maiden's Bay would have in Florida that was pressing enough to miss his own father's seventieth birthday party. But that was Dad.

"Speaking of business… I don't think it'll take long to get the hang of things." Bran took a sip and let it trickle down his throat slowly. They both knew what he was here for. The birthday party was simply the catalyst. It was time to get the details sorted.

"Maybe not." Doc pulled a chair next to his before sitting down.

Bran took the hint.

"You know, primary care, it's a bit different than trauma surgery. I have to admit I was surprised to hear you'd trade one for the other, especially having already committed three years of residency to it."

Bran took another sip, this time keeping it in his mouth a little too long, resulting in a loud gulp. "It's a family business, one you've built over decades. I can understand how important it is for you to keep it in the family."

"Let me be clear." He set down his glass, angled in a cup holder too small for it. "I want the best person for the practice, and the town, to take it over. Don't get me wrong, it'd be great if that person were you, and it indeed stayed in the family."

Bran let out a chuckle. "Well, it's not like you have people knocking on the door to buy it, right? I mean, I'm the one here, aren't I?"

Doc Bernie picked up the glass. "Not the only one."

Bran turned to his grandfather. He swore the man said something into his glass, something that didn't make sense. "What was that?"

Doc Bernie cleared his throat. "I said, you're not the only one here. For the practice."

Bran leaned his elbow on the armrest, staring the old man down. "What do you mean?"

"I mean that someone is here, that I invited, to learn the ropes of the practice to possibly take it over."

Bran shook his head. "Then, why am I here if you already have someone else?" He tried to keep his irritation in check. This was supposed to be an easy transaction. Sure, what Bran had planned for the practice would hurt the guy in the short-term, but he'd get over it. Just what was his grandfather up to?

"You'll meet her at the party tonight. Nice girl. Comes from Houston—no, wait, Dallas. I always get those mixed up, even though I know they're miles and miles apart."

"What does she know about primary care? Is that what she did in Dallas?"

"No."

"So, you invited someone with no experience, who is not in the family, to take over your practice?"

"She's a pediatric oncologist. One of the youngest and brightest in the country."

"If that was the case, what's she doing here? Why leave that?"

"Why leave the salary and excitement of trauma surgery?"

Bran opened his mouth to form some version of because you're family, but it was hard to feign the moral high ground with Scotch in his system. A tiny part of him wanted that to be the truth. He wanted to want the job for such a noble reason. But Doc didn't wait for the hollow answer.

"That's a question for you to ask her," Doc said. "Either when you meet her tonight, or when you two work together over the next few weeks."

"Work together? Few weeks?" Bran stood and walked to the edge of the deck, placing his glass on the rail. The sun hung low over the water, the days getting noticeably shorter but nowhere near the early darkness of winter.

"Couldn't put all my eggs in one basket, Bran. With your history...."

Bran nodded. It wasn't a secret he wasn't the most reliable member of the Jackson family. Most of his family was surprised he graduated from med school, let alone spent three years in one specialization.

"I'm sorry I didn't tell you earlier. If it makes you feel any better, I didn't tell her about you, either."

He turned around, back to the picturesque sunset, elbows leaning on the railing. "I don't know if that makes me feel better or makes me feel sorry for her."

Doc chuckled, and Bran gave in, too.

Bran sighed, making his way back to the chair, sitting on the edge.

"I need you—no, I want you—to try your best for this, Bran. I really would like to see you here in Maiden's Bay, helping out this town. But I can promise you this. She'll be trying her best. If you don't try your best, and maybe even if you do, I can't guarantee she won't win in the end."

Bran absorbed the news. Of course Doc Bernie wasn't going to make it easy for him. He never made anything easy. "Anything worth having is worth fighting for, right?"

"You got it."

Bran sat back in the chair with another sigh. "Then, let's bring on the fight."

THREE

THE APARTMENT ABOVE Doc Bernie's practice would more than suffice for Aubrie's stay. However long that would be. It was a modest one-bedroom, with a decent-sized kitchen with white cabinets and an island for two stools, a living area with a sofa, television, and a desk. The light gray walls were sparsely decorated—framed abstract artwork, mostly swirls of muted colors. Something to give the room a finished feeling without committing to any theme.

Aubrie reveled in the hot shower, despite having taken a quick one this morning in the hotel outside Portland. She dried her hair and let it hang freely, her near-black locks reaching the top of her shoulder blades. Her bangs framed her face, the longer locks on the edges getting to the point of needing a trim. Admittedly, her hairstyle brought out the dark brown in her eyes and even darker eyelashes. She rarely wore mascara, and tonight was no exception. Just because it was a party didn't mean she'd go all out.

Her stomach rumbled, and she finished getting ready with a pass of her compact powder, then threw on a gray rolled-sleeve blazer atop her cream blouse. She had under an hour before the start of the party, so she needed something within walking distance. Not knowing what the food situation would be at the party. Better safe than sorry.

She searched on her phone for a restaurant, and the top choice was a place down the main street in town. "Easy enough."

She bounced down the stairs and out the door onto Pearl Avenue. The vanishing sun had turned the air cooler and damper, the kind of evening chill that would be too cold for what she was wearing in a month's time. Maybe sooner.

She wasn't used to living so close to the water. The air carried a faint, low-level background sound of waves rippling along the shore. A salty breeze would carry it by, and she couldn't help but look at the water whenever the space between buildings afforded a glimpse.

Not much traffic rolled along the street as she walked north on the sidewalk. She took note of an ice cream place right next door, a tourist shop among other places, and most importantly a cafe and grocery store. Good to know where to get food.

She was half-tempted to grab something quick from Mariner's Market to eat at the apartment, but the pink neon sign of her destination, Campy's Bait and Bar, called out to her from across the street. Several cars stuffed into the gravel parking lot of the two-story building.

"Must be good."

Music from the second story hummed louder as she walked up the white wooden stairs to the top floor. The first floor housed the bait shop, which if she thought about it too long, kind of grossed her out. Sure, she had seen plenty of blood and other human liquids and solids, but something about worms—crawly, squiggly worms—sent chills up her spine.

She expected a blast of overly-loud music when she entered from the front deck, but the chatter of customers overpowered it. Booths ran along the walls with a few free-standing tables here and there. The bar sat near the middle of the room, and Aubrie made a beeline for a free stool. She slung her purse on the back of the stool and rolled her blazer sleeves up further, above the elbows. The view through the windows in the back was well worth a visit to the place. The restaurant overlooked a dock, with a scattering of beautiful sailboats among commercial and recreational vessels. To the right stood the black-banned lighthouse, and past the dock, the open water. Only the tip of the sun was left, melting into the horizon.

"What can I get you?" a young, handsome man asked from behind the bar. He had a chiseled nose and friendly face, like her younger brother who never seemed to age. She noticed his nametag—Joel. He most likely wasn't any older than her thirty years.

"Water with lemon and a menu, please."

"You got it." Joel handed her a menu and went to work on filling a glass with ice and water, topping it with a lemon wedge.

Aubrie didn't particularly care for bar food. It wasn't bad and did the job, but it usually wasn't anything great, either. She kept it safe and ordered chicken tenders and sweet potato fries. Hard to go wrong there.

Her food came surprisingly quickly, and they were some of the best breaded tenders she had ever tasted. She was about to say so to Joel when commotion broke out near the front door.

A man had entered, and several people approached him. He shook their hands, his smile handsome and face even more so. There was a smoothness about him—a suaveness—he carried with his movements, his steps. His dark hair was magazine-worthy, and he exuded charm.

"Who is that? A movie star I don't know about?"

Joel chuckled. "I believe that is a former local named Bran. I can't be sure, though, since I haven't seen him in a few years. Plus, it's hard to get a good view with the crowd around him."

"Someone well known in the community, then?"

Joel shrugged his shoulders. "Most people in Maiden's Bay are well-known, whether they mean to be or not. I guess you can say it's an event when someone returns after being gone for a while."

"I'd say it is." Aubrie returned to her meal, with a growing sense that the crowd was dissipating and the mystery figure was nearing. She all but buried her head in her dinner basket to avoid the stranger.

"Joel Reynolds." The dark-haired man stuck out a hand to the bartender. "Finally taking over this place?"

"Already have. Brothers got downstairs and *Harpeth Rose.*"

"Oh, yeah? That thing still kicking, huh?"

"I don't know about kicking. It's floating, which I guess that's all that matters."

Aubrie met eyes with the stranger for a brief moment, his crystal blues piercing.

"What can I get you?" Joel asked.

"I'll just have whatever local brew you have on tap."

A woman appeared next to the man, her long hair dyed blonde and softly curled to perfection. The woman smiled at the man, his face eventually reading recognition.

"Macy, hey, how are you?"

Her smile turned serious. "Maybe you'd know if you ever called me back."

"Yeah, about that—"

"Six months, Bran. We were together for half a year."

Bran held up a hand in defense, but Macy kept it coming.

"I know that's not forever, although maybe from your noncommittal perspective it was an eternity. But I deserved more respect than that. More than you cutting out of town without a goodbye."

Bran nodded, trying what Aubrie saw as his best to look sorry. The two would make a visually perfect couple, though, that was certain.

"I know what I did was wrong. You see, I got that residency in Seattle. And I knew if I had told you about it, if I had come to see you before leaving, I wouldn't have left at all. It would've been too hard to do it. But looking back, you're entirely right. You deserved better. Can I make it up to you?"

Macy scoffed, shaking her head. "You always were a smooth talker." She grabbed a cocktail napkin and nodded at Joel, who handed over a pen. The woman wrote down her phone number and handed it to Bran, who folded it before putting it in his pocket.

"Call me this time." Macy locked eyes with him, and he nodded. She backed away from the bar, and Bran let out a sigh.

Joel handed Bran his beer, who took it with him to the pool tables on the other side of the bar.

"That was… interesting," Aubrie said.

"To answer your question, yes. That's definitely Bran."

"I'll try to steer clear of that drama while I'm here."

"You in town a while?"

"Um." Aubrie considered it a little too funny not knowing the exact answer. "That's a good question. I've been hired by Doctor Jackson—Doc Bernie—to, uh…." Doc was supposed to announce his retirement plans at the birthday party tonight. Did that mean no one in town knew about it? Judging from what Joel was saying, the whole town probably already knew about it. But she wasn't about to take away any satisfaction Doc expected with his announcement. "To help him out with the practice."

"You're a doctor, then?"

"I am." She felt compelled to explain to him how she really didn't have primary care physician experience, that her specialty was pediatric oncology, and this was all new—the practice, the people, the town. To have someone else to talk to about it other than her mother. Her younger brother and sister were busy with their own careers and dating and life in general. She hadn't had the time to make friends, or if she did, to keep friends, working at the hospital.

"Well, that's interesting."

"Really?"

"Yeah, especially considering Bran—"

The dark-haired local celebrity returned, slipping between Aubrie's stool and the next man over. She scooted a bit away from him.

"Did I hear you just say my name?" he said.

"What?" Joel played stupid.

"It was great, Joel." Aubrie said it a little too loudly, helping out the bartender. "I was pleasantly surprised."

Joel nodded and took the basket with the remnants of sweet potato fries. "Glad to hear it. Maybe it'll bring you back to try out some of our specialties while you're here. For however long that is."

Aubrie smiled, trying not to glance at Bran.

"Let me get that." Bran took out his wallet from his back pocket.

Aubrie did a double-take. "Are you referring to my bill?"

"Yes, I am." Bran flashed a smile, an annoyingly dashing one.

"No, thanks. I'm perfectly capable of paying for myself." She handed Joel a credit card, who would process it expeditiously if he knew what was good for him. Which he did, bless the man.

Bran held up both hands. "I didn't mean to imply otherwise. I simply thought that I may have disrupted your dinner. I doubt you came here wanting someone else's relationship drama to interfere with an otherwise enjoyable meal."

Joel returned with her card, and she signed the receipt.

Aubrie took a deep breath, contemplating how much she cared to engage with the man. "That's okay. It's nice of you to offer. But maybe save it for when you take her out to dinner?" She pointed to the blonde woman sitting at a nearby booth.

Bran looked over, then nodded. "Right."

Joel covered his smirk with his arm, pretending to wipe his lip along his wrist.

Aubrie grabbed her purse. "Thanks, Joel. It was lovely meeting you, and have a nice evening."

Joel signaled goodbye with a nod.

Aubrie weaved between the tables and out of the restaurant. She got the feeling Bran was the type of guy used to things going his way, and she didn't exactly let that happen. Was it foolish of her to dismiss the offer? Bran seemed well-known in town, and if she were to stay here for a while, perhaps indefinitely, then it probably was not a good idea to get off on the wrong foot. In reality, though, how often would she see him?

Something about him rubbed her the wrong way. Like the one or two doctors she'd had to deal with in the hospital. A little overconfident, self-absorbed. Think they could win anyone over with their words and a flashy smile.

It's not something she tolerated in her old life and not what she needed in her new one. Her do-over. Restart. Whatever she should call it.

No. She dealt with him politely enough.

She checked her phone for the time. Despite the deep desire to return to the apartment and veg out in front of the television until falling asleep, she knew that would be the wrong decision.

She had a party to attend.

FOUR

BRAN STARED AT Joel before taking another sip of his beer. "Do I know her and didn't realize?"

Joel took out a row of clean glasses from the bottom shelf and placed them on the counter. "No, I don't believe you know her."

Bran nodded and stared into his near-empty glass. Sometimes he could be too forward. He knew that all too well. It wasn't meant to be a flirtation or imply she couldn't pay for herself. He had been all too aware of her presence right next to Macy, and it was awkward enough for him, let alone a stranger, to be that close to the uncomfortable encounter.

It was a shame, too. He had just seen several people he hadn't for years come and greet him at the door. It made him feel confident in returning—that maybe it wouldn't be hard to convince Doc Bernie he was the man for the job, and not some visitor from Texas.

Then, Macy showed up and treated him the way he had expected most, reminding him that not everyone forgave his leaving, his nonchalant non-goodbye to town. What was he supposed to have done? Announce his departure on the radio, on the news, praising Maiden's Bay for all it had done to support him?

The fact was that Maiden's Bay did help him in a way—by motivating him to get out as soon as he had the chance. Growing up in a small town was constricting. Everybody knew his business, and he knew theirs. Doc Bernie was such a role model and well respected by the entire town, nothing Bran did could live up to that. Even Dad felt the pressure to be like Doc, hero of the town. And when he fell short—not just anyone could be Doc Bernie—he fell into a wave of depression, which made Bran's itching to get out even worse.

"Sorry?" Bran shook out of his stupor, realizing Joel had been talking to him.

"I said, was there anything else I can get you?"

"No, this is it. I've got somewhere to be." He gave Joel his card.

Joel touched the screen of the register. "You know, there's something you should probably know about her."

"Who?"

"That woman."

"Yeah?"

"Bran!" A hefty man around Bran's age waved a hand in the air, the other holding a beer. "They said you were here." He pointed to a booth of men near the front.

"Kyle Sanders? Long time no see."

"No kidding."

They shook hands. Joel interrupted, giving the card back.

"Oh, hold on, Kyle. What was it you were saying, Joel?"

Joel looked over the two men and shook his head. "Nothing. Don't worry about it."

"Why don't you join us?" Kyle had always looked the jock in high school. But his muscular physique got softer and rounder over the years. With a noticeable gold band on his left hand.

"Are you a married man now?"

Kyle stared down at his ring. "I sure am. You remember Emmy Abrams, right?"

Bran vaguely remembered the name but couldn't pinpoint a face. "You married Emmy?"

"Going on two years now. Expecting our first."

"Congratulations." How were people his age marrying, having kids? There was still too much to do, to complete and figure out. To commit to one person right now? Yet the news hit a chord somewhere, just briefly, and Bran felt the faint hint of jealousy.

"Look, can I take a raincheck on joining you? My grandfather is having his seventieth birthday party tonight I have to get to."

"Doc Bernie, seventy years old? That's crazy."

"I know. Hard to believe."

Kyle smacked Bran's shoulder. He still had the linebacker hit to him. "Well, tell him I said hello and happy birthday."

"Will do." Bran breezed past the crowded booth, giving a brief wave before making his way out the door. The thought of Kyle starting a family kept his thoughts busy as he walked down the wooden staircase to the sidewalk on Pearl Avenue.

The party was being held at The Codfather, one of the fanciest restaurants in Maiden's Bay. Even with the limited offerings the town had, The Codfather could compete with the finest Seattle had to offer, without the exorbitant prices. Maybe it was because there was less competition for the fresh catch between restaurants, or maybe it came down to being a family-owned business, and they knew their clientele. Most of Maiden's Bay wasn't wealthy. They were hard-working, practical people who endured the seasonal tourists and rich tech-guru here and there.

Bran opted to drive to the restaurant. Situated near the top of the hill that formed the eastern arc of the town, it was quite an uphill jaunt, and it wasn't that cold to not be sweating by the time he'd arrive.

The parking lot was filling up quickly, which was no surprise given the clout Doc Bernie held with the town. Silver and gold balloons formed an archway to the front door, and large yard signs spelled out *Happy 70th Doc!* It didn't quite go with the seriousness of the restaurant, but it was a party, after all, and Doc was known to have a little fun with things.

Like not telling Bran about his competition.

Bran took in a breath before entering. Generic Italian instrumental music played beneath the chitchat of the guests.

A hostess wearing a starchy white shirt underneath a black vest greeted him with a smile. "Here for the party?"

He doubted the restaurant was open to regular patrons, so what other reason would he be here for? He shook it off and nodded.

"Both sides are open."

"Thank you."

The restaurant had two sections, split by the entryway. Bran turned left, the larger area of the two.

"Bran!" Nathaniel waved him over. Bran knew his brother had joined the rowing team in college, but wasn't expecting his long lanky bones to have put on some brawn.

"It's been too long, man." He patted Nathaniel on the shoulder. "Look at you, adulting."

Nathaniel flashed a smile. At least that was still boyish. "You look just as I remember. Want a drink?"

"Sure." How he wished he had a little more to drink at Campy's. Even though he was usually successful in coming off as friendly and confident, it took work. An energy that wasn't infinite. Though, if he had more to drink, he would've been reduced to walking up the hill. It was probably for the better.

"What'll it be?" Nathaniel waved down the bartender.

Bran didn't want to be the only one holding hard liquor, as most of the guests he glanced at on the way to the long bar spanning most of the room held wine or champagne. "I'll take a glass of red, please."

Nathaniel ordered two and tipped the bartender.

"Wait, I should be getting that."

Nathaniel grinned. "I can manage to get my big brother a drink."

"How about I repay you tonight? Head out to Campy's after this, or we can buy some beer and hang out by the lighthouse." He shook his head. "I can't believe my brother's old enough to drink."

"Thanks for the offer, but I've got plans with Gwen, then I gotta head back to campus tonight." He nodded to a young woman across the bar, who waved in return.

"Gonna go with your girlfriend over your own brother, huh? I see how it is."

"Sorry, but she drove in just for this."

"It's okay." The fact his brother connected with someone on that level ramped up Bran's envy. If no man was an island, why did he feel so much like one? "You have fun, all right? By the way, have you seen Doc yet?"

"No. Gwen and I got here right before you."

"Nathaniel!" A guy near Gwen waved him over.

"Go ahead." Bran gave him an approving smile, despite wanting to spend more time with his only sibling. Nathaniel took off through the crowd, and Bran turned the other way to look for Doc, when he bumped into someone. Wine splattered on his sweater. The woman gasped, his wine having spilled on her top.

"It's you." The woman from Campy's, the one he'd offered to pay for her dinner, set her purse down on the bar.

She examined her white blouse beneath the blazer, her shirt getting more of the brunt of the spill than his sweater. Although he did feel the coolness seeping through to his chest.

Bran hurried around, grabbing a stack of cocktail napkins.

"Here." The bartender handed him a plastic bottle of club soda.

"Thanks." He offered the napkins, and she grabbed half of them hastily. He doused the rest with the club soda but didn't dare touch her blouse with them. Instead, he stood there, mouth open, not knowing what to say, waiting for her to take them.

"I—I'm so sorry. I didn't mean—I didn't know—"

"What's done is done." She finally grabbed the wet napkins and dabbed them on the stain.

"Let me buy you a new one, or at least pay to get it dry-cleaned."

"Are you always offering to pay for things for women?"

Bran didn't know whether to laugh or scoff, slightly taken aback. "Just raised with manners. I think my grandfather would kill me if I didn't offer. Do you always turn down guys who offer to pay? I'd like to think there's still some chivalry these days."

The woman sighed, relaxing a tad, shifting her weight onto one foot. "I'm sorry. It's just that, what you did back there at the bar, turning that lovely woman's anger around with what I felt like were hollow words." She shook her head again. "Actually, it was none of my business. I shouldn't have listened in on it."

"It was probably hard not to." He half-smiled. "I don't particularly like when people are upset with me, so I tried to... make her... not upset with me." Even he knew that didn't sound great.

"Can I ask you something?"

"Sure." He spilled wine on her. She deserved however many questions she wanted answered.

"Why didn't you say goodbye to that woman, back then, I mean? Because to me it seemed like you just didn't care about her enough to say goodbye."

She had him there. She'd caught on to the truth so easily, not even knowing him. Why hadn't Macy seen that? Because his charm worked on Macy. Not on this woman. Yet again, he was delaying the inevitable with a woman and being called out for it.

"I think your lack of a response is answer enough."

Bran rolled his tongue over his cheek. Did this woman never make a relationship mistake? Who was she to judge, anyway? "Well, this has been... something. I am sorry for the shirt—"

"Bran!" Doc Bernie put his hand on Bran's shoulder. "And Aubrie! Oh, good, you're both here."

How Doc Bernie knew this woman, Bran had no idea. But any more words exchanged with her this evening were enough for a lifetime.

"Doc." Nathaniel tapped Doc's shoulder from behind. Doc's face lit with joy as he embraced his other grandson. Not quite the welcome Bran had experienced with Doc. But Nathaniel had always done everything right—dating, college, regularly visiting home. He made it hard not to love him.

"How are you doing, my boy?" Doc braced him on the arms. "Here you are getting fitter with age, while I'm doing the opposite."

"Oh, nonsense."

"Hey, how about you and Gwen come by the house afterward?"

"We'll see. Might be able to swing by for a few minutes."

"Great."

"I'd better get back. There's a few guys—"

"No, no. Go on. Have fun."

Nathaniel retreated back into the crowd, while Doc turned his focus back to Bran.

"He's a good kid, that one." Doc looked at Bran, taking a second to remember where they'd been in the conversation. "Ah, yes. Bran, this is the new hire I was telling you about, Doctor Aubrie Turnbridge. Aubrie, this is my grandson Bran."

The horror in Aubrie's brown eyes was almost worth seeing, were it not for the reason it occurred.

"Bran… Jackson, then?" Aubrie took a step back. "Joel didn't tell me your last name."

"Nor did he tell me why you were visiting Maiden's Bay." It wormed its way out of his clenched jaw.

"Oh, do you two know each other?"

"No." Bran managed to swallow the news and gave Doc a smile.

"I think we know each other enough." Aubrie gave Bran a smile, one only he could register the sarcastic tone to, before giving a warmer one to Doc Bernie.

Doc set his confusion aside. "Well, as I told you, Aubrie comes to us from Texas. So, I expect you to make her feel welcome."

"Oh, he's made me feel…." Her gaze turned to Bran again. *"Something,* all right."

"You two will be working together, so I need you to feel comfortable with each other. The quicker you can establish a rapport, the better you can work as a team to help the people of Maiden's Bay."

Bran nodded slowly. "I'm pretty sure we've established a rapport."

"Quite." Aubrie reached for her purse on the bar.

Doc tapped her arm. "Goodness, what happened to your shirt?"

"A little wine spill." She said it with good humor, though Bran knew better than to think she meant it.

Bran clutched his chest, feeling his own spillage on his fingertips. "It was entirely my fault, Doc. I had bumped into her." He stared at her less-shocked brown eyes. "I offered to compensate for dry cleaning expenses."

"It's not a big deal." Aubrie waved it off.

"That was gentlemanly of you," Doc Bernie said.

"Anyway, I should probably head out, get settled in," Bran said.

"Oh, no, you can't go before I make the announcement and introduce you two."

"What?" Aubrie said. There was that shock again.

"Happy Birthday to you—" A quartet of waiters came out of the kitchen carrying a large rectangular cake. "Happy Birthday to you."

They finished the song with a long pause between Doc Bernie's name and the last happy birthday. The crowd clapped, and Doc Bernie's joyful smile was contagious.

Until Bran turned to Aubrie for a split second.

They both turned away quickly. He was supposed to work with her, for days, weeks maybe? Hopefully her bedside manner was more polite and less riddled with judgment.

Bran turned his focus to Doc Bernie, who blew out the candles to applause. It was something that Doc was turning seventy. And it was more than something that this seventy-year-old man held Bran's future in his hands.

FIVE

THE EVENING HAD taken quite the turn. Who would've thought the man that smooth-talked his way at the bar would be the very man Aubrie would have to work with—and essentially compete against for a practice she wasn't exactly sure she wanted yet.

But she did want to be better at it than him. Yet, based on what she saw at Campy's, he was revered in the town. At the very least, well-known.

"I want to introduce my two proteges here with me tonight for this special occasion." Doc Bernie stood on a chair, which alone made Aubrie nervous for him. He was spry for his age, but her skills didn't need to be tested out on her first night on her new—albeit temporary—boss.

"This is Doctor Aubrie Turnbridge." He pointed her out below, and Aubrie gave a meek wave to the crowd. "She comes to us from Texas."

Murmurs filled the room, sending Aubrie's nerves alight. Was coming from Texas a bad thing? Did they have some grudge against Texans? Or would she be the new entertainment in town, someone different that everyone wanted to get to know?

"And of course, most of you know my grandson, Bran Jackson."

"You know you can also call *me* doctor, right?" Bran smirked, and the crowd laughed, taken by his playful banter.

"This isn't just a birthday party, although your presence here to-night has made it one of the best." Doc looked down into his drink. "I've asked these two to be here because I will be turning over the practice. As in, I'm retiring."

Some gasps echoed through the crowd, while others started in with applause.

"We'll miss you!" someone shouted from the back.

"I'll miss you all, more than you can know." Doc looked back at Aubrie, then Bran. "Which is why I want to make sure the practice will be in good hands. I will be training these two fine people in the weeks to come, to make sure they're prepared to serve Maiden's Bay as I have, if not better than I have."

"Impossible!" another shouted from a corner.

"So, please, raise your glasses in a toast. Out with the old, in with the new."

The crowd repeated the last phrase, clinking glasses and taking sips.

Interesting that Doc Bernie hadn't mentioned to the group that only one of the pair would carry on with the practice. Aubrie hadn't the time to linger on the fact too long because a young woman approached her. Her long blonde hair was fashioned in a stylish low ponytail, her eyes a soft gray and friendly.

"Hi, I'm Cynthia Pruitt." She reached out her free hand, the other holding a wine glass.

Aubrie accepted the hand and shook it. "Aubrie Turnbridge."

"Don't you call yourself *Doctor* Turnbridge?" The underlying poke at Bran wasn't lost on Aubrie. She already liked Cynthia.

"Only when necessary. Not usually at birthday parties."

The two women chuckled.

"I wanted to introduce myself when I heard you're from out of town. I know it can be a little bit of a culture shock, especially moving here from a big city."

"Are you not from Maiden's Bay?"

"Me? I am. But one of my best friends, Josie—" She waved to a woman who was laughing loudly, tight brunette curls waving with her happiness. "She moved here fairly recently. Not to say it was rough for her. Maiden's Bay can be… different."

"I understand. It's definitely a different vibe, just the size difference alone."

"What am I missing out on here?" The curly-haired woman smiled between them.

"Thought you would like to meet Aubrie. Maybe do a piece on Doc Bernie retiring, and highlight the new doctor."

"A piece?" Aubrie asked.

"That's a great idea!" She turned to Aubrie, shaking her hand. "I'm Josie Morrison with KSMV. The local TV station here? It would be a great way to get folks comfortable with the transition."

"Oh, I'm not sure...." It applied to too many things. Being on camera. Being interviewed. Taking on the job.

Someone pulled at Josie's arm. "Ah, I have to go mingle. Here, take my card. You let me know if you change your mind, or if you just want to chat. Maybe grab some lunch, have a tour of the town?"

"I'd like that." Aubrie appreciated the kindness but yearned to get out of the stuffy party air and into the bed awaiting her down the hill. She didn't want to appear rude. That was the last thing she needed for a first impression with locals.

Josie vanished in growing celebration, leaving Aubrie alone again with Cynthia.

"So, how do you know Doc? I guess most people here know him from being his patient."

"Actually, my niece, Gwen, is dating Doc's grandson Nathaniel. Bran's younger brother."

Aubrie took a second to make the link.

"And Doc's office is across from where I used to work, Bea's Bouquets." Cynthia chuckled. "Small town. Usually more than one way of knowing someone here."

"Used to? Where do you work now, if you don't mind me asking?"

"Not at all. I'm a greenhorn on *Harpeth Rose.*"

Aubrie recognized the name as something said earlier in the evening, but couldn't exactly remember the context.

"I'm a crab fisherman. Fisher*woman."* Cynthia shook her head. "You know, it's taken decades for women to be accepted in the profession, but it doesn't feel right saying anything other than fisherman."

"That's pretty impressive, whatever title you want to give it."

"Thank you. It's been interesting, that's for sure."

Aubrie took a sip of her drink, keeping an eye on Bran, who chatted with another man ten feet away.

"Would it be too forward if I gave you my number also?" Cynthia asked. "In case you want to know where to eat, or go sightseeing. Heck, just to have someone local to talk to. We can meet up with Josie, too, if you'd like. It'd be good to have someone like her on your side."

"On my side?" Aubrie's eyebrows furled. Perhaps Doc Bernie didn't have to say anything about how she and Bran were competing.

"Please. I know Doc would love to have his grandson take over, but we all know how Bran can be. Doc wouldn't have invited you here if he didn't have his doubts, either. And woman to woman, my money is on you." She lifted her wine glass and clinked it with Aubrie's.

Aubrie added Cynthia to her contact in her phone and weaved her way through the crowd out of The Codfather. The day's events had carried on longer than expected, and she longed for rest in a bed that wasn't standard hotel fare.

She fought the desire to pinpoint Bran in the jumbled crowd on her way out. Part of her wanted to stay at least as long as he did. But that was ridiculous. Was it really a competition in every aspect? As if Doc Bernie would choose one over the other based on how long they stayed at his party. If that were part of the criteria, then she would happily forfeit now.

No, it was going to come down to who had the better work ethic. Who had the knowledge, the bedside manner. Compassion for the people of this town. It was probably a good thing to have Cynthia's number, and an in with Josie, especially if they knew a lot of people and held influence in town.

Aubrie got in her car and made her way down the hill. The side streets were dimly lit, with Pearl Avenue at the bottom of town the brightest, outside of the lighthouse. It was something to see a lighthouse in operation. All Aubrie had seen was the Point Bolivar lighthouse, which was not only closed off from the public, but non-operational.

Did the lighthouse actually still help sailors? Maybe that was something she could ask Cynthia.

Aubrie parked the car on the street, making sure there were no overnight parking restrictions posted. A black Audi sat in a spot, so she wouldn't be the only one ticketed if she kept it there overnight. She scanned the key fob, opening the outer door, and walked up the stairwell. She turned the key into the door lock, but it was already unlocked.

She slowly opened the door. Music blasted from the smart speaker, and a backside greeted her, the stranger's hand on the open fridge door, head peering inside.

"Excuse me?" She barely heard herself over the jazz music.

The man turned around, and Aubrie dropped her keys.

Bran.

"What are you doing here?"

Bran cupped his ear. "What?" He pointed a finger to guide her to wait, and told the smart speaker to pause.

"What are you doing here?" he asked. "How'd you get in?"

"That's what I would like to know about you." She grabbed the keys off the floor, then crossed her arms over her chest. Only a few minutes of interaction with this man today, yet it felt like an eternity.

"This is where I'm staying. I had a copy of the key made years back from Doc Bernie."

"Well, it's not where you're staying *now.*" She jingled the keys in the air. "I was given the keys this afternoon, and it's in my contract that the position provides lodging. Didn't you see my stuff in the bedroom?"

"I haven't been back here yet. Although, I see the contract must not provide board." He nodded to the empty fridge.

"I just arrived today." She scoffed. "You know what, it doesn't matter. This is where I've been assigned to stay—by your grandfather—so you need to leave."

"With all due respect, maybe I deserve to stay here. You know, since it *is* family property."

First, the awkward exchange at the bar. Then, the wine spill, on top of being introduced as her competition. And now this? When all she wanted was to plop in bed and not wake up until Monday. And deserve? What exactly had he done to deserve her living quarters? "I traveled farther to be here." It was the first one-up she could think of. "All due respect."

"How do you know?"

"Your grandfather said you worked in Seattle as a trauma surgeon." She straightened, feeling emboldened. "Which means not only did you travel a shorter distance to be here, but you can also afford to stay somewhere else."

This time, Bran crossed his arms, pursing his lips. "Pediatric oncology doesn't afford such a luxury?"

Her throat lumped up, not having known he knew that about her. "I'm not practicing pediatric oncology now, am I?"

"Nor I trauma surgery. Although, if I were to guess, my expertise would have more practical value for the practice."

The dig hurt, despite her facade.

Bran loosened his stance and walked out of the kitchen. "Look, we obviously did not start this out right."

Aubrie held back the eye roll and kept her mouth quiet.

"We don't know each other, only what Doc Bernie has mentioned. Considering how he approached me about this situation, you were probably in as much shock as I was."

Aubrie let out a laugh, relaxing a tad. "It was unexpected, yes."

"Okay. How about we start over tomorrow? We show up and put in the work. We don't have to be best of friends, but we can get along, right?"

"There's a problem with that."

"What is it?"

"Tomorrow is Sunday." She couldn't help but have a teeny victory in there somewhere. "The practice is closed."

"Knowing Doc, he's on-call whenever he's not in the office, despite there being two other family practitioners in town. But that's beside the point."

He wanted to get a little victory in, too, didn't he? Of course Doc

Bernie was the type to be on-call. Aubrie took note she'd have to be more careful in her assumptions.

"So, Monday, then. We agree to start over?" He offered his hand, steady in the air as if it were propped on a table. Perhaps he was good at his job.

Aubrie hesitated. It was hard to trust this stranger, stranger being a loose term when she felt like she knew more than she cared to after today. But she had to try. For Doc Bernie's sake. And for her own sanity.

"Agreed." Aubrie's hand met his, surprisingly warm and soft. She had expected rough hands, ones that were dry from scrubbing day in and day out.

He squeezed her hand delicately but gave one firm shake before letting go.

She remained standing by the front door, staring at him. Bran stood in silence, looking around confused.

"Um, so I'll see you Monday, then?" It was as polite as Aubrie could muster to tell him to leave.

"Yep, Monday." Bran didn't budge.

Aubrie cleared her throat in the awkwardness. "And the apartment?"

"Oh, right." Bran snapped his fingers and jumped into action. "Sorry." He grabbed a duffel bag from the floor and patted down his pants pockets until he confirmed the keys were there.

Damn it if the guilt didn't start to build up in Aubrie's chest, tightening her lungs and constricting her throat. "Are you going to be okay, finding another place to stay?"

What if he said he wasn't? Was she prepared to share this place? Absolutely not. Yet she couldn't help feel bad he had expected to have a place to stay, and she was kicking him out.

"I'll be fine. I know a place not far from here I can go."

"Okay, great." It came out too cheerfully canned, and Aubrie wanted to shrivel into a corner. "Oh, one thing." She stepped toward him as he stopped in the doorway. "Is it okay to park out front overnight?"

"I wouldn't worry about it. But if you are worried, there's an alleyway that leads to a parking lot behind the building."

Aubrie briefly smiled. "Thanks."

Bran nodded and walked out the door.

Aubrie closed it behind him and locked it.

She briefly considered propping a chair under the doorknob. He did have a set of keys to the place after all, and who was to say he wouldn't show up randomly looking for something he'd left behind. But with her luck today, there'd be a fire, and she'd be stuck having propped the door closed.

Such doom and gloom thoughts, Aubrie. Worse than imagining such luck, she was starting to think like her mother.

"Mom!" She tipped her head back, knowing how upset her mother would be for not having called her. But Aubrie was a full-grown adult, damn it. Besides, she'd have all day tomorrow to give her a call. While she tried her best to avoid Bran Jackson.

She laughed as she corrected herself.

Doctor Bran Jackson.

SIX

HE DIDN'T WANT to admit it, but there was something about being back home, in the familiar apartment, that put Bran at ease. After the evening's drama, all he wanted was a cold drink and mindless television.

Plans that were thwarted by Aubrie Turnbridge.

They'd officially start over on Monday. But was she the type who could put aside her first impressions so easily? Maybe he had caught her on a bad day. You never knew what other people were going through. He meant what he said—she probably heard about him and the situation of Doc's retirement at her arrival today. It wasn't easy news to digest, so how could he expect her to be happy about it, happy about him?

He left the Audi parked outside the practice, next to what was most likely Aubrie's car. He only had a duffel bag with him and didn't know what parking would be like at his destination.

As he walked along the curvature of Pearl Avenue, shop lights dimmed or switched off completely, street lamps overpowering the moonlight—which wasn't much to speak of, anyway—he realized the walk was farther than he'd pictured. He had forgotten about several shops, most of which had not changed in years. He'd forgotten how Doc Bernie's office sat closer to the southern end of town, and just how long Pearl Avenue was.

Of course, it was nowhere near the size of downtown Seattle. But for once, Maiden's Bay didn't look all that small. It wasn't that confining, constricting place it had been when he vowed to leave it in high school. He relished the quiet of the night, few cars driving slowly by, a handful of walkers taking in the night on the stretch of beach.

He turned right onto Ocean Street, or O Street, and headed upward. Seattle had its share of hills, especially north of the city. But something about the hill here—its steepness, the houses looking crooked at face-value, as if everything were a gust of wind away from toppling over—made for a hard climb.

Luckily, he saw the sign, the lady overlooking the sea next to the lighthouse, before the strain in his calves warmed him up too much. Maiden's Slumber Inn.

For as long as he lived in Maiden's Bay, he had never stayed at the inn. He never had a reason to or need for it, until tonight. The famous proprietor, Constance, was about as well-known in town as his grandfather.

Bran entered the inn, the brightness of the yellow walls giving the lobby a warm, inviting look. No one sat at the front desk, a wooden counter that matched the wood of the table, which sported no legs but an anchor, nor occupied the brown leather couch along the opposite wall from the desk.

"I'll be right with you." A woman's voice carried through behind the walls.

Bran set his duffel bag down on the beige carpet and stretched out his cramped hand. Being away from surgery, even for the slightest break, stiffened his hands. As much as the fine motor skills and steadiness cumulatively improved the more he worked, they exponentially declined the more he didn't work.

An elderly yet lively lady appeared around the corner of the desk, out of whatever office or most likely living space she had been in. Her hair and wrinkles suggested eighty years old, but her pep said otherwise.

"How can I help you? Need a room for tonight?"

"I do, if you have one. I'm assuming you're Constance?"

She nodded. "I sure am. How long do you plan on staying, hun?"

Much longer than he originally thought he'd be staying in town. "I'd say a week, if you can accommodate that."

"Let me see here." She rifled through a tome of a book, handwritten notes taken on lined paper. "That should be okay. Would you like to book it out for a week?"

He didn't *want* to. He wanted Doc Bernie to give him what he came for, and go back to Seattle in a better predicament than when he had left it earlier today. A whole week in Maiden's Bay? Maybe longer? That constricting feeling came back again, the same one he had all through his teenage years.

"Sure. Better safe than sorry."

"You don't have to pay for it all up front. If your plans change, just let me know."

Bran nodded and handed her a credit card.

Constance examined it, typing the numbers into the computer register by hand. "Bran Jackson," she read off the name. Her eyes lit up, and she smiled. "You're one of Doc Bernie's grandsons, right?"

"Yes, ma'am." He didn't know why he addressed her in such an old fashion manner, but it only felt appropriate.

"I thought I recognized those eyes. They're the same as your grandmother's." Constance sighed. "May she rest."

"You aren't the first to say so."

Nathaniel took after their dad, who had a lot of the physical features of Doc Bernie. Which meant poor Nathaniel had to cherish his hair while he could. But Bran, he had Grandma Trish's eyes, and his mother's lean nose and heartbreaking smile. Looks that sometimes got him into trouble. Luckily, he had developed the art of talking himself out of it. Most of the time.

"If you don't mind my asking, why on earth would Doc's grandson need a place to stay in Maiden's Bay?"

Bran had considered his options. He could've stayed at Dad and Rita's house until they got back, but once they had, he'd end up bickering with Dad and have to leave, anyway. If Nathaniel still lived there, then maybe. Nathaniel had a way of abating Dad's disappointment in Bran, being the good son. Perhaps it was best he and Nathaniel kept their distance. Wouldn't want failure to rub off on him.

The other option was staying at Doc's house. It was going to be tough enough to work at his side every day. How could he also live with him, the man he was about to break trust with?

"You know, growing up in a house with my parents is one thing. You have to listen, obey their rules. It's another to return as an adult and stay with them."

"They still have rules, but you've had the taste of freedom, so to speak." Constance laughed a pure laugh. "Explain no more."

Luckily, she hadn't asked about Doc Bernie's place. It wasn't really her business anyway. Bran was paying to stay at her place, so why discourage a customer? On the other hand, this was Maiden's Bay. Everyone's business was up for grabs.

"Don't get me wrong. I'm happy to have you stay here." She handed him the card back, along with a room key. "Room 4, up the stairs two levels. Bathroom is at the end of your hallway. Breakfast is served between six and nine in the morning."

"Thank you." He carried his duffel bag up the narrow stairwell two flights to Room 4. The room had two twin beds with about a foot and a half of space between them. The white curtains hanging around the window on the far wall were drawn back. At least he had a bit of a view over the rooftop of the building in front of Constance's. He could glimpse a strip of water in the pale moonlight, but most of the view was of the night sky. It helped to make the room seem not so small.

What had he expected here? The building belonged on the historical register if it wasn't already, and had to be one of the oldest in town. Of course the rooms were going to be small. But Constance always had a steady flow of customers, and repeat customers from what he had heard, loyal to her. For what the place lacked in accommodations, it must've been made up for by Constance herself.

He sat on the bed closest to the window, the bed frame creaking but the mattress the right balance of firm and soft. The room lacked a television, though he noted in passing that the breakfast room had one, with two guests sitting at a table watching some game show. These days, it wasn't a necessity to have a television, considering the content was at people's fingertips on phones or tablets.

He opened his email on his phone and began reading when a call startled him. *Doctor Fredericks.*

His heart skipped at the name. Could this be news of the status of his probation. Did he want to know? Sure, he wanted to go back to his job, to do what he was great at doing and happened to enjoy. But did he want to hear the answer, on the chance that he couldn't go back?

Bran sucked in a deep breath. "Hello?"

"Bran, it's Doctor Fredericks. Did I catch you at a bad time?"

"No, relatively speaking. No."

"I just wanted to let you know that the Clinical Competency Committee had its first meeting. I can't tell you the details, but—"

"It looks bad?" Bran's shoulders sagged. "I knew it. I *knew* Sebastian had it out for me, and it wasn't how he's making it look."

"Now look, calm down. It was only the presentation of materials. You know, as your advisor, I'm going to bat for you."

"I appreciate that. I really do."

"There's a lot to unwrap here in the next meetings. It's not your ordinary questioning of competency. At least, not in the academic sense."

"Thanks for that."

"I'm only saying that it'll take some time."

They both sat in silence, the unspoken words louder than the crowd had been at Campy's Bar.

Dr. Fredericks sighed. *"I promise you Bran, I'm going to try to show them what you bring to the table. How valuable your skillset is. I've told you before, I haven't seen someone as talented as you in a long time."*

Normally, Bran would soak in the compliments. It felt different hearing them now. As if they were the cushion before the blow.

"I have to watch what I say. But can you tell me you understand that there's more at work here than the facts?"

Bran knew all too well what was at work. It had to do with money, influence. Who people knew. "As in, it'd be easier if I or my family had given huge donations in the past?"

Dr. Fredericks coughed through a slight choke. *"I can't comment on that."*

What Bran had said rang true. "Just know I've got something in the works."

"What are you doing? Bran, where are you?"

"I'm back in my hometown for a while. Maiden's Bay. Hopefully not too long."

"Probably good that you're not here, but not too far away. You can at least try to enjoy this time off."

There wasn't much he expected to enjoy. Despite having seen several folks he hadn't in years, being back in town wasn't a joyful reunion. He didn't like having to do what he planned to do, but he needed to do it. He needed Doc Bernie to hand the family business to him. He didn't want to have to stay at the inn and didn't want to have to work together with Aubrie.

He didn't want anything to do with this situation.

But he couldn't go back in time.

"I'm working on something. If I can secure it… it would be a great asset for the hospital. To expand their reach."

"Just don't do anything foolish," Dr. Fredericks said.

"It's a little late for that, apparently." It was a joke, yes. But he didn't view what he had done as foolish. It wasn't wrong based on the information he had at the time, or forbidden by hospital rules, or against any oath or patient confidentiality agreement. "Thanks, Doctor Fredericks. Again."

"Of course. I'll keep you in the loop as much as I can. You know there's only so much I can share."

"I know. We don't need you to be put under probation, too. Or they'd lose another pair of genius hands."

"Well, don't you think highly of yourself?"

Bran chuckled and appreciated the laugh on the other end. Dr. Fredericks was a fierce advocate for those he trained and served under his watch. But it took a lot for him to crack up. Laughter from the man was a rare thing.

"I'll speak to you soon." Dr. Fredericks hung up, and Bran sat in the bed, staring at the sky out the window without really looking at it. There was a lot at stake, and most of it was out of his control.

The only thing he could control was how well he did working under Doc Bernie. Which meant he had to get along with Aubrie while outshining her in every task, small or large. He'd have to go back to that mental mindset of medical school, where everyone pretended to be a part of a group helping each other out but really wanted to be the best doctor of the bunch.

Perhaps he never really lost that attitude. Every surgery he stepped into, he wanted to win. Not only to keep the patient alive, but add to their lives. To fix what he could fix, to show everyone in the room, and the patient's family—heck, all of the hospital—that not only could he do it, but he was the best man for the job.

What he hadn't considered in visiting here, in vetting for Doc Bernie's established practice, was that he could very well be the best man for the job.

But a woman may be better.

SEVEN

ALTHOUGH SHE HAD set her alarm to go off early Monday morning, Aubrie canceled it sometime between four and five AM. The impending start of her new job didn't afford her much sleep, let alone knowing she'd have to deal with a not-so-welcome coworker.

Once the blurriness in her sight cleared up with her increasing awakeness, Aubrie hit the shower. She was thankful to have had Sunday in town before starting work, giving her time to buy groceries at Mariner's Market up the road and roam around town to get her general bearings of its layout. Fortunately, most everything she needed was close by, with a few specialty shops and restaurants sprinkled in the mix up the hillside.

She brewed herself some coffee and ate half a muffin. Her nerves were still alight, anxious about what was to come. Rarely did she ever have to perform surgery on a child patient, but when she did, the same wave of nausea, hope, and fear mixed up in her.

But no lives were on the line for this. Just her livelihood.

The practice didn't start seeing patients until 8:15, but Aubrie arrived at 7:50. If anything, she could busy herself setting up the rooms, looking over scheduled patient charts, or even tidying up the waiting area if it led to that.

She walked downstairs out onto the sidewalk, only to turn back to the front door of the Family Practice of Dr. Bernard Jackson. The full name looked foreign to her. Funny she had only known him for a minute, but calling Doc Bernie anything other than that didn't feel right.

The door was locked, and Aubrie waited by the glass facade until Edith showed up.

"Good morning." She said with a smile. "You're here early."

"Didn't have far to travel." It was the truth, but not the reason she had arrived so early.

"I suppose not." Edith's keys jingled in the lock, and she held the door open for Aubrie.

"Thank you." Aubrie stepped into the dark office. Edith pointed to the light switch on the left wall, and Aubrie flicked the lights on. The LEDs lit dimly, taking their time to brighten, as if they were on the morning sun's timeline. A sun that didn't show up over the hill very well through the thick, gray clouds outside.

Edith unraveled a light violet scarf from around her neck and took off her raincoat. "If you want, I can keep your purse with mine in the desk drawer."

"Oh, sure. Thank you."

"I don't lock it, if that's okay with you. I just put it in there to keep it out of sight. No need to worry about thieves around here."

Aubrie nodded and handed over her purse. "So, what can I do to help out?"

Edith took a seat behind the check-in desk. "Well, Doc Bernie should be arriving in a few minutes. Usually, I check the phone for any voicemails left. Sometimes we get patients calling early to get a same-day appointment before I'm here to answer."

"How about prepping the rooms?"

Edith waved a hand. "No need for that. I always tidy up, replenish the paper roll, that sort of thing before leaving at the end of the day. The one thing I didn't get to was checking the supply of disposable gowns in the rooms." It was like she was thinking out loud, and when she said the words, she snapped back into the conversation. "What am I saying? You didn't get your degree and come all the way here to deal with supplies."

"It's not a problem, really. I like to stay busy."

"Hmm. I'll bet things were busy in the hospital you worked at."

Aubrie nodded. It was definitely going to be a change of pace here. But perhaps that was a good thing. Half the time at work, she didn't have time to take a break to eat. Here she could actually take breaks, get off her feet for a few minutes, and taste her food instead of scarfing it down.

"Where can I find the gowns?"

Edith smiled warmly. "We keep them in the top right drawer of the examining tables. Extras are in the supply closet at the end of the hallway, past the patient rooms. It's where you can find a lab coat, also. If you'd like to wear one."

"And scrubs?"

Edith giggled. "It's a family practice."

"Right." Aubrie's skin flushed pink. Having worked at a hospital, some things were so ingrained they had become second nature. It was going to take time to let go of them. Although, not having to wear scrubs came with a certain freedom.

She headed over while Edith listened to the voicemails over speakerphone. The supply room was a bit tight, as most of it was a utility closet. She spotted a broom and mop, a few other cleaning supplies stored in the rest of the space. She expected to see medical supplies on shelving, but then again, the size of the place meant most of that stuff probably fit in the cabinets of the examining rooms.

She bypassed the lab coat, having read too many studies on their affinity for carrying harmful microbes. Although there were other studies indicating patients were more receptive to their doctors wearing lab coats. For now, she'd enjoy wearing her business casual attire.

She refilled the folded paper gowns in each of the two rooms and checked her watch. 8:10. As if on cue, Doc Bernie came around the corner into the hallway.

"Ah, good morning, Doctor Turnbridge." He winked. "Aubrie."

"Good morning."

"How about you come into my office? We can review the schedule for the day."

Aubrie obliged and followed him to his office, taking a seat while he took off his jacket and traded it for a lab coat. Aubrie looked out the doorway. No sign of Bran yet.

"It's refreshing that you're here before me, although don't feel obligated to do that every morning."

"I like to be on time." She tipped her head in jest at the oversimplification. "Early, to be honest."

"No shame in that." He checked his watch and looked out the doorway, no doubt wondering about Bran as well. "You know, you never told me about your motivation."

Aubrie leaned forward in her chair, as if she hadn't heard the words. "Sorry? What do you mean?"

"I mean what brought you here. Why you left pediatric oncology, after becoming one of the youngest in the country, I'd imagine. Did it become too depressing?" He shook his head. "I can understand how seeing sick kids—I mean, the really sick kids and their suffering—could take a toll on the best of people."

Aubrie bit her lip. The question left a knot in the pit of her stomach. "Something like that."

Thankfully, he accepted the answer for now. This was a new day, a new job, and she didn't want to linger on the past.

"Well, this is going to be different. Sure, we see the occasional upsetting diagnosis, but for the most part, it's pretty standard stuff."

Edith walked in with two folders. "Here you are."

"Thanks, Edith." He placed the folders in front of him on the desk. "Oh, any sign of my grandson?"

Edith stopped in the doorway and shook her head. "Not yet."

Doc pressed his lips in disappointment. Aubrie focused on not showing her delight in Bran's predicament.

"All right." Doc handed Aubrie one of the folders. "Let's review these charts."

The two folders represented the only patients with appointments for the first half of the day. Doc explained they kept a few appointment slots open for same-day visits, and they accepted the occasional walk-in as long as they were not too busy, which obviously wasn't a common occurrence judging by the amount of free time Aubrie found herself partaking in.

It was clear into midmorning when Bran finally showed up. Doc Bernie didn't make a big fuss over it. He simply filled Bran in on the two patients they had seen already.

Aubrie kept herself as busy as she could. The second patient, a five-year-old boy, had tested positive for strep for the fourth time in a year. After calling in her first referral to an ENT at White Bend Hospital, she studied the recommended order of antibiotics for frequent strep, then refreshed her memory on the details of the tonsillectomy surgery itself. There were a lot of things from med school she'd have to review, having not encountered them in a while.

Bran had a harder time finding things to do. He moped about the office, surfed on his phone, and when he exhausted those things, he turned to Aubrie.

"What are you reading about?" He slipped into the chair next to her in the waiting area.

"Tonsillectomy." She didn't bother to look up.

Bran let out a half-chuckle. "Preparing to perform that in-office?"

Aubrie closed her eyes for a second, practicing patience. "Just reviewing the details. Our patient this morning will probably have to undergo surgery."

"So, again, why are you reviewing it?"

Aubrie closed the book. "I don't know how you do things, but I like to be informed as much as I can, for my patient's sake. It can be scary for a young boy to go into surgery. I like to know what to expect, to know whether or not I should refer a patient to an ENT for the procedure. And that can go for anything we encounter in this office. The more I know, the better I can serve my patients."

Bran leaned back in his chair, wide-eyed. "I see."

She opened her mouth to say more, but a woman rushed through the front door, holding a wad of fabric onto a teenage boy's head.

Aubrie shot up out of the chair. "What happened?"

Bran met her at her side.

"He fell off a ladder cleaning the gutters. I *told* my husband he shouldn't make him do it, but he wanted to teach him responsibility."

"Let me see." Bran approached the teen.

"Let's get you back to a room," Aubrie insisted. She eyed Bran, who obviously wanted this excitement for himself.

Aubrie held onto the woman's elbow, while Bran walked on the other side of the kid, holding the cloth to his bleeding head.

They sat him down on an examining table. Aubrie guided the mother to a chair along the wall.

Bran slowly released the cloth and examined the wound. "Yeah, you got yourself real good."

Aubrie stepped in front of the boy. "I'm Doctor Turnbridge, and this is Doctor Jackson. What is your name?"

"Darren."

"Good, Darren." She took out her pen light and examined his pupils. "No signs of dilation. Any ringing in your ears?"

"No."

"Darren's mom?"

"Irene."

"Irene, any vomiting after the fall, confusion?"

"No."

"Good. How about trouble walking?"

Irene shook her head.

In the time it took her to examine and question the mom and son, Bran had brought out a set of tools.

"Darren, I think a few staples should do the trick," Bran said.

Aubrie hadn't seen how well Bran examined Darren. She stepped forward. "May I?"

Bran raised his hands in the air and stepped back. "Go for it." He smirked as he folded his arms across his chest.

Her assessment of the split came to the same conclusion, no matter how much she had hoped he was wrong. Her hope vanished when she realized it was the best scenario for the patient. Admittedly, guilt struck her for even thinking such a thing. "Staples will do."

"Will *do?*" Bran scoffed. "It's the best option." His attention diverted to the doorway, and Aubrie's gaze followed.

Doc Bernie stood there, watching. Who knew how long he had been there.

"Very well, go ahead." Aubrie swallowed hard, but allowed Bran to clean and prep the wound.

"Doesn't he need to be sedated or something?" Irene asked, worry in her eyes.

Aubrie stepped over to her. "With the size of the cut and position on the head, it's not a problem. He won't feel much when they go in. Not any worse than an injection to numb it."

Irene nodded.

Aubrie turned and heard the snap of the surgical stapler. Another two snaps, and Bran was finished.

"Come back in a week's time, and we'll check to see if they're ready to come out." Bran turned to Aubrie. "Doctor Turnbridge here will give you the special care instructions to practice over that time."

Aubrie raised her eyebrows, surprised. Sure, give her the task of dispelling information. Her money was on Bran not knowing the follow-up information.

Bran helped Darren down and walked him through the hallway.

Aubrie walked with Irene and was met by Edith. "This printout covers what you need to do and be mindful of." She handed it to Irene and winked at Aubrie.

Aubrie mouthed the words, *Thank you.* "Keep watch for those signs of concussion we discussed," she said. "It's probably nothing to worry about, but call us if you notice anything or have any questions."

"I will."

After a few words with Doc Bernie, the mother and son went on their way. Bran stood incredibly happy with himself as Doc approached the two of them.

"Some good teamwork I saw going on there." He smiled at both of them. "Bran, it was nice to see some of that trauma experience come into play. Not to say it was good for the patient to experience it."

Bran nodded, hands on his hips in his smugness. "It wasn't a big deal. Head wounds can look pretty bad at the surface. A lot of blood for a little cut."

"And Aubrie." Doc Bernie turned to her. "I was very impressed with the bedside manner. You kept the mother calm and did all the examining pieces Bran missed."

"I wouldn't say *missed.*" Bran rubbed his neck. "I simply knew she'd take over that aspect, while I focused on the wound."

"You knew, huh?" The smugness hit Aubrie with Doc Bernie's compliment, and she didn't care about hiding it.

"Yeah. It's like we have an unspoken rhythm."

Darren may not have felt nauseous after his head injury, but Aubrie certainly was feeling it with Bran's nonsense.

"Whatever you want to call it, I'm proud of you two." Doc Bernie placed a hand on each of their shoulders. "We need those skills here, and it gave me some relief seeing them played out today."

"Of course," Bran said with a smile. "And we're happy to do it all over again. Right, Aubrie?" He looked at Aubrie with a twinkle of slyness in his eye.

She swallowed the thoughts before they could reach her mouth. For Doc's sake. "Right."

EIGHT

"GOOD JOB." DOC clapped his hands. "I think our first day was a success."

Aubrie's facade of a smile waned as Doc Bernie walked back to his office.

Bran wanted to apologize again for being late. But his dad and stepmom arrived back in town last night and insisted on meeting him for breakfast. Despite Bran's several warnings of having to go, Dad had drawn out the meal, deciding to drop news about how they're moving to Florida after they had finished. Not only was it a shock, but it irked Bran that they hadn't told him earlier. Not even Nathaniel thought it a good idea to pick up the phone to let him know. But he was so late, he didn't have time to ask the questions that ran through his head.

It wasn't that he cared what decisions Dad and Rita made. They had their own lives, mostly separate from Bran's, and they could go wherever or do whatever. But with Doc Bernie retiring, and now them leaving, the familial connection with Maiden's Bay was dwindling. Would that affect Doc's decision? Had he known of their impending move? Surely he knew they were in Florida during his retirement party. If Bran had called upon arrival, he would've known, too.

It didn't matter when he found out. What nagged him was the thought that maybe there wasn't enough connection to his hometown to keep him coming back. Was there a goodbye to the town for him, too?

Edith turned off the front waiting room lights and headed for the patient rooms.

"Let me help you with closing," Aubrie said.

"Oh, that's okay. It's part of my job. You go on ahead."

Doc Bernie popped his head out of his office. "You two, big day tomorrow. Make sure to rest up."

Aubrie looked back at Bran, and he shrugged. Who knew what Doc had in store for the two of them.

His stomach growled, as he had not eaten since the eventful breakfast this morning. Edith warded off Aubrie's helping hand, assuring her she had closing covered.

"Hey, Aubrie." Bran stopped her as she retrieved her purse out of the front desk. "I was wondering if you want to get some food down at Campy's?"

Aubrie didn't hide her surprise enough. He didn't mean to make her feel uncomfortable. He didn't even know if that's how she felt. But whatever it was, it was negative and not his intention.

"Come on. It's getting darker earlier these days, and you've got to be hungry by now."

Her eyebrows raised.

"I saw that meager salad you brought for lunch, and that was what, six hours ago?"

Aubrie sighed. "I don't know how you do it. You invite me to come with you, yet it also feels like an insult?"

"I'm sorry. I didn't mean it like that. I just meant... I know I'd be hungry by now, in your shoes."

Aubrie stared at the ceiling, as if looking to the heavens for guidance, before meeting Bran's gaze again. "Okay. Let's go."

"Really?"

"Are you questioning my decision?"

"You mean... like how you questioned mine back there with the staples earlier?"

She opened her mouth, apparently at a loss for words.

"I'm just joking, Aubrie."

She slung the straps of her purse on her shoulder. "I've changed my mind."

There was no winning with this woman. "Come on. We said we'd start over. At least give me a chance to—"

Aubrie held up a hand. "Fine. Can we not do this in front of…." She nodded to Edith.

He wanted to point out it didn't matter where they bickered. It'd make its way through town, back to Edith somehow. But he seized the opportunity.

"All right." He opened the front door for her, and they exited onto the street. The cool evening breeze was a relief from the office's sterile vibe. Edith had lit a cinnamon-apple scented candle at her desk to give the air some personality, but it mainly served to ignite a headache for Bran.

Aubrie closed her coat a bit tighter with the wind. Bran took the initiative to lead the way up Pearl Avenue the few blocks to Campy's.

"I understand it, by the way," Bran said. "Questioning my judgment today."

"It was a knee-jerk reaction." Aubrie kept her eyes ahead. "I shouldn't have presented that doubt in front of the patient, especially in front of the patient's mom."

"It's okay. Really. You don't know me. You've never seen me work, let alone work alongside me. I would've done the same."

"Really?" Her laser focus broke, affording a softer glance at Bran.

"Maybe?" His shoulders raised, he couldn't hold back the chuckle.

Aubrie's resolve broke, a genuine smile showing. Perhaps the first one he had seen all day. It was beautiful.

They crossed the street and went up the stairs to Campy's. It wasn't quite as crowded as Saturday, but happy hour did bring in many of the locals hitting the bar for a drink before continuing on home.

"How about a table this time?" Bran held out a hand to an open booth by the windows.

Aubrie nodded and sat down on one of the cushioned benches, while Bran occupied the other. A waitress dropped two menus for them and took their drink orders.

Aubrie investigated the menu as if she were reading the tonsillectomy text. Bran hadn't been face-to-face with her a whole lot, and now that they sat opposite each other, he noticed how her bangs accentuated the darkness in her eyes, in a good way.

The waitress came by with their drinks and took their food order. Bran had waited until the pressure of selecting was over with, as it seemed to be Aubrie's full focus. Either that, or she couldn't stand to look at him.

"So, how do you think the first day went?" He took a sip of his iced tea.

Aubrie gave a muted smile. "All right, I guess. It definitely pointed out how I need a refresher in general medicine."

"I think you did a great job covering the signs of concussion with the head wound patient."

"Darren."

"Yes, Darren." He cleared his throat, her stare one that could send daggers into a man's chest.

Aubrie wiggled in her seat and took a deep breath. "I'm just going to come out and say it. Honestly, it's why I agreed to this dinner."

"I'll take it straight." Of course she'd be to the point. Subtlety was not her thing.

"You didn't show up until halfway through the morning, without as much as an apology. What's your deal?"

Bran bit the inside of his bottom lip. "For the record, I *did* apologize to Doc. But you're right. I should've apologized to you, as well. We're coworkers, so it's only right to show you the same respect."

Her left eyebrow furled and head tilted, as if she questioned his intentions in such a statement.

"So, I apologize. There was a family thing that was, honestly, thrown on me this morning, and it made me late, despite my many warnings that I would indeed be late."

"And Darren. You seemed eager to tend to the head wound."

He nodded. "I was. My expertise is trauma, and I've seen patients lose a lot of blood with head wounds. I didn't think his would be that bad but wanted to be sure. And the quicker to get it done, the better."

She mulled this over and concluded with a head nod.

"Look, I don't mean to step on toes. I truly did want to get it closed up, and then I would've checked on signs of concussion. But I'm glad you were there to do that. Like I said, you did a great job with the patient and his mother."

She opened her mouth, but Bran beat her to it.

"Irene." He smiled, and Aubrie followed. "See, I *do* listen. And remember, too."

Their food arrived, Aubrie with a plateful of penne, and Bran his burger. It had been years since he ordered the famous Campy's crew burger, and he hoped to all hell it still tasted as good as he remembered.

"That burger is massive." Aubrie eyed the wonderful monstrosity before him.

"You want a bite?"

"No, that's okay."

"Here." He sliced a wedge out of the stacked burger. "You have to at least try Campy's crew burger once. The locals will appreciate it, trust me."

She hesitantly accepted the wedge and took a bite. "Oh, my goodness. What's that sauce?"

"Campy's sauce." He pointed out one of the plastic condiment bottles at the wall edge of the table. "And don't try to figure it out. It's the best kept secret of Maiden's Bay. I put it on their fries and chicken tenders. I've even ordered eggs late at night and covered them with the stuff."

"It's amazing." She followed it with a sip of her drink. "Here I thought Maiden's Bay didn't have any secrets."

"I see you've spoken with some of the locals, then?"

She nodded.

"I suppose it doesn't take long to realize how small of a town we are." The use of "we" struck him. As if he belonged here, was a part of the community after all these years away.

"You left to go to school, I take it?"

"That was part of it."

"And the other part?"

He wiped his mouth with a napkin. "I guess the same reason why others leave their hometowns. In the hopes of there being something bigger out there. More possibilities."

"While I was lamenting the busyness and crowdedness of Dallas."

"You grew up there?"

"Lived there all of my life."

"But you don't seem to have an accent."

She smiled. "My parents moved there from Maryland after they got married. They're still there—parents, brother. My sister and her family." She grew quiet with the last words.

"But you wanted the opposite as me, something slower, calmer?"

She nodded, though he got the sense, as with his answer, there was more to hers. He didn't want to push his luck, though. If she wanted to elaborate, she would.

"I guess it's true then, that the grass is always greener."

Aubrie set down her fork, her elbows on the table, and she leaned. "Can I ask you something?"

"Shoot."

"You left town to get your degree, live the big city life. And now you're back."

"Yes." He nodded slowly, not sure where this was going.

"Then, today, at the practice... I mean, up until the teenager showed up with his mom, it seemed like working there was absolute torture for you. That—" She sat back and exhaled hard. "I really don't mean this to be rude."

"Go on." Bran braced for whatever was coming his way.

"Just your actions, your demeanor. It seemed like you were... above the work. Above *being* there. Maybe not just the office and work. Maybe here, in town."

As much as he didn't want there to be an underlying truth to her words, there was. Not so much that he was above the work. It wasn't the type of work he wanted to do. Being back here, despite being temporary, made him feel like a bit of a failure. He knew he was good at his job, and that kind of confidence was necessary as a trauma surgeon. But perhaps he did fail in Seattle, in another way.

"I'm sorry if I came across like that. I certainly didn't mean to. I just… I have a lot going on, juggling the possible transition from Seattle to here, the family news I heard about this morning. Perhaps I was a bit antsy, uncomfortable even, being in Doc Bernie's practice again."

"It is weird—the transition, that is. I can't say pediatric oncology prepared me for this type of work."

He chuckled, his armor softening. Something about being in front of Aubrie made him feel he had to be defensive, that he had to explain himself with her more than anyone else he'd ever met. But it felt good to talk with her. A genuine conversation.

"I'll admit, seeing a trauma patient—albeit not quite the magnitude I see—was a bit of a relief."

"I knew it!" Aubrie's fist hit the table. "You wanted the wound to be deeper, didn't you? A real traumatic emergency."

"Now, that's just terrible." His pretend seriousness vanished, and he laughed.

"Doctors are terrible people sometimes." Aubrie took another sip. "We want to save lives, but in order to save lives, we need lives to be in peril."

"There's truth in that."

"Of course there is."

Bran looked at her, wondering if she was being snarky, as if she only spoke in truths. But her smile remained.

"You know, I really am sorry for today. And the other day. I'm starting to realize that maybe not everyone eats up the charm I can dole out."

"You think?" She laughed.

The warmth of it sent fire through his core. He cooled it down with his drink. The last thing he needed was to turn this coworking relationship into a different kind of relationship. Besides, despite her personality softening this evening, that didn't mean she still didn't hold him in the low regard she all but laid out the other night.

"I promise to be on time tomorrow."

Her eyes grew big, and she nodded. "Okay. I'm going to take your word for it."

"You go on ahead because it's true."

"Speaking of tomorrow, any idea what we will be busy with?"

Bran shook his head. "I thought about what the heck it could be. Some special holiday here, or event. I can't think of anything. I mean, what would keep that place busy?"

"You don't want me to answer that, speaking of patients needing to be in peril."

His mouth hung open. "Look at you. There *is* a bit of a devil in you after all."

"I'm just saying that when a doctor says expect to be busy, you'd assume it's with patients who need you, right?"

"Uh-huh. We'll go with that."

"Shut up." She giggled, and that was it. That feeling again. This was not supposed to be happening. None of this was—him returning home, taking over the practice, disappointing Doc Bernie, having this other person as an alternative that could thwart his plans. Nothing would thwart his purpose here more than a romantic fling.

But Aubrie was different. She saw right through him, from the very instant she met him. No one, no woman, had ever made him feel so uncomfortable, out of place, and well, like such a jerk for doing some of the things he did and saying some of the things he said. There was no hiding with her.

Hopefully, he could do a better job at hiding what he felt in this moment than all of the other things she had figured out about him.

Because that internal gut reaction, those butterflies, that connection... they were hard to hide.

NINE

Tuesday, September 18

TO SAY AUBRIE was surprised with Bran last night would be an understatement. When he peeled off the facade and finally started being real, there was a relatable person in there. They were both highly-trained doctors in difficult specialties, and shared similar experiences. But most of all, he made her laugh. They joked with each other, and he could take the jabbing. He wasn't that into himself that it hurt his ego, which contradicted her judgment when they first met.

Although they had agreed to start over yesterday morning, today felt like the actual reboot. She arrived early again for work—too curious about what would keep them busy—to wait out the extra half hour she had after getting ready in the apartment. Even though Edith brushed off Aubrie's offers of help, Aubrie helped out anyway, making sure the rooms were tidy while Edith made copies of a form.

When Bran showed up before Doc Bernie, her heart skipped a beat. "Ah, so you *can* show up on time."

"Excuse me. I'm not on time. I'm *early.*" He grinned slyly. "And I brought some pastries from Crescent Cafe."

"Oh, don't mind if I do." Edith checked out the flaky, buttery goodies in the white box. "Thank you, Bran."

"Yes, thank you," Aubrie conceded. She couldn't help but indulge in a chocolate chip croissant, using her other hand to catch the flaky crumbs before they landed on her blouse.

The windows afforded a view of Doc Bernie hustling down the sidewalk toward the office.

"He's in a hurry." Aubrie looked at Bran, again anxious about what was in store for them.

Doc walked through the front door. "Morning." He eyed them eating the pastries. "Oh, good to see you eating. You'll need that energy."

Bran crossed glances with Aubrie again. "About that, Doc. What exactly are we doing today?"

Doc shook the raindrops off his coat and folded it in half, hanging it over one arm for the time being. "We've got two crews lined up for their annual physicals."

"Two?" Bran's shocked face worried Aubrie.

"Crews?" Aubrie was confused.

"Fishing crews." Bran stuffed his hands in his pants pockets.

"That's right," Doc Bernie said. "It's hard to get them to come in for checkups throughout the year due to their schedules. So, when they know they'll be in town, I just go ahead and make it a day."

"But two?" Bran asked. "I'm hoping the smaller boats?"

"*Harpeth Rose* and—" Doc clicked his fingers, as if the sound activated his memory. Aubrie caught a slight shake in them. Perhaps he was anxious for the busy day ahead. "*Midnight Gully.*"

Aubrie shook her head almost in sync with Bran's reaction.

"Why are you shaking your head?" Bran asked.

"I've heard the name *Harpeth Rose* a lot since arriving. I met one of the crew members, Cynthia, at Doc's party." She grabbed a napkin to wipe the butter off her hands. "Why were you shaking your head?"

"You've heard about *Harpeth Rose* because it's the most famous fishing vessel in Maiden's Bay. And I was shaking my head because it's one of the longest, with the largest crew."

"Shouldn't be too bad. Twenty or so patients today."

"Twenty?" Aubrie calculated the time in her head. Depending on the extent of the physical, and if any of them had underlying conditions to go over, each one could take twenty minutes or more. That was nearly seven hours of work right there.

Edith waved the stack of papers in her hand. "I made twenty-five copies of our standard physical form, just in case."

"I can't imagine it'll be worse than a busy night in Seattle, Bran. Or full day's work in Dallas." He looked at Aubrie.

"No, I guess not," Aubrie agreed. "But the earlier they get here, the better."

As if on cue, three people entered the practice. The oldest wore a purple UW cap, his unshaven face sporting stubble a few days old. The man beside him had lighter hair, but a thick beard, and wore boots over his sweatpants. The third was none other than the woman Aubrie had met Saturday night.

Aubrie approached her. "Cynthia, you didn't tell me you'd be in this week."

Cynthia smiled. "I didn't know myself. Captain told me last night that since we're all here, we need to have our physicals."

"Personal policy," the older one said. "I like to make sure everyone stepping on my ship has the okay from Doc, here."

Doc Bernie shook hands with the man. "I hope you'll entrust your crew with my two proteges."

"If you trust them, that's good enough for me."

Doc turned around. "Nick Campbell, this is my grandson, Doctor Bran Jackson, whom you may already know."

Nick touched the brim of his cap briefly in greeting. "I believe we've crossed paths here and there."

Bran nodded in agreement.

"And this is Doctor Aubrie Turnbridge."

Aubrie reached out a hand and shook the rough, strong hand of Nick Campbell.

"This is my brother Ben, and it sounds like you know our greenhorn, Cynthia, already."

The greetings ended, and they stood in awkward silence. Nick rubbed the back of his neck. "We thought it best if we arrived in smaller shifts instead of all at once. My crewmembers don't particularly like waiting around."

"Which is ironic," Ben said, "since that's most of what we do on the ship."

"Yeah, when you've chosen where to set pots," Cynthia chimed in. She lightly elbowed Ben, who sneered at her in jest.

"All right, let's not keep our patients waiting," Doc Bernie said. "Nick, I can see you in my office. Ben and Cynthia, go ahead and pick a room."

Aubrie was about to offer to take Cynthia when Doc spoke up. "Aubrie, go with Cynthia. Bran, Ben."

Aubrie was certain Cynthia wouldn't have cared who performed the physical. She had to live with a group of men for days on a ship, after all. The things Cynthia had to see or hear were outside of Aubrie's imagination. But when there's a woman doctor available, why not make her a little more comfortable? At least Doc Bernie had the same idea, which made Aubrie feel better.

The first round of physicals took about as long as Aubrie had anticipated. Another five men were in the waiting room when Aubrie and Bran finished around the same time. They each took another, and as the day went on, it seemed like the crewmembers multiplied.

She worked as fast as she could while remaining thorough. Some of the men explained the physicality of their jobs, and the extent wasn't lost on Aubrie. She agreed with Captain Nick. No one should be out on the boat doing that kind of work if they had any major issues to worry about.

By one o'clock, Aubrie's stomach growled. The pastries Bran had brought were long gone, which Aubrie guessed were consumed by the waiting patients. She went out to the lobby for the next patient, catching Bran in the middle of a conversation with one of them.

"We just want to be able to see all of you today. I know you won't want to have to reschedule."

"Take one of these others." The young man pointed to the other three waiting.

"What's going on?" Aubrie asked.

The young man's hostility melted into a smile.

Bran huffed, turning to Aubrie. "This fine gentleman insists on being your patient."

Aubrie eyed Bran. For a second her stomach turned. It wouldn't be the first time a creepy man tried to get close to her. Being in med school, especially at that younger age, there were men who made snide remarks and even tried to touch her during rounds. She appreciated Bran's effort to talk the patient into being seen by him.

Aubrie looked over the patient. Nothing screamed ax murderer or creep externally. In fact, his five o'clock shadow gave him a handsome ruggedness, and he glanced at her with a little embarrassment.

"It's fine," Aubrie said. "I can take him."

"Are you sure?" Bran raised his eyebrows, genuinely concerned.

She leaned closer, whispering in his ear. "I'll knock on the wall if I'm in any trouble."

Bran hesitantly nodded and accepted the next patient to volunteer.

Aubrie signaled for the young man to follow. "Your name?"

"Garrett Philhouse."

"Doctor Turnbridge. But you can call me Aubrie."

He nodded and smiled as they entered the exam room. Garrett took off his worn ball cap. He sported a longer cut, a few locks having escaped the confinement of the hat before taking it off. He ruffled his hands through it. Indeed a handsome man.

But Aubrie needed to get through this. She instructed him to change into the gown and returned a few minutes later. She nearly broke in laughter at the site of the man—handsome eyes, gorgeous hair, and at the bottom of his legs, green socks with a pattern of brown fish on them.

"Those are some socks." She inspected them closer. "Bass?"

"Trout. I go fishing on my off-time, too."

"Hmm. I've never been good at identifying fish."

"I can teach you." He gave a smile again, and Aubrie refocused on the task at hand. "I'm sorry," he said. "If I made you feel uncomfortable. That wasn't my intention. It's just that—well, when I saw you, you kinda took my breath away."

Aubrie felt her face reddening by the second.

"I just thought, I have to talk to her. I couldn't leave here thinking I didn't even bother to introduce myself."

Aubrie exhaled, her nerves feeling a little more at ease. The patient, however, remained quiet, perhaps embarrassed with his words.

She performed the exam, listening to his chest, checking his ears and throat, pulse and blood pressure.

"Well, looks like you're a healthy twenty-eight-year-old. Let Nick know you've got the okay from me."

He nodded.

"You can change back and leave whenever you're ready."

"Yes, ma'am."

Aubrie filled out the rest of the physical form and handed it to Edith to enter into the system. Garrett walked out of the room and headed for the lobby, Aubrie not far behind to call back the next patient.

"Okay," she said to the three men waiting.

Bran arrived at her side, giving her a nod. She knew it was a question—asking if she was okay.

"It was fine," she said.

"I'm sorry." Garrett turned away from the front door. "I'm usually not this forward, but… I was wondering.…" He took off his hat again, ran his hand through his hair. "Would it be too much to maybe go out for some coffee or a drink or something some time?"

One waiting patient whistled, while another let out an "ooo."

"Come on, give the guy a chance," the whistler said.

"He's a good one, that Garrett," said the other.

Aubrie was flattered, staring at her feet before looking up at Garrett again.

"You're not actually considering this?" Bran said, out of the corner of his mouth.

Aubrie wondered if his expression was that of being appalled or… was it jealousy?

"You're new in town, right?" Garrett asked. "Maybe we can go for a walk, show you the town?"

Aubrie bit her bottom lip. Dating was not something she anticipated doing here. Nor was competing with another doctor for the position. But she didn't know many people. And despite the initial awkwardness, Garrett had only been polite and sincere. It didn't hurt how good looking he was.

"Okay."

The men waiting cheered, and Garrett stood there with a grin.

"Call Edith, she'll give you my number."

Garrett nodded and left with an extra bounce in his step.

"I can't believe you agreed to that," Bran said.

"Why not? Am I not allowed to meet people? Go on a date here and there?"

Bran's chest swelled with his deep breath.

"Besides, aren't you supposed to call… Macy, is it?"

Bran held up a hand. "That's an entirely different situation."

Aubrie chuckled. "I couldn't agree more."

Bran's expression turned scornful, though he didn't hold it for long. "It's different because she's not my patient."

"Neither is Garrett. For all I know, this was just a one-time exam."

Bran huffed a few seconds more before calming down. "All right. Do what you want. But don't say I didn't warn you."

"Warn me? About what?"

He leaned in closer to her, his whispering breath tickling her neck. "These fishermen. They're different. Yeah, they're tough, but fishing will always come first with them."

"Several of the men were wearing wedding bands. Including Ben and Nick. Cynthia even told me Nick is married to that news lady I met, Josie."

"So, you were scoping out Captain Nick, then, too?"

Aubrie's jaw dropped, and she let out a scoff. "No, I was *not*. I'm observant, that's all. My point is, many of these guys are married, and it works out for them."

"Well, just be prepared to hear more than you want to know about crabs and squid and fish. Pretty gross if you ask me."

"I didn't ask you, did I?"

The men waiting eyed the two of them. Aubrie wondered if they heard every word.

"I just want you to be aware. They're not here all year."

"That can be a good thing."

"They come and go on their own schedule, and you'll have no say." He shrugged.

"Where is this coming from?" Her voice grew louder than a whisper.

"Just someone I knew."

Aubrie's eyes grew wide. "I think I see now. This is about you, isn't it? Let me guess. You dated someone, or wanted to, but they ended up dating a fisherman. Am I close?"

Bran cleared his throat, adjusting his lab coat around his collar. "That's silly. It was a high school into college thing. Went our separate ways. You know, why am I telling you this? It doesn't matter."

Aubrie bit her tongue, but her grin wasn't so easily concealed. Bran had been hurt. Who knew he had it in him? But this wasn't all about him. He was concerned for her wellbeing. He had enough respect for her that he didn't want to see her hurt.

And no matter what her past thoughts on Bran were, she had to admit that she was flattered.

TEN

DOC BERNIE HAD been correct. The day was long—one continuous chain of walking patients to and from the exam room, going through the process of the physical, filling out the form, and doing it all over again. Bran hadn't even realized they'd gotten to the second crew until mid-afternoon, when he had said something about Captain Nick and the crewman corrected him.

The time was quickly approaching five o'clock, and Bran needed to wrap this up. He walked his latest patient back to the front lobby, and luckily no other patients were waiting. Doc and Aubrie were still with theirs.

"Could that be the end of it?" he asked.

Edith looked up from her desk. "Looks to be." She let out a sigh, her relief on par with Bran's. "I can lock the door while we have the chance." She giggled.

Bran checked his watch again. He didn't want to leave prematurely, but he also didn't want to be late for his appointment. It was tough enough convincing a lawyer to stay at the office after five and charge the standard rate.

Doc Bernie's office door opened, and the man spoke a little too loudly to his patient. "And that's when he said, but it's not mine, it's my wife's!"

Both men broke out in laughter, and the patient shook Doc Bernie's hand before walking out into the lobby. The patient nodded to Bran, who nodded back, and then he left the practice.

Doc Bernie handed Edith a clipboard, then stretched and fisted his hand quickly before slipping it into his pocket. "All done for the day?"

"I believe so," Bran said. "I think Aubrie's finishing up with the last patient."

"Very good. This would've been a three-day event had you two not been here this week."

Bran faintly smiled. "Happy to help." Though now he needed to get going, and fast. "Anything like this planned for tomorrow, or anytime soon for that matter?"

"No, no. This was something special, and again, I'm glad it could be done while I had your help. As for tomorrow, who knows what it will bring."

Edith raised her hand. "Three patients are scheduled for checkups."

"Oh, well, there you go." Doc Bernie smiled.

Bran didn't want to seem in a rush, as if the small-talk wasn't important, but it was hard not to look in a rush when one was indeed exactly that. "I guess I'll be off for the evening, then?" He wasn't going to leave without Doc Bernie's okay. Even if it meant the attorney had to wait.

Aubrie's voice carried out of the hallway, and she arrived in the lobby with her last patient. "Have a good evening."

"You, too." The man put on his coat and left the office.

"Yeah, that should be okay." Doc Bernie gave him the go ahead.

"Headed out already?" Aubrie asked.

"Well, funny thing," Bran said. "This patient, James I think his name was, asked me out for a drink."

Aubrie shook her head. She was smiling, though, so she didn't take it too seriously. "Very funny."

Bran returned the smile but snapped back to his plans. "No, I do have something scheduled, so I'd better get going."

"Okay." Aubrie's glance turned to her feet. Was that a hint of disappointment? Had she expected—heck—*wanted* to spend time with him?

Edith got up from her desk. "I'd better get to tidying up back there. You have a good night."

"You, too. To all of you." Bran put on his jacket, quickly checking for the presence of the envelope he'd tucked inside, and walked out of the front door with a brief wave to the other three. The cloudiness gave a darkness to the early evening hour. He popped his collar slightly and raised his shoulders, his ears and neck getting the brunt of the September wind bite.

His thoughts walking along Pearl Avenue wandered from the day's busyness to Aubrie. He had definitely caught something from her reaction to him leaving. But she was asked out by one of the men today and had agreed to see him. So, why would she be disappointed if Bran was going somewhere without her tonight?

Maybe she simply viewed him as a colleague. Or a friend. That was a good thing, right? Yet why did either label not sit right with Bran? What exactly did he expect from her?

He threw the thoughts away for another time. He checked behind him as he turned away from the sea and worked up the hill for two blocks. The office of Mitch Henderson sat on the corner of N Street and Falmouth Drive, near the outskirts of the main set of businesses in town. Yep, two blocks wide, up the hill, was enough for Maiden's Bay's shops. Not many people wanted to roam about town window shopping if they had to go too far from the flat portion of Pearl Avenue.

Not that he thought Doc Bernie or Aubrie would've followed him, but he didn't want them to see where he was headed. If they did, then they might ask questions, the answers of which were not exactly good no matter how he'd try to frame them.

He peeked into the front windows of the law office, the lights still on, thankfully. If Mr. Henderson had canceled, Bran would have to make up another excuse to either miss in the morning or leave work early.

He walked in, the dark cabinetry and carpeting like that of an Ivy League library. A dark-haired woman, a few years younger than him, sat at a desk in the lobby. Her hair was tied back in a sleek ponytail, and she held up a finger for him to wait as she spoke on the phone.

"No, I am aware. Mmmhmm. Yes, tomorrow. Have a good evening." She hung up the receiver and stood, straightening her gray jacket matching her pencil skirt. "For your sake, I hope you're Mister Jackson." She reached out, and Bran shook her hand.

"Yes, Bran."

"Chloe Reynolds."

"Are you meeting with me?"

"Oh, no. I focus mostly on maritime law. It'd be a bit of a reach for your needs."

Bran nodded. "I see."

"But go on back. Mister Henderson has been expecting you."

"Thank you. Nice to meet you."

"Likewise." Chloe grabbed her purse and headed for the front door.

The fact no one was in the office besides him and Mitch Henderson fluttered his insides. It's not that he wanted this meeting to happen. He needed it to happen. That didn't mean he'd like it.

Bran approached a door matching the rest of the dark wood. It sat slightly ajar, and he knocked before stepping any closer.

"Come in."

He entered the office, situated in the back corner of the building. The window facing north let in the little evening light remaining, unlike the east window covered by Roman shades.

Mr. Henderson stood, a sleek, thin man a good two inches taller than Bran's five-foot-eleven. The sleekness carried through his frame to his face and even down to his nose. He had the lanky body type of a basketball player, though judging from the framed pictures, model airplanes, and Civil War history books on the shelves, he wasn't much of a sports guy.

"You must be Bran Jackson." The men shook hands. "Nice to meet you. Mitch Henderson."

"Thanks for meeting me like this." Bran took a seat in front of the desk following Mitch's lead. He fixated on a framed photo of the man, in a woven top and large headdress, amid many others dressed in the same fashion.

"Coast Salish," he said.

"Excuse me?" Bran diverted his attention back to Mr. Henderson.

"Coast Salish on my mom's side, many generations back."

There were several descendants of many tribes living in the area, some more known than others. Bran had heard of Salish, considering the Salish Sea bore their name.

"How about we get to it?" Mr. Henderson shifted two binders from the side of his desk to the middle. "I did much of the preliminary work you asked for." He opened a binder and turned it around for Bran to see. "It took some digging, but I got lucky with your grandfather's accountant, who owed me a favor. I've laid out the estimated value of the property, equipment, furniture, payroll info, the trajectory of the pool of patients, et cetera." He pointed to a number at the bottom of the list in bold. "That is the estimated valuation of the practice."

Bran nodded, the number about fifty grand more than what he estimated offhand.

"Of course, this doesn't include estimates of intangibles."

"Intangibles?"

"Loyalty of patients, for one. Doc Bernie practicing on Sundays even though officially the practice is closed. Those kinds of things can add up. Also, with you being a trauma surgeon, that could potentially add quite the asset, not to mention how much that would do for this town to have someone like you so close by." Mr. Henderson leaned back in his chair. "That is, if you mean to expand the practice and use those skills."

He waited for Bran's reaction, but Bran had no intention of telling this attorney his plans. It was on a need-to-know basis, and Mr. Henderson need not know.

"All of this laid out, I should say, is under the assumption you will resume what the practice already is. So, of course, any changes will affect that bottom number."

"I understand." Bran briefly scanned the itemized list again. "And transferring it to my name?"

"That's a grayer area. Without speaking with your grandfather, I'm not sure what his intentions are. I can only guess that if he's not outright selling you the business up front, then he will ask for a percentage moving forward." Mr. Henderson shrugged. "Or maybe he'll gift it to you for all I know."

Gifting would be the optimal scenario, but Bran didn't want Doc Bernie to go without supplemental income during his retirement. Certainly he expected some sort of monetary compensation for handing it over.

"And let's not forget, all of this is contingent upon Doc Bernie choosing you as his successor."

It was the first acknowledgment of Aubrie, of someone else within finger's reach of owning the practice, and it tightened Bran's throat.

"Oh, don't be so surprised," Mr. Henderson said. "I know about that bit of competition he has you two undergoing. Announcing at his birthday party set that in motion. Too many gossip worker bees there to not spread the word wide." He leaned forward, elbows on his desk. "Can I ask you a personal question? Not lawyer to client, but with that confidentiality attached."

Bran sucked in a breath. "Sure."

"Do you really want this place? The practice?" He leaned back again, this time placing his hands on his head, elbows spread out like wings. "I know we don't personally know each other, but I know of you. You left town, became a successful trauma surgeon at a prestigious hospital in Seattle. I mean, why, of all the places and occupations to change to, you choose this family practice in Maiden's Bay?"

Bran opened his mouth to sound a canned response, but Mr. Henderson wasn't done.

"I mean, if it was about loyalty to family, there wouldn't be competition, would there? The fact your grandfather has you vying for this against a stranger, someone from halfway across the country… sounds to me like he doubts the strength of the family ties."

It was too much to listen to. The fact he was relying on Doc Bernie's trust, their familial connection, made it worse. Bran was playing off of it to secure his place in the world, or at least that of the trauma center at Seattle University Hospital. He had kept the secret long enough and wanted to shout it out to this attorney he'd known for a few minutes. He needed this practice to hand it over to the Seattle University Hospital system, which was looking to expand its program of creating smaller community centers across the state. That Bran was an asset not only with his skills, but was able to procure a new location that already had the lion's share of patients in town. That patients with further needs could then be transferred to Seattle, rather than the smaller, local hospital in White Bend.

Not that he was guilty of what triggered his probation. But surely with this practice under his belt, the university would not hesitate to reinstate his position and let him continue to rise in the ranks at the hospital.

But all of that involved, to put it as it should be put, screwing over his grandfather. There was no way of sugar-coating it. He would betray Doc Bernie's trust and create a larger rift between himself and the family. Himself and the town. It would be a blow to the town to hurt Doc Bernie. Bran couldn't ever come back after that.

There was an added layer now, which his thoughts pulled him to as he sat in the attorney's office of Mitch Henderson. And that was of Aubrie Turnbridge. The woman whose trust in him was building, the woman who occupied his thoughts more frequently and raced his heart.

Mr. Henderson awaited an answer, and Bran pulled up the closest lie to the truth he could muster. "Because I couldn't not choose this practice. That's why."

Mitch handed over the binder, his face blank. Why did Bran care what he thought? He was paying for this man's services, and the relationship was purely transactional. Bran carried the binder to the front door, Mitch seeing him out.

"Have a good evening."

"You, too."

Bran exited, stopping on the sidewalk down the street when he reached the first blue mailbox. He retrieved the two sheets of paper from the binder that were required and placed them in the stamped envelope with the other materials he'd gotten ready this morning. He looked side to side, as if someone were to catch it was addressed to Seattle University Hospital Health Care Real Estate Group and rush over to stop him. He slipped it in the box, double-checking it disappeared from the metal door.

As he walked away, he couldn't help feeling the envelope wasn't the only thing he'd left behind.

ELEVEN

Wednesday, September 19

AUBRIE WOKE UP confused and a little disappointed in herself. Disappointed because she agreed to go out on a date with Garrett, someone she had known for a whole five minutes. On the one hand, she wasn't here to date, and such personal drama could affect her focus on the practice. On the other hand, she did come here to start a new life. Why couldn't dating be a part of that?

The confusion hit worse than the disappointment. She should've been flattered with Garrett's compliments, yet Bran's jealousy stuck in her head. How was she supposed to interpret that? Was it simply her competitive spirit, finding amusement in the fact she was asked out in front of him? Or was it something deeper?

"No matter." Her breath emanated in the air in a white wisp, the morning greeting her with a bite. She was thankful for the limited exposure as she entered the office. The lights were on, and Edith was busy at her desk.

"Good morning." Edith looked up over her glasses. "May want to keep that jacket on." She turned her sights toward Doc Bernie's door.

Aubrie pulled her halfway-off jacket back on her shoulders. "Why? What's going on?"

"Good morning!" Doc Bernie clapped loudly. Aubrie was beginning to see it was one of his habits whenever he had news or wanted to guide the discussion. "Special assignment for you today."

"Something to do with outside, I take it?" Aubrie glanced at Edith for confirmation.

"A house call," Doc said. "Grace Donchik."

Edith grabbed a bag behind her desk and a file folder, handing both to Aubrie.

"She's a patient of mine with a heart condition. I check on her every one to two months. She lives a bit of a ways away, and I don't feel comfortable having her drive out here on her own."

Aubrie skimmed through her file. "She lives by herself?"

"She has two sons that visit on and off."

"Husband passed away last year, poor thing." Edith shook her head, melancholic eyes behind her glasses.

"Cardiovascular syncope," Aubrie read. She flipped through the pages, checking out the meds and history. "She's had several episodes in a short period of time." She looked up at Doc. "Has she been to a cardiologist?"

Doc let out a long sigh. "Well, Grace isn't exactly, how do I put this kindly…?"

"She's doctor averse." Edith followed up with a strong nod.

"That's one way to put it." Doc Bernie opened his hand, wriggling his fingers. Aubrie wondered if the colder air stiffened his joints. "I keep telling her to. I suspect it's heart valve disease. You'll hear for yourself, most likely."

"That's quite serious." Aubrie was no cardiologist, but she knew enough to know the severity of the issue.

"Maybe she'll take to you better than me."

Aubrie had her share of difficult patients. More so difficult parents of patients. Ones who downplayed their child's diagnosis, or didn't believe in the possibilities of modern medicine and how they could be helped. It was frustrating to say the least, but a part of the job.

The front door opened, and Bran breathed into his hands. "Whoo, first real bit of a fall blast out there."

"Cold front," Edith said. "It'll last only a day or two."

"I don't know why I bother with a smartphone when you're around, Edith." He winked at her, and Edith turned a darker pink than her pale blush.

"Don't get too comfortable." Doc Bernie grinned. "You can join Aubrie on the house call."

"House call? People still do those things?" Bran looked at Aubrie, who could only give him a shrug. "You have a black medicine bag?"

Aubrie waved the red duffel bag in her hand.

"Should we prepare to be ready for bloodletting, too?"

Aubrie chuckled, but Doc Bernie didn't seem to appreciate the joke, folding his arms, mouth in a straight line.

"I'll text you the address." Edith typed on her cell phone, and Aubrie heard the ping from her purse. "Aubrie has the file of the patient. Just a simple check-up on her."

Aubrie handed the file over to Bran, her fingers grazing his briefly, sending a warmth through her chest. She hesitated, hand held in the air for a second, meeting Bran's blue eyes.

"Hello? Any other questions, you two?" Doc must've asked the question moments ago, but all sound, breathing, had been blocked out of Aubrie's mind.

She snapped to. "I think we're good. I can call if there's anything we need to ask."

"Good. I'll see you guys this afternoon."

"Afternoon?" Bran asked.

"It's about an hour and a half drive out there. Might as well take your lunch break before coming back to the office."

Aubrie and Bran met stares again, this time Bran breaking it by heading to the door. "I'll drive," he said. "If you're okay with that."

"What about looking over her file?"

"You can give me a summary, right?"

Aubrie scoffed but took it in good humor. Other than the fact that the patient probably needed surgery to fix her problem, the visit should be pretty straightforward.

She accompanied Bran on the walk along Pearl Avenue. "Didn't drive to work?"

"I'm staying at Constance's. Technically Maiden's Slumber Inn, but everyone calls it Constance's. Just up the road."

They passed Crescent Cafe, the aroma of warm buttery pastries a little too enticing, then past Mariner's Market on the corner. Aubrie had come to appreciate, in a short amount of time, having everything she needed a short walk away. Texas was known for big everything, which tended to be true. But that meant sprawl as well, and living in the city there felt far from this experience.

She looked across the street, down a little ways at the Campy's sign. It wasn't lit this early, but she wondered if they didn't want to serve breakfast, or kindly didn't serve breakfast so that other places like Crescent Cafe could take that share of the market. It was the kind of town she could imagine business owners doing such a thing.

Bran turned east onto a side street, and Aubrie followed, the road rising up steeply. "So, you found a place okay?"

"Ah. You ask now that it's"—he pretend-looked at his wrist with no watch—"three days after you kicked me out of the family apartment?"

She *tsked*. At first she didn't feel that bad for claiming her stake in the place—it was where Doc Bernie had assigned her, after all. Where else was she supposed to go? She doubted the job would cover alternative housing costs if she refused the place provided. But after a day or two working with Bran, the guilt escalated. "I'd been meaning to ask."

"I'm just kidding." He nudged her elbow with his. "It's fine. The room is small, but the breakfast is good, and Constance is a sweetheart."

Aubrie was taken aback.

"What?" Bran asked.

"A sweetheart? It's just not the way I've heard you talk about someone before."

"Are you jealous I find a woman to be a sweetheart? A woman who may well be in her hundreds, with plenty of years left in her?"

"That's not what I meant." Her skin flushed with color and heat. So much that she started to doubt what she said was the truth.

"Well, she is, and maybe you don't know me well enough to know how I talk about people." His eyebrows raised as high as his mocking smugness.

"Maybe you're right." He most likely was right. She had judged him before knowing him.

"I'll take that. As good as it'll get from you." He smirked and nodded his head to one side. "Over here."

She recognized his Audi parked in a narrow alleyway next to Maiden's Slumber Inn. He unlocked it, and she sat in the passenger seat.

"Pretty nice car." It definitely was a step, or three, above Aubrie's Accent—Bluetooth device connection, black leather seats. Even the visor had a tech-savvy mirror. All that mattered to her, though, was if a car got her from one place to the next. She knew other doctors who signed new leases every two years on the latest models. It just wasn't her thing.

"It's not my dream car. But it's reliable."

She was surprised to hear the words. "Is that what matters most to you in a car?"

"Doesn't that go for everyone?" He looked at her briefly. "I'll admit, it looks nice, too."

"There we have it. The truth."

They both laughed.

They pulled out of the alley parking, Bran's driving surprisingly cautious. Aubrie connected her phone to the car's display, and they took off heading north. She had never been this far north in Washington State, let alone the country. It was a bit exciting to be out of the office, even if they didn't have time to explore.

"That's not being vain, by the way. Liking nice things. Or wanting nice things."

Aubrie wondered if she was being too hard on him. Probably. Why did she always jump to the worst conclusion with him? "As long as it doesn't interfere with the necessities, I guess there's nothing wrong with that." If she could afford it, would she buy a car like this? Maybe.

"Is there even a road to get to this place?" Bran zoomed out on the monitor's map, getting a better look at the destination. "She is a bit of a ways, isn't she?"

"I barely know Maiden's Bay and almost nothing up this way."

"I almost forgot you're not from here."

"Is that a good thing? Like, I fit in well here?"

"Depends on what you think of the local folk." He grinned, then turned his focus back on the road. They crested the northern curve of hill that closed off Maiden's Bay from the rest of the world. Bran followed the directions, turning east. The landscape changed from a few rough hills to rolling greenery. She had heard the rain helped Seattle stay green, with some of the best flowering displays in spring. This area didn't look too far off from what she pictured, the road cutting through forests of hemlock and firs, cedars and pines, but without any city in sight.

"They're good people, for the most part," Bran said. "Locals."

Aubrie nodded.

"I say for the most part because, well, my dad wasn't the best at being a dad, if you know what I mean. But I can't blame that on the town. I guess we'll know for sure soon enough. He's moving down to Florida. That was that big thing he had to tell me on my first day with you and Doc at the clinic."

"So, that's why you were late."

"Yeah. In typical Dad fashion, not only could he not get back in time for Doc's birthday party, but he had to cut into my work time to tell me the news."

"Well, despite how it was delivered, I'm sure it was big news for your family."

"Big news for anyone in town, really. It's not a frequent occurrence to lose people that grew up in Maiden's Bay, especially ones still with family there."

"Do you understand why that is? I mean, I haven't been here but a minute, but even I can see the benefit of a small community."

Bran looked at her, a warm smile growing. "I'm starting to understand better."

The look set off a fire in her, and she did what she could to quell the flame.

Diversion.

"It is pretty isolated out here. I'm getting to understand why Missus Donchik sees Doc Bernie."

"Not a whole lot of medical care to speak of out here. Actually, the hospital I work for, Seattle University Hospital, has started an initiative to open up clinics in these smaller communities." His face turned… different. As if the fact he just shared upset him in some way.

"That seems like it could be good. Then again, if patients like Missus Donchik aren't willing to listen to people like Doc Bernie, they may not take well to professionals coming from Seattle."

"Yeah." He said it faintly, as if his stomach turned sour and he wasn't feeling well.

They were the last words spoken until they pulled into a long, narrow dirt road leading through farmland. A two-story white house sat far back on the property, a matching white fence lining both sides of the road all the way back.

"Oh, shoot. I guess I should've asked for the summary of our patient. Missus…?"

"Donchik. Grace Donchik."

"Grace. Okay."

"She's shown signs of cardiac syncope, with several fainting spells. Doc has tried a series of medications to help prevent recurring episodes. Currently, she's on a beta blocker."

"Any cause found?"

Aubrie shook her head. "From what Doc said, I don't think she's seen a cardiologist."

"Jesus." Bran stared off ahead, as if his thoughts went well past the dashboard. "I know she's out here, but some of the world's best cardiologists are right there in Seattle."

Aubrie shrugged. "Doc was hoping maybe we could convince her to be seen? But it sounds like an uphill battle."

"Yeah, I know the type."

"So, you have them in the trauma unit as well?"

Bran turned to her, slowing the car. "Are you kidding? On one end, we get the patients who think we can literally attach any body part back on to perfection. On the other end are patients who don't want us to touch a goddamn thing. Never mind having their chest impaled with a javelin."

The picture in her head sucked the breath out of her. "Man. A simple yes would've sufficed." She chuckled but also wondered if that happened for real, and if so, how the heck did it happen?

Bran pressed on the brakes, and Aubrie jolted forward, bracing the dashboard.

"What was that for?" She looked at him, his stare focused on something ahead.

"Grab the medical bag. Quick."

Aubrie turned her eyes to the front of the car. A young man was running toward them, arms flailing in the air for their attention.

She looked back at Bran, adrenaline coursing through her veins.

"Looks like Missus Donchik won't need convincing."

Aubrie's hand gripped a strap of the red duffel bag tight as she bolted out of the car.

TWELVE

BRAN RAN NEXT to Aubrie along the dirt drive toward the house. The young man was faster than either of them, gunning to the left as they neared the front porch. A garden of leafy greens and tomatoes sat to the side of the house, four boxes neatly soiled and cared for.

A gray-haired woman slumped on the ground between two of the boxes, holding a fist to her chest.

"My goodness." Aubrie dropped to the ground next to the woman and opened the duffel bag.

Bran's breathing from the running was fast, but the sight of the woman in cardiac distress tightened his chest. His face felt on fire, and he couldn't get enough air in his lungs.

"I take it this is Grace Donchik?" Aubrie looked up at the young man, a thin guy wearing cargo pants and a sweater one size too big with the sleeves rolled up.

"Yes, ma'am."

"And you are?"

"Tim. Timothy Donchik."

"Okay, Tim. I'm Doctor Turnbridge, and this is Doctor Jackson. We were sent on a house call by her doctor, Doc Bernie. Can you tell us what happened?" Aubrie grabbed the stethoscope, eyeing Bran. He stood frozen, his breath uncatchable.

"I'm visiting for a few days, and she asked me to help with the garden. She was fine for maybe ten minutes, and then…." He shrugged. "She just yelled out and rolled on her back."

Aubrie changed the position of the scope from the woman's back to the chest. "How long ago?"

"Couldn't have been a minute before you arrived. I was running to the house to call for help when I saw your car pull up."

"Bran? Wanna help here? Take blood pressure?" Aubrie stared, but Bran barely registered. The woman's face morphed right in front of him, a heftier, younger woman. The white house and garden vanished, replaced by the tile floor of the diner, the glossy menus, and smell of burnt coffee. Screaming out, a man holding him back, others hovering over the limp body.

The hallucination sucked out the last bit of air in his lungs. His legs buckled, and he fell to the ground, his name a muffled shout in the distance.

It must've only been for a few seconds.

He opened his eyes, blinking away the blackness.

The young man's fingers pressed against Bran's neck.

"What—what are you doing?" He swatted Tim's hand off of him.

"We lost you there," Aubrie said.

"Sorry. I'm okay." He sat up, head pounding and mouth dry.

"Tim, why don't you get him a glass of juice? Or soda? Something with some sugar in it."

Tim nodded and ran off.

"You okay?" she asked.

"I'm fine. Just give me a minute. How's our patient?"

Mrs. Donchik still clutched her chest, but her breathing leveled out since their arrival.

"She needs to get to a hospital," Aubrie said. "At least have an EKG, Echo."

"Is she stable enough to move her?"

"Are *you* stable enough to help move her?" The worry in Aubrie's eyes killed Bran. It was embarrassing, fainting like that. It had been a while since the last time he was reminded of her, of seeing what he had seen, and it overtook him.

"I told you, I'm fine."

Tim appeared with a glass of orange juice.

"Drink it," Aubrie ordered.

"I'm not diabetic or anything." He took the glass anyway, seeing as his mouth felt like it was cracking under its parchment. That and not wanting to fight Aubrie over a glass of orange juice.

"Tim, your grandmother really needs to go to a hospital. There's not much here we can do to help her, and I'm afraid she'll have another spell sooner rather than later."

Tim nodded. "Should I call an ambulance?"

Bran stood, legs a little shaky, but he did his best to hide it from Aubrie. "By the time they get here and take her back to a hospital, we could've done it ourselves."

"I can drive, then." Tim asserted himself with a nod. "Where to?"

Bran eyed Aubrie, but then remembered he was the local expert here. She wouldn't know what was closest or best for Mrs. Donchik, who now sat upright, having her back lightly rubbed by Aubrie.

Bran weighed the options. They could drive an hour back to the west, to take her to White Bend Hospital, but they didn't exactly have a stellar cardiac unit. Even though the alternative turned his stomach, it was the best option.

"Seattle University Hospital. It's half an hour's drive longer than going to White Bend, but they have one of the best cardiology teams in the country."

"Can you stand?" Aubrie helped Mrs. Donchik to her feet. Once there, the patient gained her confidence back.

"I'm not going anywhere," Mrs. Donchik said. Her voice was shaky, but held an authority to it. "Tim and I are going to finish with the gardening."

"Gram, these doctors—"

"I don't care what these doctors say." She wriggled out of Aubrie's loose grip.

Tim approached her, stopping directly in front of her. "Gram, listen to me. I just witnessed you buckle over, not being able to get back up. You couldn't stand, walk, or communicate with me. Now, I don't even like digging the soil for the seeds. Do you think I want to have to dig your grave?"

Bran eyed Aubrie. You never knew who or what could reach a stubborn patient, but he hoped for Mrs. Donchik's sake, it was her grandson.

"We're going to take you to get tested. If you're fine, we'll be right back. If there's a problem, then it's about time we get it fixed."

Tim and Mrs. Donchik faced off in what looked like a staring contest. A power of wills.

Mrs. Donchik pursed her lips together. A menacing look, Bran would give her that.

Tim didn't back down. Bran felt a hint of pride for the kid, though he had only just met him. And something else—a longing, or a sadness. Would there be anyone in Bran's life to do the same for him when he was older?

"Fine," she said. "But the lady doctor rides with us. I don't trust this one with a pet bunny."

Bran sighed with relief. "I'll follow behind you."

"I don't think so." Aubrie glared at him. "You just stay put."

"Excuse me?" Bran set aside his astonishment at her assertiveness to help Mrs. Donchik in the back seat of the car.

Aubrie buckled the woman up and closed the door. She faced Bran and took out her pen light.

"Oh, please." He deflected with his hands.

"Don't be a baby." She looked at his pupils, then checked his pulse.

"You want to take my blood pressure, too? Check my ears?"

"This isn't funny. You passed out."

"I fainted, and barely. It's not a big deal."

Aubrie stepped closer, close enough to catch the floral aroma of her hair. Hyacinth? Rose water? He had never been great at distinguishing such smells. He just knew it was pleasant and dizzying.

"Taking a lesson in stubbornness from Missus Donchik, are we?"

"No, that's not—"

"Then tell me what happened back there," she said. "And not something like you locked your knees by accident for too long. The truth."

Bran took a deep breath, contemplating how much to tell her. It had been years since he last spoke of it. Heck, he barely spoke about it after it happened. Although he didn't know Aubrie for long, something told him to tell the truth, to let it out. Something other than Aubrie's orders. He looked around to see if Tim was in earshot, but he had moved to the driver's side of the car and started it up.

"My mother," Bran said. "I was there when she had a heart attack. One that she never recovered from."

Aubrie's shoulders slumped, her defiance softening. "And this brought that all back?"

Bran nodded. "I was eight at the time. Not exactly something I wanted to see, or should've seen. We were just out for breakfast, me and her." He couldn't stop his lips from moving, stop the words spewing out. "She was sitting across from me in the booth, and I had asked if she could sit next to me instead. The air conditioning was freezing, and—" The lump in his throat grew. "She got up, and I remember hearing the silverware clink from her hand gripping the table. And then she was on the floor."

Aubrie reached out to his arm with the slightest touch. "I'm so sorry. I didn't know."

"Of course not." His face scrunched in a wince. "Not many people do. It's my fault, really. It's not something that ever feels appropriate to bring up in conversation."

"I get it," Aubrie said. "I really do."

Bran nodded. "The irony is that she's the reason I got into medicine in the first place. Yet I can't handle seeing patients with heart conditions, apparently."

Aubrie smiled mildly, withdrawing the comforting hand. "I won't tell anyone."

Bran wanted to hug her, hold her, do something.

Tim stuck his head out of the car window, eyeing them.

"We'd better go," Bran said.

"Yeah." Aubrie snapped back to the health emergency at present. "Are you sure you're okay to drive?"

"It'd be better than riding in their car. Poor Tim would have to look over two patients." He managed an awkward chuckle.

Aubrie reluctantly agreed with a nod. "You'll tell me if you feel dizzy or sick?"

Bran crossed his heart. "Promise."

Aubrie got in the back with Mrs. Donchik, and Bran walked around to the driver's side.

"You know where you're going?"

Tim gave a thumbs up.

"All right. I'll be right behind you. Doctor Turnbridge here has my cell in case you need me. Otherwise, I'll see you there."

Bran returned to his car and reversed out of the long dirt drive, back to the road. He waited for Tim's car to take the lead, then followed him.

He turned on the heater, not realizing he had been sweating, the dampness in his clothes chilling his skin. He had been honest with Aubrie. His mother's death wasn't something he talked about with anyone. Not his brother. Not even his dad. Or especially his dad. There was always a piece of him that thought Dad blamed him for her death. As if an eight year old could and would purposely cause his mother to have a heart attack. It was just another reason why he and his father didn't tend to get along.

It didn't help that Dad remarried in what felt like record time. As if Mom's life, Mom's devotion to him, meant nothing upon her death.

But Bran vowed to help other people. He didn't want other eight-year-olds to go through what he did. He chose to specialize in the field that saw the worst, most gruesome and damaging injuries. The ones that usually came out of nowhere, that took people by surprise but didn't take their lives. Because he was there to help them.

He hadn't told a soul why he had—not his family, friends. Not even in an admissions essay to get into school. Until today.

Until Aubrie.

He turned the radio on, as if tuning to a station would tune out the thoughts of Aubrie. She had the ability to get the truth out of him, to open him up like cracking an egg, a swift flow of information running out of his mouth. What was it about her that got to him?

As much as he didn't want to linger on thoughts of Aubrie, he certainly didn't want to think about where they were headed. Yes, Seattle University Hospital was the best place in the western half of the United States, if not the entirety of it, for Mrs. Donchik to be examined for her condition. It was also the place he wasn't supposed to be. But he was bringing a patient who was obviously in need of care. What were they going to do?

The thoughts—of Aubrie, of returning to the hospital, of Doc Bernie's practice—they all jumbled into a worry soup, churning his gut and causing the onslaught of a headache. He decided to focus on the car in front of him, a maroon Chevy Cavalier with two holes of rust above the Washington State license plate.

His gaze wandered up to the back window, the silhouette of Aubrie next to Mrs. Donchik. Hopefully, she wouldn't have another incident in the car. Judging by Aubrie's concern, the woman's condition was serious. Aubrie hadn't freaked out or warned Tim how bad it could be but simply stated they needed to go to the hospital. The longer he was around her, the more he saw she was a good doctor. And a good person.

There you go again. Thinking of Aubrie.

As they cruised along I-5, his nerves wavering more, his cell phone rang. Aubrie. He answered through the dashboard monitor.

"Hey, I just wanted to run it by you. Tim was going to drop me off with Missus Donchik and park so we can get her checked in right away. But I didn't know if you wanted to come in with us, if you think that will make a difference?"

It will make a difference all right. Just not the kind Aubrie was thinking of.

"No, that's fine. You go ahead in with her, get the process started. I'll make a call and let cardiology know the situation."

"Okay, sounds good."

It probably did sound good, and best case scenario, Mrs. Donchik would be seen, they'd discover what was causing her issue, and they'd come up with a plan to treat it. Worst case scenario looked much uglier.

He put the greater odds toward the worst case scenario. There was no way of knowing for sure, but he was about to find out.

THIRTEEN

BETWEEN MRS. DONCHIK'S condition and Bran's unexpected passing out at the house, Aubrie's nerves were frayed. The car ride to Seattle University Hospital felt like an eternity. As much as she took in and appreciated the scenery on the way to Grace Donchik's home, she cursed it for never ending, the first hour of driving a monotonous loop that stretched for miles. As they approached the city, excitement and anxiety crept in. Mrs. Donchik had kept alert during the car ride so far and did not put up a fight about where they were going. That didn't mean she wouldn't once they arrived.

Bran's behavior on the phone was indecipherable. He seemed both helpful and hesitant, which could've been because of what he had shared with Aubrie. Experiencing a traumatic event, like the death of his mother at a young age, stayed with a person. Even the patients she had managed to care for through their cancer experience had to deal with the mental health aspect of it for sometimes years afterward.

"Just pull around the ER entrance there." Aubrie pointed to a U-shaped drive in front of the ER's glass sliding doors.

Tim stopped the car and turned around. "All right, Gran. Doctor Turnbridge is going to take you in."

"Where are you going?"

"I'll park and be right in."

"Oh, no, you won't. I'm not going in there without you."

Aubrie met Tim's stare.

"It's okay, Tim. Valet will park." Aubrie got out of the car and waved to the valet driver standing by a podium. The man jumped to attention and jogged to the driver's door. Tim was already at the rear door, helping Mrs. Donchik out of the car.

"Nice and easy," Aubrie said. She didn't know how readily the elderly woman could have another spell. It may have been induced when she got up quickly from gardening for all Aubrie knew. She and Tim helped Mrs. Donchik into the building, and Tim worked out the check-in with as much information as he could provide.

Aubrie eyed the front door for signs of Bran. Maybe it was all too much for him. That he couldn't bring himself inside, be reminded of his mother's death. It tugged at her heart, that he had lived through something like that. But when Bran came running from around the corner into the hospital, her tensed body eased with relief.

And something else that took her by surprise—she smiled at the sight of him. It was absurd what her body did without her permission.

"Doctor Jackson! Long time." The triage nurse stood, a muscular black man half a foot taller than Bran. The two exchanged a friendly fist bump.

"How are you doing, Stan?"

"The question is, how are *you* doing?" The undertone with which he said it implied that something was wrong or had been wrong with Bran. But maybe Aubrie was imagining it.

"Ah, don't worry about me. Right now, we need to worry about Missus Donchik, here."

The patient, already with a hospital armband, was wheeled back through a hallway past a locked door, with Tim accompanying her.

"I'll go," Bran said.

"You sure?" It made sense to Aubrie, since this was his former place of work. But she had to be certain he was in the right mind to help.

Bran clutched her elbows in a gentle grip. "I promise. I know the cardiology team. Let me do what I can."

Aubrie nodded. "I'll call Doc Bernie, let him know what happened."

"Good idea. He'll be curious when we don't show up after lunch." Bran's hands slipped away. He tapped the square button on the wall, giving Stan a nod, and went through the doorway into the hall after Mrs. Donchik.

Aubrie stepped aside, close to the front windows of the waiting room. Around a dozen people waited, not a whole lot considering how big the city was and what she was used to seeing going to work. She didn't always pass the emergency room, but sometimes she took the longer way around the outside of the hospital and would peek in the windows, gauging just how busy they were. Nighttime was the witching hour, at least in Dallas. More car accidents, fights, occupational accidents, alcohol poisoning. If it happened during the day, it happened exponentially worse at night.

She faced the corner of the room and dialed Doc Bernie's office. Edith answered.

"Hey, Edith, it's Aubrie. Is Doc Bernie available?"

"He's in with a patient right now. Is it an emergency?"

"Sort of." Aubrie weighed telling Edith or waiting to tell Doc. Who knew when he'd be done. "You know how we visited Grace Donchik this morning?"

"Of course."

"Well, when we got there, she was on the ground, having an episode. We've taken her to Seattle University Hospital. She consented for me to share her file, and Bran is speaking with the cardiology unit as we speak."

An older man held up by two younger men walked through the glass doors, a staff member assisting them with a wheelchair. The way he clutched his chest suggested a heart attack patient. No knowing how many patients cardiology was dealing with right now.

"Oh my word," Edith said. "Yes, I will let him know right away. I'm sure he'll be happy to know, though, despite the not-so-pleasant circumstances, that you got her to see a specialist."

Of course Edith knew the ins and outs of Grace Donchik. Not only was she present when Aubrie and Doc were talking this morning at the office. But it was Maiden's Bay. Apparently, the remote outskirts were not remote enough to escape gossip's reach.

"Have him give me or Bran a call when he's available."

"I most certainly will. You two be careful coming back, and take your time. At least appointment-wise, this afternoon looks slow."

"Thanks, Edith." Aubrie hung up and slipped the phone in her back pants pocket. She stared at the door leading to the other parts of the hospital, as if Bran would come running through there with good news at any moment. If they were to stay with Mrs. Donchik, this most likely would be an all-afternoon event.

She approached the triage desk a minute after the last patient in line was processed, wanting to see if she had the okay to join Bran and Tim. She stopped when she heard the private conversation happening farther back from the desk.

"I can't believe he's here, though." A female nurse spoke with Stan. Aubrie pretended to ignore their conversation, not staring at either one of them.

"He was with a patient under cardiac duress," Stan said. "What was he supposed to do?"

"I don't know. Go to Seattle General?"

"We both know cardiology here is much better."

"Still," a second woman said. "To have done that, with a *patient* nonetheless, and come back here while on probation? Is he even allowed to be on the property?"

"Probation?" Aubrie blurted out, grabbing the attention of the three gossipers.

"Sorry, is there something we can help you with?" Stan asked.

"Yes, I'd like to know what is going on with Doctor Jackson."

"We can't discuss that," one of the women said.

"Seems like you were okay discussing it a second ago." Aubrie dialed back the snarkiness. "I think I should know. I definitely think his grandfather should know, considering Bran is currently working for him. If he's on probation, we'd need to know why. For the safety of our patients, at the very least."

Stan eyed the two women, no doubt annoyed they had put him in this position with their chitchat.

"He slept with a patient," the second woman blurted out.

"Nancy!" The first woman stared in shock.

"She *does* have a right to know. Don't you think any subsequent employers should be made aware of his behavior?"

"That's not up to us to decide," Stan said.

The woman ignored him. "Not only did he sleep with a patient. He had an ongoing relationship with her."

"Of course, it wasn't secret for long. Once Doctor Hycliff found out, Doctor Jackson was immediately put on probation."

"And the investigation is still ongoing." Stan folded his arms. "We don't know the whole story, although you two would love to condemn the man any chance you can get. Don't think I don't know about your past endeavors with him, Sofie."

Sofie scoffed and rolled her eyes. "It's completely inappropriate. That man is inappropriate and shouldn't be allowed to be around patients. Especially female ones."

"First off, that's a doctor you're speaking about," Stan said. "And he is the best damn trauma surgeon I've seen in my years here."

"That doesn't excuse his indiscretions," Sofie said.

"All around the hospital," the other woman said.

Aubrie's stomach turned. Her first impression of Bran was that he was the type of guy to have his fun and end it when it wasn't fun anymore. But she thought she was getting to know him beyond first impressions. That he was actually a deeper, more thoughtful person. These two nurses had her doubting her judgment all over again.

Whether they told the truth about why the probation happened, and whether those things actually happened, didn't matter as much as the fact that Bran hadn't told her—or likely Doc Bernie—that he was on probation in the first place. Probation was no joke. Worst case scenario, his license could be revoked, and any hopes of practicing in his grandfather's footsteps would be demolished.

Another thought, more concerning, lingered in her head. If he were on probation, that meant he was still employed by Seattle University Hospital. Had he not told them about taking over Doc Bernie's practice? He had said he didn't know about her presence in Maiden's Bay and what Doc Bernie did, pitting them against each other. So, why would he keep his affiliation with the hospital? Maybe probation had to be sorted out first. She was fishing for any logical explanation she could catch.

The thoughts overwhelmed her, swirling in her head to a nearly dizzying effect.

The desk phone rang, and Stan picked it up. "You can go head on back now."

"Me?" Aubrie was pulled back into the moment.

Stan nodded. "Down the hallway. Elevators on the left. Fourth floor is cardiology."

Aubrie was a stew of emotions. She wanted to confront Bran, to find out the truth. She also feared it. As much as she felt leery about Bran upon first meeting him, she didn't feel that way anymore. At least, not until now. She wanted to believe there was more to him, the pieces that she had seen the past few days. Those reflected the true Bran. Not the superficial, fake-facade Bran.

She entered through the door and followed Stan's instructions to the elevator. She pushed the up button and checked her watch. Damn. There was a slim to no chance they'd make it back by closing to Doc Bernie's.

Her stomach sank as the elevator doors opened. She had nearly forgotten about her date with Garrett tonight. It was the last thing she felt like doing, yet canceling didn't sit right. Garrett seemed the type who would understand if something had come up. Heck, he was a fisherman, and from what she'd learned, they didn't have a precise schedule they stuck to outside of when to head out.

It was more important to see how things went over here first. Mrs. Donchik took priority. Not Bran's behavior or probation. Not the date with Garrett. The *patient.*

She shared the elevator with two men in lab coats who stood in silence—too quiet for Aubrie's comfort. Dallas General had been a busy place, but friendly. Most staff greeted each other and engaged in small chitchat. These two made the space feel like a church, or a library, but less enjoyable.

The doors opened at the fourth floor, and Aubrie approached the main desk ahead.

"Can I help you?" a woman asked politely.

"I'm here for Grace Donchik. She's a patient of mine, along with Doctor Jackson. Doctor Bran Jackson." She didn't know why she had repeated his name like that, as if the staff here wouldn't know him, or if there was another Dr. Jackson in the hospital. Perhaps she shouldn't have said his name at all, given the information she learned downstairs.

"She's being assessed right now. Doctor Jackson should be with her around the corner, Room four-thirteen on the right."

"Thank you." Aubrie pulled herself together, rearranging the order of the list in her head of what she wanted to ask Bran. But Mrs. Donchik came first. After that, there were too many questions for Bran.

She approached Room 413. The door was open, a woman standing near it. Mrs. Donchik lay in the bed, hooked up to a monitor, while Tim sat in a chair beside her, holding her hand.

"Sorry, I didn't mean to intrude." Aubrie smiled at the woman. "I'm Doctor Turnbridge. I helped bring Missus Donchik in and brought her file."

"Oh, yes. I'm Doctor Madan." The woman held out a hand, and Aubrie shook it. "Can we talk out here?"

Aubrie agreed, and Dr. Madan stepped into the hallway.

"We are going to run some tests on Missus Donchik. So far, her EKG indicates an irregular heartbeat. With her history, I have my suspicions it's a heart valve defect, but I want to do a thorough workup to make sure." Dr. Madan peeked through the door's window, Mrs. Donchik visible through the sliver. "I will say it's good you brought her here when you did. I can't believe she hasn't been seen by us or any other team until now."

"From what I know, she wasn't exactly keen on coming here. Even after her incident in front of her grandson today."

"Well, we will take good care of her. I don't see reason to stay unless you want to. We have all of the information you've given us, and her grandson is with her."

"Thank you for letting me know. I'll pass on the info to her PCP." Aubrie looked around the hallway. "Have you by any chance seen Doctor Jackson?"

"I haven't seen him since we brought her into the room."

Yelling emanated from farther down the hallway.

"Stop it, you two!" a woman yelled. Footsteps sounded, pounding harder and closer. A woman rounded the bend.

"A fight!"

"What?" Aubrie and Dr. Madan followed the woman around the corner, and they both stopped, in shock at what they were witnessing. Two men were on the ground, yelling, grabbing, clutching, hitting.

Three men in brown scrubs wrestled the fighting men apart.

Dr. Madan looked at Aubrie. "Well, we seem to have found Doctor Jackson."

Aubrie stared down the two men. One in his thirties with dark hair, a bloodied sharp nose, in green scrubs. The other twenty-eight years old, blue eyes and dusky brown hair, with a bloody lip and red splotch near his eye.

"Hey, Aubrie." Bran huffed for breath on the floor, licking his lip. "How's Missus Donchik?"

FOURTEEN

"WHAT IN GOD'S name is going on here?" Dr. Madan demanded.

It was exactly what Bran was worried about, returning to the hospital knowing Doctor Sebastian Hycliff would most likely be here. Although he hadn't expected there to be an actual physical fight.

"Do I need to report the both of you to—"

"No, it's fine." Bran's sparring partner raised a hand, stopping the wrath of Dr. Madan. "Isn't that right, *Doctor* Jackson?"

Hycliff's inflection on "Doctor" indicated he either thought the title for Bran was a joke, or a reminder of how Bran should've been acting. As if the same standard didn't apply to him.

"Yes, Doctor Madan. We're all done here." Bran eyed Hycliff, who was making his way up off the floor, wiping his scrubs and checking his wounds.

Bran could barely look at Aubrie, who folded her arms across her chest, awaiting an explanation. He shuffled himself up off the floor and tipped his head toward the corridor. "Care to update me on Missus Donchik?"

Was it brushing off the fact he had a physical altercation with another doctor? Yes. Did he care about Mrs. Donchik's health? Yes. But he also wanted to speak with Aubrie, away from the others who were around.

Hopefully, he hadn't disappointed her too much. They had been getting along so well up to now. She uncannily got him to open up about Mom, for goodness' sake.

Aubrie sighed. "Let's clean you up."

"I don't want to see anything remotely like this again, you two. Are we clear?" Dr. Madan was not appeased until the two fighting doctors met her gaze and affirmed with a nod.

Bran looped his arm beneath Aubrie's elbow. "Come on." He pulled her away from the scene. He was happy to leave it behind them, but sensed Aubrie's irritation that he took charge now.

"I don't need much cleaning up, do I?" Bran stopped in the hallway, checking out his reflection in a window. It wasn't as useful as a mirror, but good enough to see that his face looked pitiful, the bruise near his eye swelling and a lip twice the size it should be, affecting his speech.

"Speaks for itself, doesn't it?" Aubrie said.

"Fine." He deserved her anger or resentment or whatever negative emotions she felt and cared to dish out. "In here."

He led her to a small examining room, an empty one used for overflow storage near the floor's front desk. There were unopened boxes stacked near the walls, with a sink in the corner and an examining table wheeled to the side next to it. He kept the lights off, the side window allowing enough light in to make out everything but giving the room a blue-gray aura.

Aubrie checked the boxes and cabinets by the sink for anything to help, to no avail.

"There's a real supply closet two doors down." Bran dabbed his lip with the side of his hand.

"Wait right here." Aubrie walked to the doorway and stopped, swiveling back to face Bran. "I don't want to come back and find you in a tussle with someone else, you hear?"

"Yes, ma'am."

Aubrie could procure all the supplies she wanted from that closet, but what his face most needed was ice.

Bran exited the room and worked his way down the hallway, back to the main desk on the floor by the elevators. Two nurses worked behind the desk, with the addition of Dr. Madan. The conversation stopped, and they all glanced up, Dr. Madan resting her fist on her hip while she looked Bran over.

"I was wondering if I could get some ice?" Bran looked at each of the staff members, their mouths unmoving and eyes on him.

"I can get you some." A younger woman stiffly smiled and disappeared through a door behind her.

"You need to vacate the premises immediately," Dr. Madan said. "If Doctor Fredericks finds out what happened, and you're still here with the bruises to prove it…."

Bran knew, no matter how well the facts might be supporting him against probation, that this would be enough to oust him. "I understand. As soon as Doctor Turnbridge patches me up, I'll be out of your hair."

The young woman returned with an ice pack.

"Thank you." Bran gave a nod and hurried back to the makeshift storage room. Despite Dr. Madan's anger—urging him to leave the hospital before Fredericks saw him—was she protecting him? Was she Team Bran in all of this?

Bran washed his hands, trying to wash away the bloody proof as much as he could.

Aubrie returned with gauze, cotton swabs, and antibiotic ointment. "Come sit." She said it with a coolness. An authority to it.

He dried his hands off in paper towels and sat atop the examining table. "How bad does it look, Doc?"

Aubrie pressed her lips tight before answering. "Is this some sort of joke to you? You were in an outright brawl with another doctor." She dampened the cotton balls with the ointment and pressed it to his lip. Bran suspected she didn't feel bad about it burning.

"No, it's not a joke. Although it wasn't exactly unexpected."

Aubrie shook her head, annoyed. "Here." She grabbed his hand and placed the ice pack in it, then guided it to the side of his face. "You're going to tell me what that was all about." She worked through another cotton ball until all of the blood cleared up. "But before you do that, you're going to tell me all about your probation."

The word *sucker* punched Bran in the gut. How much did she know? Had she been talking to staff? He averted her gaze, tipping his head down. She was bound to find out about it, right? Did he really expect she'd step in this building and not hear whispers?

She touched his chin and lifted his head back in front of hers. "Silence is not an option here, Bran." Even with her frustrated, and who knew what else with him, her touch sizzled.

"It was the risk of bringing Missus Donchik here. But I thought I'd take it, as it was her chance at the best treatment."

"What's going on?" That was Aubrie for you. To the point, no frills. No bullshit.

"There was a patient, a young woman. She came in with multiple fractures from a car wreck." He could picture her, blonde hair dampened through with sweat. "She had to undergo multiple surgeries, which meant a lengthier time in the hospital. But over that time, I got to know her better."

"I have a feeling where this is going."

"It's not what you think. Well, not exactly." That was the problem, wasn't it? His prior behavior. Everyone knew of his escapades, his dalliances with this nurse, with that staff member, that woman from the bar. "Nothing happened. Did she flirt with me? Yes. Did I flirt back? Maybe." He shrugged. "I don't know. But I knew not to get involved with patients."

"Did you, now?"

He knew how he was perceived and why. But he took the boundaries of the doctor-patient relationship seriously. "Look. I'll admit that I've had my dalliances here and there among the staff. A nurse or two, physician's assistant. But never have I crossed that line with patients."

Aubrie's confusion read as clear as the red *EMERGENCY ENTRANCE* sign at the front of the building. How could he expect her to believe anything now, when he hadn't told her or Doc Bernie about the probation in the first place?

"What happened?"

Bran shook his head. "It was later. About a week after she was discharged, she contacted me. Came to see me here. I didn't know at the time, and I should've connected the dots, but I didn't."

"Know what?"

"The other guy in the fight, Hycliff? She was his fiancée."

"Oh, Bran."

"Yep. She didn't tell me, and I didn't even question why I saw him stop by her room once."

"So…." Aubrie's hesitation worried Bran. "Something happened, then. Between the two of you?"

"You're asking if we slept together?" He raised an eyebrow, and a slight grin grew. She cared about his answer. He turned serious again. "Just once."

"And this Doctor Hycliff found out."

"Firsthand."

"Oh, Jesus, Bran."

"The thing about it is, obviously, if I knew she was his fiancée, I wouldn't have done it. But that part doesn't matter right now. It was after she had checked out. Outside of the hospital, at her apartment."

"But Doctor Hycliff reported otherwise?"

"He was upset, of course. So he reported that I was having an inappropriate relationship with her during her stay, which carried on after."

"Surely they'd find out that wasn't the truth."

He lowered the ice pack to his lap, the bruise already changing from red to hints of blue and purple. "It's under review currently. But there's another thing you need to know about him. He saw me as competition the first day I walked in here. Not only that, but his family is a bit of a legacy around here. There's a Hycliff Building in the College of Medicine, if that doesn't tell you everything you need to know."

Aubrie's shoulders slumped, and she shook her head.

He knew the weight of it. If there was a worst man to cross, Bran had done it. "Now you see it's an uphill battle."

"Is that why you returned to Maiden's Bay?"

"You can put it that way." He stared at the window. "It sounds cliche, but it's such a dog-eat-dog mentality here. And don't get me wrong, I was all for it. I welcomed the competition, the pushing of each other to get better in our fields, with our skills, our hands, our knowledge. But after a while—"

"It gets old. It weighs on you."

She had said it so quickly, knowingly. He stared at her, holding onto their common understanding.

"I wouldn't think there would be a lot of that in pediatric oncology."

Aubrie raised her eyebrows. "Maybe not so much, but in med school? Sometimes I think I had been so happy to be rid of those shark-infested waters that I didn't fully think of the downsides of pediatric oncology. What it could do for the spirit, for the psyche."

Bran saw in her eyes, the weight she carried was entirely different. But a weight, nonetheless.

"I need to have my name cleared, Aubrie. Whether I end up returning here or not." He stared into her eyes, her gaze fixed onto his. He didn't deserve her gaze, her time. Or the pull he felt ringing him in, pushing them closer. He needed to know she believed his words. "You believe me, don't you?"

Her eyes looked down at her hands. "What matters is what your probation review committee believes."

"That's not completely true." He reached up to her cheek, edging the back of his fingers lightly on her skin. She gasped, the sound knocking the wind out of him. "I care what you believe." It came out in a whisper.

Footsteps sounded in the hallway. Aubrie snapped to, grabbing the ice pack and placing it back near Bran's eye. "We'd better get going."

Bran whipped himself out of the oddly perfect moment. "Yeah, Doctor Madan said as much."

"If it's any consolation, I get the feeling she's on your side."

"Doctor Madan's a good woman. A great doctor."

"Come on."

Bran hopped off the examining table.

"You okay? Dizzy at all?"

"Nah," he said. "He did look worse, though, didn't he?"

Aubrie shook her head and chuckled. "What started it with you two? Did someone throw the first punch, or did the sight of each other throw you into a testosterone frenzy?"

"Hey, now, I'm not one to get into bar brawls."

Aubrie took enough time to stop and give him a look of *yeah, right.*

"I'm not. If anything, I'm too friendly sometimes. You witnessed that when we first met."

She chuckled again. "Okay, maybe you're right on that front. So, what was it?"

Just the thought of Hycliff rounding that corner, giving his sly smirk. He hadn't charged at Bran. He wasn't even angry.

"When he walked by me, he whispered something into my ear."

"A whisper? You're telling me he said something, and that set you off? What was it?"

"He said, 'Don't worry, I put her back in her place.'"

Aubrie gasped, stopping in her tracks.

"Exactly."

"What an *asshole.* Sorry, I'm not big into using that language, but—"

"It's accurate in this case."

"You should report him."

"And then what? The fact that I swung at him first would come out, and then it's over for me."

"He knew that. He knew it would rile you up. Do you think he actually did anything to her?"

Thinking of that man hurting any woman made his mouth taste of bile. "I sincerely hope not." Bran shook his head and met Aubrie's eyes once more. "It's not that I'm in love with her. I was never in love with her. I...." Need to shut up. He didn't want Aubrie to think he had feelings for the former patient. Maybe in the beginning, yes. But Aubrie needed to know that his heart wasn't taken.

No, that wasn't true. His chest felt tight, a compression like Grace Donchik must've felt, his heart under a grip. It quickened his breath, clenched his throat, and hinted at excitement over a paralyzing fear. Walking behind Aubrie, this woman who'd helped him, listened to him, always given him a chance to explain himself, he realized something he'd been denying all this time. Hiding it deep down, not letting it surface, until now.

His heart was taken.

FIFTEEN

THE RIDE BACK to Maiden's Bay felt like an eternity. Aubrie stared out the window as Bran kept the radio on, persistent background noise to overshadow the silence. It wasn't that she hated him, or was even furious with him. She was upset he hadn't said anything about probation and his predicament with Seattle University Hospital. Once she did hear what happened, it was understandable he didn't tell Doc Bernie.

Also wrong of him.

As for the incident with Dr. Hycliff, well, that was unfortunate. Not that she ever condoned violence, but it sounded like the man deserved whatever punches Bran landed.

Now, her behavior with Bran afterward… the intensity in his eyes, his fingers caressing her face. She very nearly kissed the man.

She had to expel that from her thoughts as she showered and readied herself for her date with Garrett. The one-time patient, as she tried to justify it. It was either the last thing she needed after the day's events, or the exact thing she needed.

She leaned toward the former as she straightened her blouse beneath an unbuttoned sweater jacket outside of Iwaki House. They had agreed on something not too formal, a one-story hibachi grill up the hill but toward the middle part of town. The reasons why she had agreed to any of this flew out of her memory. Her nerves begged her to turn back, but her stomach had suffered enough, given she hadn't eaten since breakfast.

For a second, Aubrie thought she had walked into the wrong place.

Three white walls boxed in waiting patrons, a large landscape painting behind the front desk. A short woman with a tight ponytail greeted her.

"Hi. I'm meeting someone." Aubrie peeked around the corner, the sizzle of the grills and chatter of diners easing her tension. Just as she was about to check the opposite side, she caught a handwave.

Garrett.

"I see him." Aubrie smiled, and the woman followed her, carrying an awkwardly large menu.

Garrett sat in one of two chairs at the shorter end of a hibachi grill. The longer side sat four, and another two directly opposite Garrett. The chef nodded in greeting, and Garrett stood, offering Aubrie the empty seat.

"May I get you a drink other than water?" the woman asked.

Aubrie scanned Garrett's choice, a glass of beer with enough sweat to show he'd been here a while.

"I'll take a glass of white wine, please." Aubrie smiled politely at Garrett, who took a sip from his glass.

"Sorry for ordering a drink before you got here," he said after a gulp. "I was a little nervous."

Aubrie's body shifted, shoulders lowering and jaw relaxing, as if she let out a sigh no one could hear. "It's okay." She tucked a lock of hair behind her ear. "To be honest, I was—am—pretty nervous myself."

"But you're a doctor. I didn't think doctors got nervous."

She chuckled. "We may have nerves of steel when it counts, but dating? That's something different, for sure." Her glass of wine arrived, and she took a sip. "I tend to plan what I can for situations in order to reduce anxiety as much as possible."

"Oh, yeah? You planned out tonight?"

She shrugged. "I thought this place would be good since we wouldn't be sitting directly across from each other. It can be awkward."

"Yet here we are, turned to one another. Should I look the other way?" He swung around in his seat, back facing Aubrie.

"No, no." She touched his shoulder, and he playfully returned. "We're good."

His genuine smile melted what remained of Aubrie's nerves. This was a nice guy, she just felt it in her gut. And cute.

"So, how are you liking Maiden's Bay? What all have you seen so far?"

Aubrie took a breath to answer, a breath that was knocked out of her as the greeter filled the two nearest seats with guests. A beautiful blonde woman in a tight floral dress sat catty-corner to Garrett, and a dark-haired man next—

Aubrie choked on her wine.

Bran.

"Are you okay?" Garrett handed her a napkin, and she accepted through her coughing.

"No, yeah, I'm fine. Went the wrong way." As this evening, no, entire day, was going. She traded the wine for the water glass, eyeing the couple over the rim.

"Hey, I recognize you." Garrett pointed at Bran. "You were the other doctor, the one who wanted to give me a physical."

"What's that?" The blonde woman eyed Bran.

Aubrie scanned the seating at the other hibachis. Were there no other empty chairs?

Bran leaned closer to the woman. "We had two fleets of fishermen in for physicals this week."

"Name is Doctor Jackson, but here you can call me Bran." He reached out a hand across his date to Garrett, who shook it. "You're…." Bran snapped his fingers. "Greg."

"Garrett."

"That's right." He put a hand on the woman's back. "This is Macy. Macy, this is my colleague Doctor Turnbridge, and her date, Garrett."

"Please, call me Aubrie." She exchanged smiles with the modelesque woman.

Macy. Of course. How could Aubrie forget? The woman at Campy's the first night she met Bran. She threw aside the fact he had asked Macy on a date. What mattered more was, why were they here? Had he figured out where she was going to meet up with Garrett?

Or was this pure coincidence?

"Rough day with a patient?" Garrett asked.

"What?" Bran took a second to register his meaning, then rubbed his swollen lip. "Yeah, this, no. Would you believe it if I said rough day with a doctor?"

Garrett chuckled.

Bran joined in, then sneaked a glance at Aubrie. "No, this... not a big deal."

His face may not have been, but him being here was. "Bran, can I speak to you for a sec?" Aubrie nodded away from the table. Toward anywhere but here.

"Sure." He placed a hand on Macy's shoulder. "Excuse me."

Aubrie led Bran to the lobby, then swiveled on her heel, meeting him face-to-face. "What the hell are you doing here?"

"Whoa, calm down."

"How did you find out?"

"Are you serious right now? I had no idea you were coming here with Greg tonight."

"It's *Garrett*. And after what happened today, you're going out with *Macy?*"

"Oh, so it's okay if you go out, but not me?"

Aubrie rolled her eyes.

"Look," Bran said, "there were two things I wanted. To eat and to drink. And Macy's number was laying right there on a napkin on my nightstand." He straightened. "Wait, is this because I asked Macy out?"

"What?" Aubrie's voice turned a little too high. She closed her eyes, shaking her head. "Of course not. What you do on your own time is your thing."

"Exactly. Thank you."

"But you're disrupting *my* thing. Do you know how long it's been since I've been on a date?" She immediately regretted saying it. And hadn't noticed the handful of customers waiting for a table around her until now.

Bran sighed. "What would you have me do, Aubrie? There are

no other tables here at the moment. Would you like me to take her somewhere else?"

"Yes." Aubrie's mind flashed to Bran taking Macy to his place at the inn. It was a split second, a freakish thought that shouldn't have bothered her. Shouldn't have even appeared in her thoughts. "I mean, no. It's fine."

"It's fine?" Bran said it with doubt.

"Yes, it's fine." It came out with a streak of irritation.

"Okay, fine then." Bran gave one nod and waited for Aubrie to lead the way back to the table.

They returned, Aubrie more aggravated than she was before their talk. Garrett had Macy giggling up a storm as Aubrie took her seat.

"He's a charmer," Macy said to Aubrie.

Bran slipped a hand behind Macy's waist as he sat back down. "What did we miss?"

Aubrie met Bran's glance. Her eyes must've betrayed her because he mouthed the words, *You said fine.*

"It is fine." The out-loud words silenced the group, their eyes on Aubrie. She cleared her throat. "I—I've heard just about everything on here is good." She held up the menu to block out Bran's gaze.

Garrett pulled her out of her anger bubble with a touch to her wrist. "I was thinking maybe we could get one of the samplers and split it. Try out a few different things."

Aubrie took a deep breath, taking in the man sitting next to her. His scruffy locks and golden smile. She was on a date, for crying out loud! And Bran wasn't going to mess it up.

"Yeah, that sounds great."

She hadn't meant to, but she glanced at Bran, whose expression had turned more serious. It wasn't anger or annoyance. She couldn't quite place it.

"Let's have a toast." Macy raised her cocktail glass. "To relationships, old and new." She smiled at Bran, who returned it with his own.

Aubrie clinked glasses with Garrett and nodded to the reunited couple. Although she didn't see how they were a couple, considering

Bran had ditched Macy years ago and didn't want to tell her the truth about why.

"You didn't drink." Garrett's full attention was on Aubrie.

"What?"

"After a toast, and the clinking, you're supposed to take a sip."

Aubrie stared at the glass raised in her hand. "Oh, right." She took a sip.

Garrett leaned closer, the scent of cedarwood helping Aubrie escape her reality for a second. "Be honest with me."

Aubrie's heart skipped. Had he sensed something was up with her and Bran? No, that was silly because nothing was up with her and Bran. They were colleagues. Who happened to be on a double date this evening.

"You were afraid you were going to choke again, weren't you?" He glanced at the wine glass, then back at Aubrie. It took her a second to process the words, and when she did, she chuckled.

"You got me there."

The hibachi chef spun a spatula in the air and caught it, to the applause of the others at the table. "Everyone ready to order?"

He went down the line, starting with Aubrie and Garrett, then Macy and Bran. A group of four ladies rounded out the table, Aubrie catching some of their chatting about their kids off to college.

"How about we check out the fish tanks while we're waiting?" Bran asked Macy.

Her reaction of confusion seemed about right. "But it's hibachi. They basically perform while they prepare our food."

Bran smiled, then leaned to her ear and whispered something. She frowned slightly, but let him take her hand. Aubrie caught his glance. Thank you, she mouthed.

Bran gave a nod and guided Macy to the fish tanks on the opposite side of the room.

It brought about a minute of relief for Aubrie. "I'm so sorry about that." She placed her hand on his knee. It felt natural, and he didn't seem to mind. "I didn't know he was going to be here."

"It's okay." Garrett shrugged. "I see my crewmates all the time when we're back in town. Granted, not as much as I see them when we're out at sea."

"Do you get sick of any of them? I can't imagine being in such tight quarters for… how long are you guys out there?"

"Sometimes weeks."

"That's…." She giggled, and he matched with a laugh.

The hibachi chef flung a sizzling shrimp onto the top of his hat, and the women at the other half of the table cheered.

"It's a lot, for sure," Garrett said. "Of course, we get on each other's nerves by the end of it. But we'd also risk our lives to help each other. As long as we have that, we're good."

"Now you're starting to make it sound enjoyable."

He chuckled and placed his hand on top of hers on his knee. It sent her heart fluttering. If only they could be by themselves and have a chat.

"Thank you."

"For what?"

"Being okay with this." She pointed with her free hand to the empty seats, which were going to be filled again at any minute. "Here I was worried we'd be alone, staring at each other with nothing to say."

"Really, it's okay. I mean, unless you two have something going on."

Aubrie's hand froze beneath Garrett's. She tried to pass off the wave of panic that arrived with his words. "What? No."

Garrett nodded. "I just didn't know for sure."

"What do you mean?"

"The other day, at Doc Bernie's. He was pretty adamant not to let me see you."

"Well, in his defense, you were pretty adamant to see me."

Garrett laughed and raised his hands in defeat, her hand missing the touch. "I admit. I'm guilty."

"He was just looking out for me, that's all. You know, like your crew does for each other."

"Okay. Maybe it was more me being insecure. I didn't think you'd go out with me, and now you're sitting right here." His smile could've melted the coldest of hearts.

"That's right. I'm here. With you." She tipped her glass to his, and they clinked again. She wanted to take this all in. To be happy in this moment. The first date she'd been on in ages, and he was sweet, funny, and outrageously adorable.

But then Bran returned, pulling her out of what this date could have been. Dropping the bottom out of her stomach and messing with her thoughts.

"What did we miss?" Macy furled her eyebrows in disappointment. "I heard cheering." She gave a dramatic frown.

"Oh, nothing. A few shrimp theatrics." Aubrie's hand lay on the table, and Garrett took it in his once again.

Aubrie smiled at him, squeezing his hand briefly in response. Macy grinned, as if admiring the pair of them.

While the look on Bran's face had returned. The one Aubrie couldn't identify earlier. But this time, she was pretty sure she deciphered it. Not anger. Not irritation.

Jealousy.

SIXTEEN

Thursday, September 20

"GOOD MORNING." BRAN entered Doc Bernie's practice, hoping he beat Aubrie in arriving.

"Morning, Doctor Jackson." Edith greeted him with her usual smile. Even though it was routine, Edith's smiles were real.

But Bran caught her staring at the purple bruise around his eye, and her smile faded.

"My goodness, what happened?"

"Oh, a misunderstanding yesterday. Not a big deal." He reflexively pressed his lips together, the fattening decreased from yesterday. With his eye, the swelling had gone down a bit, but the color took on a personality of its own.

He shed his coat and thin scarf, Edith eager to hang them up for him. It was something he could do on his own, but Edith made it clear she'd be offended if he didn't let her do her job. He wasn't going to argue what her job entailed or didn't entail.

Bran cleared his dry throat, nervous about seeing Aubrie after last night. "Is Doctor Turnbridge here yet?"

"Oh, yes. Aubrie went into Doc Bernie's office a few minutes before you arrived."

Bran nodded. Of *course* he didn't beat her here. Aubrie considered herself late if she arrived less than fifteen minutes early.

There were things he needed to clear up with her, and conflictingly wanted to get it over with and skip all-together. As the morning progressed and patients rotated in and out of the practice, it was obvious

Aubrie was perfectly happy immersing herself in work and ignoring him. She seemed to always be going in the opposite direction when he crossed her path, and while she acknowledged his presence with a brief upright flinch of her mouth, she didn't stop as much as to say hello.

When lunch had come and gone without having seen her leave by herself, Bran took the opportunity during an afternoon lull to address the trout in the room.

Bran scanned the hallway and waiting room before walking right up to her. "Hey."

"Hey." She messed around on her cell phone, standing by Edith's desk. Edith had a way of busying herself to seem as if she wasn't paying attention, but Bran knew better.

"About last night...." He nodded away from the desk, and Aubrie reluctantly set down her phone and stepped closer to him.

Aubrie spoke in a whisper. "I thought we resolved this well enough last night."

"I know, I just—" He wanted to tell her why he invited Macy out. It wasn't to date her, to rekindle some flame that barely burned years ago. In fact, it was because of Aubrie that he took the initiative to call Macy. To apologize for his past behavior, to buy her dinner, as a friend. He even told her that he wasn't looking for a relationship—or a fling, to be frank. He genuinely wanted her to know her friendship was valued, is valued, and that he has changed. It was nice to hear how well her career has been going.

"I said last night, it's fine. You had your date, I had mine. We ate our meals."

It wasn't fine with a cloud of awkwardness hovering over them the entire dinner. "I realize my presence made it hard to focus on your date." He meant it in the most innocent way—that he had interrupted her time, but realized after the words came out how poorly they sounded. "I mean, you had a hard time paying attention to him." Nope, not better. But it was true. He had watched her throughout the evening. It was hard not to, seeing her dressed up, smiling and flirting with what's-his-name. Garrett.

Aubrie put her fingers on the bruise around his eye. While the puffiness had gone down, the tenderness still lingered. "And you have a hard time not ticking people off, you know that?"

He let out a brief chuckle. "I suppose I deserve that."

Aubrie crossed her arms, eyebrows furled in satisfaction.

"For many reasons."

"I just don't understand you, sometimes. Or maybe it's me."

"What do you mean?"

"For some reason, the men around me act so childish sometimes."

"You should've seen him as a kid." Doc Bernie handed a file to Edith. "He was never one to follow rules."

"I think that still goes." Aubrie gave him a widened stare.

"He'd come around looking like—" Doc Bernie paused, smirking. "Well, like he does today. Remember that scuffle with the Crinton boys?" Doc shook his head, all too happy to reminisce. "Broken collar bone, a few stitches to the ear."

Aubrie stepped closer, investigating his left ear.

"It's the other one," Bran said. "And there's not much to see. The scar all but faded." He switched his attention to Doc. "To be fair, they came after Nathaniel."

"True, true." Doc switched to Aubrie. "I heard Bran jumped right in the middle of it. Took the brunt of the fighting and never threw a punch."

Bran's cheeks felt alight with heat.

"I'm sure whatever this was—" Doc Bernie waved his hand in the vicinity of Bran's face—"there's a good justification for it."

"Thanks, Doc."

"Of course." He turned to Edith. "I'm off to grab a bite." He gave a loose salute, his fingers not quite straight and hand shaky, as he exited.

Aubrie scoffed. "Of course your grandfather is going to stick up for you."

"He's a wise man, regardless of being my grandfather." Bran didn't hide the smirk until he remembered what they had been talking about before Doc's interruption. "But in all seriousness, I am sorry."

Her hands moved to her hips. "For which part?" She leaned closer, speaking in a low whisper. "Crashing my date, or getting in a brawl? No, for not telling Doc Bernie about your probation?"

At the sound of the word, she turned her attention to Edith, whose head remained down. Bran caught her eyes drifting, betraying her pretend unawareness.

"For all of it."

"Then you'll tell Doc Bernie what's going on when he gets back?"

Bran rubbed the bump on his lip. "It's not that simple."

"Sure it is."

"Aubrie, please. There's more to it than—"

The front door swung open, a woman holding it while a hefty man carried an infant in his arms.

"She's burning up and not moving." It was Ben, one of the Campbell brothers who had been in not long ago for his physical. His face beaded with sweat, his t-shirt wet from the damp towel wrapped around the infant.

"Bring her back." Bran rushed to the back, through the hallway to the first examining room. Aubrie said something to who Bran suspected was Ben's wife. They met up in the room as Bran took off the little girl's onesie and pants, leaving nothing on but the diaper.

"How old is she?" He grabbed a stethoscope and listened to her heart. Her skin was hot. "Aubrie, temp?"

Aubrie's eyes were glazed over, as if in another world. She was pulled back with his words, and she nodded.

"She's going on nine months," Ben said.

"When did this start?"

"103.1." Aubrie's voice was weak.

"I went to do her feeding before nap time, but she wasn't latching. And I felt how warm she was. About an hour ago."

"Did you give her anything?" Bran gazed over the two parents, and they shook their heads.

"Her fever was escalating, and we wanted to get here as soon—" She broke down, Ben holding her in his arms.

"It's okay, Ange, we got her help."

Amid the frantic couple, just behind them, was Aubrie. Her face was stone, eyes moistening. Bran wanted to reach out to her, but she backed out of the doorway and bolted down the hall.

Bran focused back on the parents. "That's right," he assured them. "What's this little angel's name?"

"Annabel," Ben said.

"All right. Wait right here."

Bran stepped out into the hallway to the front desk. Aubrie sat in one of the waiting room chairs, biting her thumb and forefinger, focusing on who knew what.

"Edith, I need your help."

"You got it."

"I'm going to need some children's acetaminophen, some fresh wet cloths, and some formula if we got it."

"On it." Edith ran to fetch the items, while Aubrie continued to stare at the wall.

"Aubrie?"

She turned her head to him. "I—" All she managed was a shake of the head.

"It's okay. You just wait here, see if we get any other patients."

She nodded, as if relieved to be given a responsibility other than the imminent one.

Bran made his way back to the room. After looking for obvious signs like rash, he administered the acetaminophen and changed out the cool cloths. "You were wise to use the cool compresses."

It was the first bit of relief he saw in Ben's eyes since arriving.

After a painfully long thirty minutes, Annabel's fever came down, and her alertness improved. He briefed the parents about caring for Annabel at home, and when to call him or 911 if her condition worsened.

Ben and his wife left after another thirty minutes, just to be safe, and thanked Bran with hugs.

He walked them out to the waiting room. "I know it can be scary, the first time your child is sick. As it's most likely a virus, it's mainly managing symptoms and keeping her comfortable. You let me know if she starts screaming, tugging at her ears. We don't want that mucus getting into her ears, causing an infection."

"Will do." Ben looked at his wife. "I'm going to be heading out again soon. I'm trying to take on less fishing trips."

His wife rubbed his back, then patted Annabel's head.

"Would you mind following up with Angela? My reception will be in and out."

Bran nodded. "No problem." He could see the pain it caused Ben, having to leave his wife and sick daughter on their own. It was their way of life, one Bran couldn't see for himself. But if calling Angela every day over the next week alleviated Ben's worry, then that's what he was going to do.

"Thank you, Doc."

Bran held the front door open for them and watched as they walked off. He turned back to the waiting room, Aubrie out of the chair.

He was going to ask Edith where Aubrie had gone to, but Edith merely pointed at the doorway as Aubrie walked an elderly gentleman to the waiting room.

"Every day, Mister Guzman. No skipping this time."

"I know." The man waved the order away and exited.

Bran wanted to get Aubrie before she had time to run off or pretend she was too busy with whatever. He nearly pushed her into the hallway, the concern unavoidable in his voice. "What was that?"

"What was what? Mister Guzman?"

"No, not Mister Guzman. With Annabel?"

She stood silent.

"The little girl? You froze. What's going on?"

"It was… nothing."

Bran scoffed. "I see. When it's me freezing, it's something, but when you do it, nothing."

Her resolve began to return. "In all fairness, you passed out. I didn't."

She was good at turning the tables. He'd give her that. "You may not have passed out, but you flipped out. I could've used you in there."

"But you managed just fine, didn't you?" Her eyebrows nearly met in anger. If anything, he should be the one upset, not her.

"Luckily, she's likely fighting a common virus, and we got her fever under control. Taking fluids. But if it had been something else—"

"Well, it wasn't something else, so we're good."

"What's going on out here?" Doc Bernie stopped short of the hallway entrance. Bran hadn't noticed he'd returned from his meal break.

Aubrie's glare could've cut through metal. "Maybe you should ask Bran." Her steeliness gave in to pleading.

"I asked the both of you, but okay. Bran?" Doc Bernie nibbled on an oatmeal cookie, not ready to hear what Aubrie wanted Bran to say. When would Doc ever be ready? Aubrie didn't even know the half of it.

"The Campbells were in here, while you were gone. Brought in little Annabel."

"Everything okay?"

"She is now." He returned the glare to Aubrie. The seconds ticked by before turning back to Doc Bernie. "We'll need to call Angela, just to follow-up, over the next couple of days."

"Okay." Doc Bernie said it hesitantly, as if unsure of the whole thing. "I'll have Edith put that in the schedule. Helps to remember when it's in writing."

"I agree." Bran gave a brief smile.

The three of them stood there, Bran and Aubrie facing each other, Doc Bernie the third wheel looking in on them.

"Okay… well, how about we get back to it, then?" Doc Bernie pointed to his office entrance, no doubt eager to escape the tension in the air.

"Gladly," Aubrie said.

You sure about that? is what Bran wanted to say, but he also didn't want to prolong the battle of the stare-downs.

What was it about that patient that bothered her? Surely, as a pediatric oncologist, she had seen much worse. So, why the negative reaction? Why freeze up?

It wasn't so much the freezing up as it was that she refused to tell him why, after he had been so open with her. He hadn't told anyone about his mother like he had done with Aubrie. Why was it hard for her to open up to him?

It led to one thought, a thought that last night had helped nurture. And that was how much she cared for him. He swore she kept eyeing him last night. Not really even him, but Macy. That she didn't like him being together with Macy, despite her sitting next to her date.

Perhaps he read her all wrong. If she did care about him, beyond whatever level of friendship they'd call themselves at this point, she would open up.

The frustration kept the knot in his stomach tight, long past the end of clinic hours and well into the night.

SEVENTEEN

"I'M HIKING."

"Did someone tell you to go take one?"

"Mom!" Aubrie's breath had barely quickened a few minutes into her walk up Sentinel Hill before her mother called. Why she decided it was a good time to pick up the phone....

A little piece of her hoped the call would drop, to have an excuse to end it early.

"No, I'm off for the morning, but Doc Bernie wants me in later. He'll call me if he needs anything earlier." Yes, another valid excuse to end the conversation. It's not that Aubrie disliked her mother. She loved her dearly, and the fact Aubrie wasn't around in Dallas anymore for family dinners or outings wasn't lost on her. She would miss them, too—for the most part. It was that Mom was never going to approve of Aubrie's decision to move to Maiden's Bay, which had nothing to do with the location—like it would with the average parent not wanting to be far away. No, her mother wouldn't have approved a move to Houston.

"Has it kept you busy? Such a small practice?"

What Mom didn't understand—at least one of the things—was Aubrie's pursuit to slow down. "I think you'd be surprised how busy it's been all week. We had an entire day dedicated to performing physicals to two fishing crews in town."

She could picture Mom's repugnant facial reaction. Like she caught a whiff of rotting fish. *"Oh, Aubrie."*

"It's fine, Mom. I know you think it's not important work. That I'm wasting my skills. But the practice, me being here, does benefit the community. There was a woman with a heart problem that lived in the middle of nowhere, who really needed specialized care. Bran and I drove her to Seattle University Hospital to take care of her. It's a different way to practice medicine, a more personal one that bleeds into the community, not just inside the practice."

The response took seconds longer than expected. *"Who is this Brian fellow?"*

Aubrie slumped her shoulders, shaking her head. "His name is *Bran*. He's Doc Bernie's grandson. He's also a doctor."

"In town for a visit, or…?"

Aubrie avoided telling Mom the exact situation. That she had come all the way here not knowing she'd compete for the position. And that "the position" was actually taking over the practice. It was enough to handle the guilt of having quit her job and giving up her place. Were all mothers gifted with laying on the guilt?

"He's actually from Seattle University Hospital. It helped that he knew the cardio team there. Made me feel comfortable knowing the patient was in good hands." Luckily, not the hands of that Dr. Hycliff.

Aubrie felt a tinge of pride having given an inexact answer to Mom's question.

"Is he handsome? If I Google him, will he show up?"

Aubrie's successful deflection of work only led to the other of Mom's favorite topics. Relationships.

"He's rather debonair."

"Stop joking with me."

"What do you want me to say? Bran is good looking, and from what I've seen so far, a good doctor. But he's also—"

"Aubrie?" A voice rang out from behind her. A man stood amongst the trees, in gray hiking pants and boots. His crystal blue eyes matched his rain jacket.

Bran.

Aubrie nearly dropped the phone from her ear. "Mom, I gotta go."

"Is everything okay? You sound—"

"Yeah, it's fine." The words sounded short. "Promise. Just met up with someone, that's all."

"Met up? Who is it?"

"I'll talk to you later, Mom."

Aubrie hung up the phone and held it in her hands, not knowing whether to put it in her pocket or chuck it through the woods. She wanted to run, hide behind a tree. But Bran clearly stood in front of her. Hiding was a no-go.

"What are you doing here?" She fiddled more with the phone, taking the corner of the protective case off and back on. Over and over.

"I imagine the same thing you're doing here. Minus the cell phone." He pointed to her fidgeting hands.

"Right. I should've left it back at the apartment."

"Hiking 101." He smiled.

"I'll remember it for next time." She nodded, the conversation going as smoothly as the craggy top of the hill ahead. "Did you, um, happen to hear any of that?"

"What?" He feigned confusion, then overemphasized understanding. "Oh, you mean the phone call? No."

"Okay." The relief helped calm her worries.

"Except for the good doctor part."

"Oh." Not so bad. "Well, it's the truth. Like I said, so far as I've seen. You've performed well with the patients."

"Thank you." His grin grew, and he scratched his jawline by his ear. "And was the good looking part true, too, or…?"

His smugness made her smile, despite the embarrassment of him hearing the worst of it. "I was speaking to my mother. Who doesn't know about this situation here." She waved her hand between them. "With taking over the practice."

"I see. So, she doesn't know about the competition Doc Bernie tricked us into?"

"Nope. No she doesn't. And I want to delay that knowing as long as possible, so I deflected into more of the"—her words became more spaced out—"personal aspects of you. She took the bait, which meant I had to go into your looks."

He slipped his hands into his rain jacket pockets. "Which are good."

"You're really enjoying this, aren't you?"

Bran chuckled. "I'm sorry. It's none of my business. I was surprised, though, to see you up here. Didn't know you were the hiking type."

She shrugged. "Not a lot of hilly terrain in the Dallas area. Thought I'd give it a try."

"You on your way down or up?"

It was tempting to say down, and be done with the whole thing. But it didn't make much sense not holding off the phone conversation until the parking lot a hundred yards away.

"Just started."

Bran walked off and stopped at a split in the trail. He turned around. "That way takes you on the other side of Sentinel Hill to Frasier's Pond. They call it a pond. Some days you can catch ducks floating on a bit of water, others you can search all you want and won't find it." He pointed his thumb behind him. "And this way up to the summit. Hope you're carrying bear spray. It's a ton more useful than the phone."

He gave one nod before resuming his trek along the path ahead of him. Aubrie stood there, letting the seconds tick by, in disbelief that he'd walked off. When she couldn't see him after a bend in the trail, she hurried to the split.

"Are you serious?" she shouted.

Bran was simply going to bump into her and not walk with her? Was this some reverse psychology he was using? Or did he want to be on his own?

Aubrie wanted to be on her own when she first started out. But she hadn't thought of bears, or what would happen if she sprained an ankle out on her own. The whole idea of hiking seemed dumb now.

Bran retraced his steps back to where she could see him. "What, about the bears?"

She spread her arms out and dropped them in frustration. She didn't know if she was asking about the bears, or if he really meant to leave her on her own.

She traversed the distance to him, trying to shake off the feeling that every step was under scrutiny. No, hiking wasn't something she'd done often, but how hard could it be? Whatever she needed to figure out, she would. She went to med school, dammit. She can work out hiking.

"Were you really going to leave me to hike by yourself?" It was hard to read him, despite knowing him better over the last several days. It was much easier to assume everything he did was for himself, but she knew him enough to know that wasn't true.

He chuckled, biting the swollen bit of his lip.

"You know that's not going to heal if you keep irritating it."

He looked at her quizzically. "Now, why on earth would I want to hike by myself when I could have the joy of such helpful company?"

She chuckled. "Okay, I get it. Be on your merry way."

"I'm kidding. I figured"—he squinted into the sky—"a full minute before you realized you'd want my company."

She put her hands on her hips. "Why do you make it so hard to be with you?"

His eyes flinched, as if a spark had ignited a flame only to be burned out instantly. "Aubrie, would you like to join me up Sentinel Hill?"

It was her turn to pretend. She sighed, looking up at the sky. She looked over her shoulder, toward the start of the trail.

"And *I'm* the one who's hard to be around?" Bran gave a stare in mock seriousness.

"Okay. I'll join you."

"Great." He gestured for her to walk ahead.

"Thanks."

"Oh, that's just so the bears get you first."

She stopped walking and pivoted on her heel.

"I'm kidding again. Sheesh." He caught up with her and took to her left, the trail wide enough to accommodate the both of them unless someone came down their way. "The bears are true, by the way. Black bears, at least. Grizzlies are on the other side of the state."

"Good to know. Ever seen one here?"

"No. You'll hear about sightings every now and then. But me, never personally."

"You seem to know your way around."

"I hiked more as a kid. Used to come up here with my dad. He liked the view at the top, pointing out all the places down below. Then, after my mom died, he stopped coming. I did, too, at least at first. Once I got a little older, I was able to ride my bike around town, and I found myself coming here. I think when something like that happens, it's good to have somewhere to escape to."

"Healthier than other things."

"That's one way to look at it."

It was then that she saw him for his age, the start of wrinkles at the corner of his eyes, the strand or two of grays in his hair. He didn't bring a backpack, but there was a definite weight in his steps.

"I'm sorry. You don't have to talk about what happened if you don't want to."

"No, it's all right. I've told you most of what there is to tell."

As the trail turned upward, conversation faded. They made the ascent, a series of switchbacks that turned rockier the higher they reached. Every muscle in Aubrie's legs ached as she urged them to move on. Bran shed his jacket but wasn't breathing as hard as Aubrie. He stopped every so often for a water break, which she suspected he did for her out-of-shape sake.

"Nearly there." He offered his water bottle.

Aubrie shook hers in her hand. "I've still got a little."

He led the way to the top, the trees clearing into short, wheat-colored grass. To the right was a cliff made of boulders, as if they stood atop a mound of enormous rocks covered in a tarp of dirt and grass to accommodate the climb.

The wind whipped the bangs and loose tresses along Aubrie's face. "It's beautiful."

Maiden's Bay sat below, the sea beyond. They were higher than the restaurant of Doc's retirement announcement, higher than the outskirts of Maiden's Bay. A handful of rooftops dotted the curved hillside to the right, a good hundred feet below.

"It looks so tiny, yet so vast from here." The Ferris wheel she had noticed this morning that appeared overnight sat on the southern rim of shoreline. She looked over at Bran to ask about it but held back. He surprisingly looked content, as if he could stand there all day. "You like it here, don't you?"

His smile remained. "I think I do. More each day." His eyes met hers, a rush of flutters catching her off guard.

Aubrie smiled back. "It was worth the climb."

"Despite being with me?" Bran joked.

Aubrie nudged him with her elbow. "You got me up here quicker than I would have on my own."

"I wasn't going to say anything."

"Stop." Aubrie laughed.

The wind died down, as if out of respect for the silence they now stood in.

Bran turned away from the view, toward Aubrie. "Look, about the other day—"

Aubrie held up a hand. She didn't want to go into all of it. Not now, this nice moment, just the two of them, no one else in the world. Standing at the top of it.

"I just—"

Her phone buzzed in her pocket. "Sorry, hold on." She checked the caller. "It's Doc."

Bran gave a nod.

"Doc Bernie, everything okay?" She held a finger to her free ear, the wind picking back up again.

"I need you to get over here. I called Bran as well but keep getting his voicemail."

Aubrie looked over at him. "He's with me. Doesn't have his cell phone on him."

"Good. I could use you both. It's an emergency." Doc hung up before Aubrie could respond. She stared at her phone in disbelief.

"What is it?"

"Doc says we need to come in now. Some sort of emergency."

"What kind?"

"He didn't say. Hung up before I could ask."

"Then we'd better go."

Aubrie nodded in agreement, and they started their descent, steps quicker from the urgency and the easier downhill.

"I told you," Bran said as they rounded a switchback.

"Told me what?"

"Never bring a cell phone hiking."

EIGHTEEN

THE DESCENT DOWN Sentinel Hill was the fastest Bran had ever trodden. When they hit the parking lot, he felt the strain on his knees and hips. The aftermath would be worse tomorrow.

They decided to take their separate cars to the clinic. The drive on a Saturday normally would've taken about fifteen minutes, but he pushed past the speed limit when he could. Aubrie had no problem keeping up behind him.

It had only been ten minutes since Doc Bernie had called Aubrie when they arrived, though every second felt like an hour. Was there a fishing vessel injury? A car accident? Neither of them had been able to see any disruption in town from their vantage point on Sentinel Hill.

They both parked on the street in front of the clinic, next to an open-air Jeep hastily parked sideways. Bran held the door open as Aubrie raced in.

"What's going on?" she asked.

Bran scanned the waiting room. A young woman in a thick red jumpsuit received a cup of hot liquid from Edith. Next to her was a man in the same outfit, sitting on the ground, arms resting on his bent knees.

"There was an incident on a whale watching tour." Edith spoke low. "Doc wants you two back there."

Bran led the way to the first patient room. A woman, her jumpsuit unzipped down to the waist, paper gown draped over her torso, lay upright on the examining table. Doc Bernie busied himself placing leads on the patient for an ECG.

"Doc, what's up?" Bran stood next to Aubrie, ready to jump in.

"She had a seizure out on the water," Doc said. "No history of seizure. At least one ambulance is on the way from White Bend. Should be any minute now."

"At *least?*" Aubrie asked.

"I need you two to check on the other patients."

Bran and Aubrie met glances before moving to the second patient room. One patient lay on the examining table, another on the floor. Only their heads were exposed, while their bodies were buried under mountains of blankets.

A third man stood up from the chair in the corner. "They helped her out of the water."

"What?" Bran stuck a hand out, slowing down the explanations that weren't explanations at all. "Tell us what happened out there."

Aubrie approached the patient on the table, lifting up the stacked fabric over his feet.

"We were in the middle of a whale watching tour, when that guest started convulsing. She lost grip of the raft... it happened so fast."

"She fell overboard." Bran pieced it together. "And these two jumped in after her."

The man nodded, rolling his wool cap in his hands nervously.

"What's your name?"

"Terrence."

"Okay, Terrence. We're going to help. How long were these passengers in the water?"

"I don't know. Maybe three, five minutes? But it took us a good twenty minutes or so just to get back to land."

"Bran." Aubrie said it with worry. "They all still have their wet clothes on."

"Terrence, I'm going to need you to help us get their wet clothes off." Bran pulled the layered blankets off the patient on the floor, hastily unzipping the wet jumpsuit. The patient lazily eyed him, but didn't say a word.

Aubrie and Terrence worked on the other patient.

"Any idea of the water temp out there?" Aubrie asked.

"Sub fifty where we were."

Bran caught the worry in Aubrie's eyes. He checked the patient's pupils and pulse, and examined the body for any discoloration, especially in the extremities.

"Aubrie." He nodded for her to speak with him by the doorway. "I'm not seeing anything overly concerning with mine."

She shook her head. "Mine whispered he couldn't feel his feet. But his fingers and toes check out, as far as I can tell."

"I still say we keep them under the blankets. I'm going to turn up the thermostat, as well."

Aubrie nodded in agreement.

"If more than one ambulance arrives, let's send them just in case. If not, keep them here for a while." He turned to Terrence. "Would you mind staying with them a bit longer?"

He shook his head. "No. My boss Brie's here, too. She'll understand."

Aubrie turned to Bran. "Where are you going?"

"Out to the waiting room. Come on."

He glanced in the first room, Doc Bernie staring at the ECG readout, as he walked to the waiting room with Aubrie following. The seated woman leaned her head back on the wall, eyes closed. The other man remained on the floor.

Bran walked right up to the pair. "You must be Brie? I'm Doctor Jackson. This is Doctor Turnbridge. It's my understanding one of your passengers experienced a seizure and fell overboard. Two other passengers then jumped in the water, retrieving the first. Is that correct?"

Brie nodded. "Yes. Isaac"—she pointed to the drained man next to her, damp from the boots to the waist—"and Terrence back there helped carry her offboard to a transport vehicle."

Aubrie crouched to Isaac's level. "How are you feeling? May I?"

"I'm fine. Just a bit tired."

She slipped his sleeve up to check his pulse. "You'll let me know if you start to feel unwell? Something like this can come as a shock. Everyone handles it differently."

"I'll let you know."

Aubrie smiled. "Good. You might want to take off your outer gear. Edith can help you with a blanket."

"I'm fine, really."

"Doctor! We need help back here!"

Bran and Aubrie ran back to the hallway. Doc Bernie stood in the doorway of the first examining room, waving them over to the second.

Terrence was stripping off his jumpsuit, pulling off a thermal shirt over his head. He threw it on the floor, face red and body full of sweat.

"What's going on?" Aubrie asked.

"He just started fanning himself." The covered patient on the examining table sat upright. "Then breathing hard."

Bran turned the thermostat back down a few degrees. Aubrie checked Terrence.

"It's not that, Bran."

"What do you mean?"

"Terrence, you're having a panic attack. I want you to sit up here on the counter. Can you do that?"

He nodded, eyes watering with tears, and propped himself up.

"Look at me, Terrence. Follow my breathing." She took a deep breath in for several seconds, exhaling out for more. "That's right, keep going." She grabbed a wad of paper towels and wet them at the faucet. "Here, put this on your chest or neck, wherever it feels good."

Bran stood between the two hypothermia patients, tending to them, though he couldn't keep his eyes off Aubrie. Panic attacks weren't uncommon in the trauma center. If they happened, it was usually experienced by a relative or friend of the patient, who had witnessed or been a part of the accident, or saw the severity of the injury, or both. But did Aubrie have experience with panic attack patients? Didn't seem like something she'd encounter a whole lot in pediatric oncology.

Yet she knew exactly what to do, how to speak with him soothingly yet firmly to calm him down. When she was thrown into action, it was like a switch turned on, and she did everything right.

Except yesterday, with Ben's daughter Annabel. Some other switch had been flicked. One that made her run from the situation. He thought she was about to open up about it at Sentinel Park, but then Doc Bernie called them in.

"I'm going to give you some space, check on Doc Bernie."

Aubrie gave him a quick glance of affirmative, and Bran moved to the room next door. The patient was sitting up, alert, chatting with Doc Bernie.

"Everything okay in here?"

Two EMTs, led by Edith, rushed the room. Doc briefed one of them while the other helped the patient off the examining table. They walked her out to the gurney in the corridor and rolled her out of the clinic.

"Is it okay if I stay until the other passengers are cleared to go?" asked Brie, standing outside the doorway.

"Of course." Doc Bernie led her out of the hallway to the waiting room. "Edith here can get you anything you need in the meantime."

Bran found himself alone with Doc Bernie as he returned.

"Everything okay with the other patients?"

"Yeah, one is back on his feet, the other is on his way there. One of the tour employees experienced a panic attack, but Aubrie has that covered." Bran rubbed his chin. "Actually." He touched Doc's elbow. "Can I speak to you in private?"

Doc led him into his office and sat at his desk, stacking a pile of mail on top of another mishmash of papers.

Bran closed the door most of the way and remained standing. "Is there something I should know about Aubrie? Something that maybe led her to work here?" The guilt crept up, the irony of his unspoken secrets not escaping him. "I don't mean to sound rude or sketchy. It's just, she was really great with that patient in there during his panic attack. Yet, yesterday, when Ben came with his daughter Annabel, something about it changed Aubrie."

"What do you mean, *changed* her?"

This was all wrong. He shouldn't have brought up her behavior. It made him look like he was trying to "win" over her in this crazy competition. Had Aubrie told Doc Bernie about his passing out the other day? Not that he knew of. Nor had she said a word about his probation.

"I'm sorry. I shouldn't be talking to you about a coworker, especially in this situation." He pinched the bridge of his nose.

"Correct me if I'm wrong." Doc Bernie stood, walking around his desk and leaning on it, close to Bran. "But it sounds like you might care for Aubrie?"

"Care is a relative term." Even he could hear the fluster in his words.

"Is it?"

"Care, in as much as her being a doctor, at my grandfather's clinic. She's a coworker, and it's good to have each other's backs."

"Mmhmm." Doc seemed to enjoy Bran's discomfort too much.

"I just thought maybe you knew something I didn't."

Doc Bernie rested his hand on Bran's shoulder. "Bran, there are many things I know that you don't. And I'd assume vice versa."

Bran chuckled. "You're right."

"But maybe you two can work that out this afternoon."

Bran's interest piqued, the adrenaline from the unforeseen emergency returning. Another one of Doc Bernie's plans? "Why? What's this afternoon?"

"That's why I had you two take the morning off. But you can see how that goes sometimes. Let's grab Aubrie."

Bran waited in the office as Doc Bernie went to the patient room. He heard a little of their conversation, Aubrie hesitant to leave the patients in the room. But Brie was in there, and Terrence had calmed down, while the hypothermia patients were improving last he checked.

Doc Bernie returned with Aubrie and sounded his usual clap, the one that signaled an announcement.

"First, thank you both for coming this morning. Obviously, unforeseen circumstances. But." He held up both hands, forefingers in the air conducting his announcement. "I was having you come in today so I can offer the afternoon up to you, to go to the Crab Festival. Aubrie being new in town, I thought it would be a good way to meet more people, have your face out there."

Bran's feelings jumbled. A bit of sadness, hurt even, that his father didn't invite him to go, knowing Bran was in town. It was one rare family affair they had carried through Mom's passing, up until Bran left. Add to it a pinch of excitement at the excuse to spend the afternoon with Aubrie, outside of the clinic.

Aubrie tucked her loose strands behind her ear. "What is the Crab Festival? Do I have to go crabbing, or touch a crab?" She winced. "I'm not sure that's my thing."

Bran's enthusiasm grew. "No, nothing like that, though there are plenty of vendors selling crab everything to eat." He tapped her arm. "Come on, it'll be fun. The whole town will be there, and what else are you going to do the rest of the day?"

He knew he had her. Either that, or she felt obligated because Doc Bernie all but assigned them to it as a job. But it wouldn't feel like a job. Not with Aubrie. Just like working with her in the clinic never felt like actual work.

"Okay, fine." She looked at Bran, and he knew the elation showed on his face. He didn't care. She pointed in his face. "But I'm not touching a crab."

Bran showed his palms. "I get it, no crabs. Only cooked crabs. And we'll use a fork."

She punched his arm lightly, and they both smiled.

Bran would have to thank Doc Bernie at some point.

This was going to be fun.

NINETEEN

THE WARM WATER hitting Aubrie's back was divine. After rushing down Sentinel Hill, then dealing with the heightened pressure at Doc Bernie's with the whale watching patients, she needed the clean slate.

She had recognized the signs of the panic attack right away. It wasn't hard, considering the number of attacks she had experienced the past year. The spike of fear. Flash of heat through the body. The sense of drifting away from Earth, nothing anchoring her to the ground.

The hope was that the move would help alleviate the frequency of attacks. That eventually they'd go away. For some time, it was working—she hadn't gone through an attack in Maiden's Bay.

Until Ben brought Annabel in.

Obviously, she didn't hide it well enough, despite following her coping steps of removing herself from the trigger, using her breathing techniques, saying the alphabet slowly backward in her head. Bran knew something was wrong and tried to get her to open up. But her problems were her problems. He couldn't fix her, nor would she want him to try.

Her phone buzzed. Bran. As if he knew she was thinking about him at that moment.

Out front. Take your time.

She slipped on a long-sleeve shirt and jeans with boot cuffs and brown boots. She slung her purse across her body, grabbed her favorite sweater, an oversized cream cable knit with brown buttons, then headed down the stairs.

Bran stood on the other side of the glass door in a brown plaid flannel shirt beneath a brown jacket, hands in pockets. She didn't pin him for the flannel type, but he wore it well.

"All set?" Bran held the door for her exit. "You look nice."

"Thank you. Same." It was the truth, but why was it so hard to hear it coming out of her own mouth? "I'm guessing the Crab Festival is on the south side of town?" Aubrie closed her sweater tighter, as if that would close off her thoughts from leaving her mouth.

"What gave it away?"

"Oh, I don't know. Something about the giant Ferris wheel that was erected overnight down that way?"

"I thought you were going to say the wafts of boiled crustacean you caught permeating the air."

She sniffed the air for a moment and shook her head. "I don't catch anything different."

"You will." Bran smiled. "Shall we walk to this thing? By the time we find parking, we'd probably end up close by here, anyway."

She looked down Pearl Avenue, and Bran was right. The parking spots filled up since they had rushed to the practice earlier, and a line of cars headed south. It was the first real traffic she had seen in town.

"I'm up for walking."

"Great." Bran walked by her side along the sidewalk heading toward the southern tip of the crescent that was town.

"I haven't been out this way much so far." Aubrie took in the window display at Bea's Bouquets as they passed. Golden yellow and orange leaves were strewn about a table covered in a mahogany brown tablecloth. Bright yellow sunflowers burst out of an oversized glass vase in the center of the table. "But I've been loving the displays at the flower shop."

"That's Bea's," Bran said. "Been around for quite some time. In fact, most of the shops have been here since I can remember."

"That's not a bad thing, is it? I think it'd be nice, knowing when you're gone that you'll come home to what you're used to."

"That's one way of putting it."

She slowed her steps, taking a good look at him. "I take it you have another way of putting it?"

"Well, I've been gone for a good part of three years. You'd think something would change. Doesn't a town need progress to keep itself alive, to be relevant?"

"Maybe. But where I'm from, it's sink or swim. Stores and restaurants pop up all the time but could be gone and replaced in a year. Months even. That just tells me the newest, hippest thing may not be what's needed. And to be honest, it's hard for a place to feel like home when it looks different every time you blink."

Bran's skeptical look melted.

Aubrie pointed to his smiling lips. "I've convinced you, haven't I?"

He chuckled. "I admit, I never thought of Maiden's Bay like that. I always thought it was resistant to change, a town slowly dying because it didn't want to embrace the new."

"But…."

He elbowed her lightly. "Perhaps you're right. A part of me does appreciate the familiarity of it all."

Noise grew as they continued down the curve of Pearl Avenue, the open sea beyond the bay appearing in glimpses between houses and shops. Music played under a sea of voices and even a few delightful squeals from the Ferris wheel. Cars crowded the entrance of a parking lot too small to accommodate the visitors.

"Looks like this is a pretty big deal in Maiden's Bay."

"Oh, yeah. The Crab Festival is the only one of its kind within a hundred miles of coastline. At least, that's what they say on the advertisements. But I do know people come from Parkside, White Bend, even farther out."

The end of Pearl Avenue was closed off with barrels and cones, a white banner with red lettering hung above a makeshift entrance. 67th Annual Crab Festival, a crab reaching up to the text, its claw making the V in festival.

They walked through, the aromas in the air a platter of seafood goodies. There were food trucks galore, each with their own specialties—fried crab cakes, buttery boiled crab legs, crab burgers. They walked by two trucks with large skillets, grilling butternut squash and zucchini, late season corn on the cob, even pumpkin.

"This is amazing." Aubrie stopped in front of a truck called A-peeling Desserts, an exclusively apple dessert establishment with apple pies, fritters, and crumbles.

"Here." Bran nodded toward the truck. "They've got great candy apples." As he said it, Aubrie noticed a glass display separate from the baked goods. The apples were enormous, some covered in caramel, others chocolate or red candy. The toppings were endless, with nuts, chocolate chips, sprinkles. A truck attendant was busy rolling one in Lucky Charms.

"I didn't even have lunch." Aubrie's stomach growled in retaliation.

"Um, hello? An apple a day?"

Aubrie laughed. "I don't think they mean *this* kind."

He said something to an attendant and turned back to her. "Yeah, but this kind's good for your mental health."

She shook her head, eyes growing big when the attendant handed Bran a sliced caramel apple larger than any apple she'd ever seen.

"Come on. You know you want to try one."

"I didn't say otherwise." She grinned and selected a slice. The tart juicy apple collided with the butteriness of the caramel, which stuck to her teeth. "That's one of the best things I've ever tasted."

She finished the first slice and went for a second, Bran smiling in delight, a string of caramel stretched past his lip.

"Here." Aubrie touched his cheek with her thumb to wipe the caramel away.

"Oh." Bran's hand met hers, and they stood frozen for a second, her hand touching Bran's. She caught a glimpse of his blue eyes. "Thanks."

She pulled back and gave a nod, her hand aching for the contact again. She cleared her throat, as if clearing the past moment, and noticed a white tent set up next to a parked ambulance.

"Hey, is that the medical tent?" She pointed to the white canopy. "Think we should see if they need help?"

"Yes to the first question. And no to the second. I'm sure they're fine." He took another bite of an apple slice.

"Come on, you're not even curious what kind of staffing they have? Supplies, expertise?"

He exaggerated his enjoyment of the candy apple, closing his eyes dramatically. "Mmm," he said with a stuffed mouth. "So glad Doc Bernie gave us the afternoon off."

"Just for a minute? I'm going to check it out, with or without you." She walked away, the disappointed grunt from Bran audible.

"Fine." He caught up with her as she entered the tent.

Two uniformed EMTs sat in folding chairs at a table, one with his arms crossed, the other looking over several food truck flyers.

"If they need any help here," Bran whispered, tickling her ear and sending a thrill down her spine, "it's breaking the boredom."

She nudged him playfully.

"Hey, I know you guys." The folded arm guy pointed at them. "At Doc Bernie's, right?"

Aubrie recalled his face. "That's right." She ran through events back to the day she first arrived, which seemed ages ago. Not in a days-have-been-torturous kind of way. She had gotten to feel comfortable here so quickly, she had forgotten just how fresh she was to town. "You helped with the appendicitis patient."

The man nodded.

"I—*we*"—she eyed Bran—"wanted to see if you needed extra hands here."

"Nah," he said. "It's usually slow at this thing. We get the occasional kid sticking his hand where he shouldn't, getting a finger pinched. Or the tourist who didn't realize they were allergic to shellfish."

"Have you tried any of these?" The other EMT held up the food truck menus.

Bran leaned toward the man. "I'd try the apple dessert one." He showed off the remains of the candy apple.

"Thank you for stopping by, though," the first said. "Do you know any kids who may want a sticker?" He held up one from a stack, the sticker reading *Don't be a crab, get the jab*. "They're from last year's vaccination awareness campaign."

"No," Bran said.

"I'm sure we could use them at the clinic if you don't mind."

"Go for it." He handed her a stack, and she put them in her purse.

"Thank you," she said. "See you around."

"Hopefully not." He chuckled. "At Doc Bernie's, at least. You know what I mean."

"I do." Aubrie waved and followed Bran out the tent. She stopped just outside, halting his footsteps farther into the fair. "Was that so bad?"

He tipped his head back, staring at the sky, like a teenager who had been told to do his chores, which made her giggle. He smiled back. "Is there ever a moment you're not thinking about medicine?" He pointed to her purse, housing the stickers. "About helping people?"

She hadn't thought about it before. How much did she think about work? "It's not exactly the type of job we can walk away from at the end of the day."

He sighed. "I know. But it seems like you bleed medicine. Like it's what gets you out of bed and keeps you going."

She shrugged. "Is it not that way for you?"

He rubbed his chin, as if a beard were there to scratch. "Don't get me wrong. I love what I do. But, with people like you, like Doc Bernie, you live medicine."

A thought was born, one that grew a smirk on her face.

"What?" he asked.

"Are you trying to say that I'm like Doc Bernie? You know, since I'm like him, I'd be great to take over the practice?"

"Wha—I—" He hastily scrambled his hand through his hair.

"I'm joking, Bran."

"Of course."

They started walking to who knew where. It didn't matter, as they were in the middle of the busyness that was the Crab Festival.

Bran stopped, another thought apparently striking him. "You would be great to replace my grandfather. For real."

"Thank you," she said, walking slowly beside him again. "Why do I feel there's a 'but' in there?"

"It's just that, with your mind focused on work all the time, you forget to have fun."

She stopped and turned to him. "Do you really think that of me? That I don't know how to have fun?"

His shoulders nearly touched his ears. "I mean, Doc Bernie's party, hiking, this festival. They've all led to you talking or thinking about work, haven't they?"

She thought over each one on his list. "I guess eventually. But work isn't everything."

He raised an eyebrow.

"What? I can have fun."

Bran swiveled on his heel, looking smug. "Then prove it."

"I don't have to prove myself to you."

"Because you can't."

She felt compelled to slap him, the innate reaction she always held back when someone told her she couldn't do something. She also wanted to show him he was wrong—the reaction she usually acted on. But why did she care what he thought? She questioned whether she didn't know the answer, or didn't want to face the answer. "All right, I'll play your little game."

"No talk of work the rest of the afternoon."

She placed her fingers over her chest. "Promise. No work talk." She couldn't fight the smile forming on her lips as she stepped away from him, walking briskly to a sign up ahead.

"Where are you going?" he shouted behind her.

"To have fun."

TWENTY

BRAN COULDN'T REMEMBER the last time he enjoyed himself as much as he did today. Aubrie had vowed to not talk about work and kept her promise. They worked their way through the food trucks, sampling the finest seafood Maiden's Bay had to offer. They played ring toss, threw darts at balloons, and learned knot-tying from the fishing experts.

It wasn't the activities themselves that amused him. It was the fact he was there with Aubrie, seeing things from her out-of-town perspective. She held such enthusiasm and wonder, like a kid going to the movie theater for the first time. He had been to the Crab Festival several times growing up, but after Mom died, it didn't hold the same excitement. Despite the annual visit being the one tradition Dad had continued.

"You're not afraid of heights are you?" He stood next to her in line for the Ferris wheel. It was something he had wanted to do back when they entered the grounds, but he waited until closer to sunset to suggest it.

"Heights? No." She looked up at the wheel, holding her hand over her brow. The sun reflected off the metal structure, the red, yellow, and orange seat colors nearly indistinguishable in its golden glow. "Other things, yep. But not heights."

Without the talk of work, he had been able to keep it out of his mind, too. But now he wondered about her fears. Did they have something to do with Ben's visit yesterday? As his mind strayed to Doc

Bernie's practice, the guilt of his plan—what he actually planned to do—crept in. The best part of him knew not to carry on with Aubrie. Not to long to touch her cheek or feel the soft strands framing her face or build a stronger connection.

But that's what they were doing, and he didn't want it to stop. He wanted more. He wanted everything of her, to know what she was thinking when she wasn't saying a word, to hold her tight at night and again in the morning. He knew enough how others saw him, that it was all sex and no real emotions. Had there been times it was all for the fun? Sure. Had he wished for something more meaningful? Of course.

And now that opportunity was here, in his hometown. Right in front of him. Why, then, did his head keep saying to run? To leave her be, to let her find someone worthy of her love. Because he sure wasn't.

Aubrie deserved better.

"Are you?" She looked at him quizzically.

He snapped out of his downward spiraling thoughts. "Afraid of heights?" He shook his head. "No."

"I didn't think so."

"Why's that?"

"You seemed pretty comfortable this morning, during the hike, atop Sentinel Hill. My brother, who is almost debilitatingly afraid of heights, wouldn't have crossed the clearing at the top or taken in the view, let alone stand within thirty feet of the cliff's edge." Her eyes nearly glowed when speaking of him. She looked so genuinely happy.

"I get the feeling you're close with him. Your face lights up when you talk about him."

Her cheeks flared red, and she looked down at her shoes.

"Any other siblings?"

"A sister." Her joyous expression faded.

They moved up in the line a few paces and reached the front, Bran thankful for the task interrupting the devolving conversation.

They sat in a red cart, Aubrie to his left. Bran pulled the safety bar into its locked position. The wheel creaked backward, and Aubrie clenched her fists around the metal bar.

"I thought you weren't afraid of heights."

"I'm not," she said, giving him a stare. "Doesn't mean I fully trust old fair rides."

He chuckled. "Point taken. I've certainly seen my fair share of ride accidents—"

Her hand clutched his forearm. "No talk of work. Especially that kind of talk." Her softening scowl reassured him she wasn't upset or put off.

"You're right." He laid his hand on hers, and she didn't pull back. He could leave it there all night as long as she accepted it.

The ride sped up a touch and brought them around to the top. The town of Maiden's Bay sprawled out before them, the setting sun sending streaks of fire light across the water, bouncing off the windows of the shops downtown. The lighthouse stood in its nobility, a commanding beacon that would rotate its beam any minute now.

"Such a wonderful view."

He took in the silhouette of her face, her dark tresses, bangs nearly touching her long lashes. "Sure is."

"I don't think there's a bad view in any of Maiden's Bay." Her attention turned to him, and he swung his stare back out to the north.

"The views from the first floor of rooms at Maiden's Slumber Inn aren't much to look at."

"Oh, no. That's where you're staying, right?"

"It's okay. I have no complaints."

"Except that the stranger from out of town, competing for the favor of your grandfather, is occupying your family's apartment." She smirked.

"You're not a stranger." He smiled as they descended to the bottom of the loop. "And I'm glad you came here. Even if it's to whip my butt in medicine."

She bit her lip, the pink returning to her cheeks in the dying sunlight. "I wouldn't say I'm whipping your butt."

"No?"

"I mean, I'm obviously doing better than you, but—"

He dropped his jaw in half-shock.

She elbowed him and laughed.

"Okay, Miss Competitive. I've got something for us to try. See who's better once and for all."

"Oh, yeah? If it involves catching crustaceans…."

"No. Something a little more fun."

After waiting for two carts to unload, they finally exited the Ferris wheel. Bran grabbed her hand, more to help stay together through the growing evening crowd. But he'd be lying to himself if it didn't feel amazing, to be connected to her, her soft yet skillful hands, the instruments for her talent. He wanted to protect them and her, not let this town or anyone give her cause to worry or feel sad or angry. She deserved to feel as happy as she did this night, for every night.

The sun's final rays disappeared, the evening's cool blues taking over. Strands of lights flicked on, some tiny and sparkling like Christmas lights, others big bulbs as if they were at a carnival. They weaved through the crowd, toward the coastline. A wooden platform was set up on the short beach, a stage that supported dancers and a live band.

"Oh, no." Aubrie tugged at his arm, shaking her head. "You're not taking me up there."

"Come on, it's just dancing." He gave a mock pout, a desperate attempt at puppy eyes.

"If it means you'll stop making that face."

"Yes!"

"Let's be clear. That wasn't victory. That was me saving you the embarrassment of that awful frown. Even I know how this town talks."

He chuckled and led her across a few feet of sandy beach and onto the dance floor. The bay waves lapped the shore some twenty feet away. The moon took over the night sky, casting its silver shadows along the windows of downtown stores along the shoreline.

Bran spun her around, taking the lead. Despite her hesitations, she was a good dancer, catching the beat and following his lead. The quick music ended, and Aubrie let out a sigh with her bottom lip, blowing her bangs lightly off her forehead. She took off her sweater and tied it around her waist.

"I can get you a drink if you'd like." Sweat formed on his brow, and a drink didn't sound bad to him right now.

"No, it's okay."

The crowd grew on the dance floor, pushing them closer to one another. The band kicked into a slow song. Without having to ask, Bran's left hand met her right, their other hands wrapped around each other's backs.

"You know," she said, her warm breath on his neck.

He willed his knees not to buckle.

"I'm sorry."

"For what?" He pulled her in a tad closer, her hand to his chest, afraid she would let go. That she was going to leave him standing alone on this dance floor, coming to her senses.

"For judging you when we first met." She pulled back to look at him. "You're not at all what I pegged you for. I assumed the worst, and obviously, I was wrong."

He moved his hand further up her back, reeling her in closer. "You don't have to apologize. You weren't all wrong."

The weight of his intentions swelled to his mouth, right at the tip of his tongue. He wanted to tell her everything. Confess how he was about to hurt Doc Bernie, all for himself. But she was staring right into his eyes.

"Hey, what is it?" Her hand caressed his face, and he closed his eyes. It was too much to bear, yet not enough of her.

"Aubrie?" The voice of the man next to them pulled Bran out of his push-and-pull conscience. He danced with a child no more than seven or eight who was all smiles and pigtails.

"Garrett?" Aubrie's body froze and broke away from Bran.

That was it. That was the closest he was going to get to Aubrie. And it was more than he had deserved.

"Didn't expect to see you here." Garrett smiled, which turned south when he recognized Bran. "This is my niece, Cora."

The blonde girl gave a nod, holding onto Garrett's hands, feet atop his.

"Bran, can you give us a second?" Aubrie's eyes read pity. Surely for him.

"Sure, go ahead."

"Miss Cora." Garrett gave her a bow, and she giggled before running off the dance floor.

Aubrie walked through the dancers behind Garrett. Bran followed their trail a distance behind. He stood next to a vendor selling seashell jewelry, making out the silhouettes of Aubrie and Garrett alongside the dance platform on the beach.

He couldn't hear anything and didn't want to be caught staring. But it was hard not to wonder what they were saying to one another. There were arm touches, and Aubrie rolling her head back in a laugh. And then they hugged.

Bran felt the fool for thinking Aubrie may feel anything for him. Just look at him. Obvious remnants of his fight in his purple bruise and split lip. He touched it as if it had split open again, the swelling down but not gone.

He wanted to walk away. No, run. Far from the festival. From Doc's practice. From Maiden's Bay. Despite feeling more at home here than he ever felt in his past, he wasn't Maiden's Bay material. He had broken hearts. Broken or bruised a few bones of Sebastian Hycliff, most likely. And he was about to break Doc Bernie's trust, which was tough enough. But now Aubrie's trust was on the line. How could he do either? What sort of person could hurt the people he loved?

He pressed his hands above his eyes, wishing all his past away. Wishing he could be better. Do better.

There had to be another way. A way for everyone to get what they wanted without hurting anybody. What that was, he didn't know.

"Bran?" Aubrie touched his shoulder from behind.

He swung around. "Yeah? Are you... going with Garrett? It's okay, I mean, I can walk back by myself."

Aubrie shook her head, smirk growing. "No, Bran."

"Oh. I thought I caught you two hugging."

"Spying on us, now?"

"No, I—"

"Bran, I'm kidding. Again." She laughed. "You really have to lighten up, you know that?"

"I'm the one who has to lighten up?" Somehow she had done it. Returned the smile on his face and made him feel like the most important person in the world. "So, then... the hug...?"

"I didn't want to make enemies in Maiden's Bay off the bat, so I told him how I felt."

"Which is?" Bran cleared his throat and scratched the back of his neck. "I'm sorry, you don't have to tell me."

"No, I want to tell you." Aubrie grabbed his hands in hers. "I told him that while I had a good time on our date, I didn't feel a connection beyond friendship."

"Oh." Bran sighed and squeezed her hands a smidge tighter. "How'd he take that?"

"Just fine. I think it was early enough not to hurt too much. We wished each other well, and that's that."

"That's that."

"Mmhmm."

Bran touched her cheek, wrapping his fingers behind her ear, along her neck. He pulled her in close, her lips near yet too far away. Beneath the festival air was the sweet smell of her, of flowers and vanilla. She closed her eyes, and he wanted a snapshot of her like this, open and honest and all things Aubrie. She was beautifully dizzying.

The band's music stopped, and the feedback of the microphone rang in the air. "Thanks everyone for coming out tonight, for our sixty-seventh annual Crab Festival."

The crowd cheered and whooped. Bran slumped his shoulders, and Aubrie smiled. He leaned his forehead to hers.

In another life, Aubrie Turnbridge.

He wrapped his arm around her back as they faced the stage.

"Is that the Master Crab?" Aubrie looked at him with a grin. "You know, the MC?"

Bran chuckled. "Either that or the King Crab."

"Wow," she said. "That was worse. *Definitely* worse than mine."

"Oh, come on!"

"Thanks to all of our food trucks, vendors, and entertainment. Stick around for our fireworks show. It's sure to be the best one yet!"

There was applause and hoots, and the band started up once again.

Bran turned. "You want to stay out for the fireworks? We can stay here, or head out to Campy's and watch from the dock. A bunch of people gather there. It's actually a better vantage point."

"Where do they set them off from?"

Bran leaned in closer, his face almost touching hers. "You see those lights sort of bobbing on the water there?" He pointed out to the middle of the bay, and Aubrie nodded. "They do it off that ship. Just safer for the crowd, plus less likely to start a wildfire in these parts."

Aubrie stared out at the water, biting her lip.

"What? What is it? I know that look."

"What look?" Aubrie snapped out of her trance.

"The one where you're thinking up something."

She huffed in amusement. "I think I have the perfect place to watch them."

TWENTY-ONE

AUBRIE TRIED TO remember how the apartment looked this morning when she had left it. Funny how the morning felt like it was days ago. First the hike, then Doc Bernie calling them in. Then, the festival.

It was sometime between the hike and festival that she realized what her heart wanted. It wasn't the polite and handsome Garrett. She was sure he'd treat her right and was a genuinely good man. But seeing him on the dance floor confirmed her feelings. She had to tell him they weren't right together.

Because she was falling for someone else.

Aubrie led Bran up the stairs to the second story apartment. Luckily, it remained tidy, minus a bowl or two in the kitchen, which she promptly put in the sink.

"Make yourself comfortable. After all, you know where everything is." Her hands shook as she reached for a wine glass in an upper cabinet. Maybe this was a bad idea, having him over. "Would you like a glass of red? I'll open a new bottle."

"Sure." Bran stood, hands in his pockets, looking out the window.

She got another glass, uncorked the cabernet sauvignon, and poured it into one glass. After taking two gulps for herself, damn nerves getting the best of her, she poured some in his glass and brought it over to him.

"It is a good spot to watch the fireworks." He turned, accepting the glass. "Thank you."

"You said Campy's gets busy. I don't know, with today's events, the crowds at the festival… I could use a bit of space."

"No, I get it." Bran held his glass in the air. "What are we 'cheers-ing' to?"

"Hmm. I always feel like whatever I come up with is cheesy."

"It is an odd custom, isn't it?" He stared out the window a second, then back to Aubrie. "Well, since we're here for the fireworks, why not to fireworks?"

She lifted her glass. "To fireworks."

They clinked glasses. She took down another gulp, the alcohol warming and relaxing. The feeling of Bran holding her hand on the dance floor, touching her back, her face, burned into her skin's memory. It happened naturally, a progression throughout the evening that left her wanting more. Now, standing alone in the apartment, there was an awkwardness. A pressure to fill the silent air with conversation, to ease back to where they had left things off.

"You know, the stairwell goes all the way up to the roof." Bran stared into his glass before his gaze moved upward to her eyes. "If I'm remembering right, there are some extra blankets in the chest at the foot of the bed."

Getting out of the growing stuffiness and silence of the apartment seemed like a perfect idea. Aubrie set her glass down and rummaged through the chest, finding two heavy, fluffy folded blankets. She checked the bedroom door, Bran respectfully waiting in the living area. She hurried to the head of the bed, straightening the sheets.

"Find any?" Bran shouted.

Aubrie stopped her fussing, grabbed the blankets, and returned to the living room. "Two enough?"

"That should do." He took the blankets out of her arms, still holding his glass of wine. She followed him out of the apartment, snatching her glass and the open wine bottle, and into the stairwell. She hadn't been up to the roof during her stay. It wasn't something she would normally explore. The stairs alerted her to the growing soreness of her muscles from the morning's hike.

Bran held the door open for her, and she walked out onto the roof. The ascent was worth the aches.

The roof put her high enough over the shops across the street that she could almost see the breaking waves on the coastline behind them. The crescent moon's reflection rippled on the water's surface, while a light but crisp breeze blew in from the sea.

"Here." Bran arranged one of the blankets on the roof, comfortably enough from the western edge of the building. He held a hand out to hold her wine glass as she sat down.

The blast in the sky jolted her muscles to tighten.

"It's just the fireworks starting."

"I wasn't ready for that." She giggled, crossing her legs and sipping her wine.

Bran took the second blanket and covered her shoulders. She scooted closer to him for it to stretch across his at the same time. Her bent knee rested atop his thigh.

The fireworks boomed more frequently, giant sparkles of crimsons and gold and royal blues. In their radiance, clusters of people watched from the road and dotted the rooftops. The biggest fanfare came from the right up Pearl Avenue, which she assumed to be from Campy's.

Bran drew nearer, the warmth of his body overpowering the magic of the wine. He whispered in her ear. "Do you hear that?"

She sat still, looking out to the sky, straining to pick up whatever he did. She thought she made out the faint sound of music, but the fireworks washed away anything before she could cling to it.

"I don't think—" She turned to him. He wasn't looking out at the light show, or leaning to hear anything. He stared right at Aubrie, a hunger in his eyes, lips slightly parted.

He moved slowly, a smoothness to his actions, as she had pictured him to be in the most serious of emergencies. Cool and calm. Steady and determined.

He took the glass out of her hand and set it down. He touched her hand, the initial sensation reflexively pulling it back, but she fought it, embraced it. She wanted the touch.

He pulled her hand to his chest, his heart racing beneath his jacket, beneath the flannel. "I thought maybe you could hear how crazy you make me."

"Bran."

"I don't deserve to be here, in this moment, with you, so I'm going to cherish every second, every millisecond, I get."

"How could you say that?" She touched his cheek, other hand frozen on his chest. There were many reasons not to move forward. How long it had been for her, how she wasn't completely healed from the trauma of a year ago, how he was the reason her future in Maiden's Bay wasn't set. That she didn't know him for long enough.

But she had seen enough of him. How she had been wrong about him. How he was a good person.

He closed his eyes, shaking his head. She held onto his cheek and pressed forward, meeting his cabernet-laced lips, the sweet and bitter an intoxicating mixture. He let out a soft moan, hand traveling up her neck, cupping her hair. She felt his chest, then around his shoulder, muscles taut and warm.

"Should we go back downstairs?" She let it out in short breaths between kisses.

He nodded, not letting go of her lips with his.

She made the move to stand, both of them a balancing act, refusing to let go of each other.

Bran kicked over one of the wine glasses. "Oh, shit."

Aubrie pulled on his collar, giving him more kisses. "It's okay. Don't worry about it."

They managed to work their way through the door, back to the stairwell. Aubrie pulled away, holding onto his hand and racing down the stairs. She turned to the apartment door, and Bran turned her around. His body pressed up against hers, her back against the door. He kissed her neck, collapsing all resolve in her legs, melting away any and all doubts.

"Let me get the door," she giggled. She finagled the handle and managed to open it, the two of them nearly falling into the apartment.

She rolled Bran's jacket off his shoulders, and he shuffled with taking it off, hands stuck in the sleeves. Finally, he flung it, the jacket hitting the floor. Aubrie took off her sweater, walking backward to the bedroom.

Their bodies met again, his sweet lips an addictive candy, soft tongue sending shivers down her neck, her spine, past the heat rising in her core, down to her toes.

She fell back onto the bed, Bran atop her. He kissed her neck again before pulling back.

Aubrie opened her eyes, meeting his stare.

He looked at her like she was the only thing he had ever desired in the world. "Aubrie, I don't want to rush this."

Aubrie sat up halfway, on her elbows. "You want to slow down?"

"God, no. But you deserve to be loved. The right way. I don't want you to think this is something I do." His breathing quickened, and he lowered his gaze. "I mean, I know my past actions would say otherwise. But I want you to know you're…." He clung to find the words.

"Hey." She touched his cheek, Bran cherishing it with closed eyes. "It's okay."

He opened his eyes, taking her hand in his. "I don't want to mess this up. Because I care about you. More than I can say."

"Bran, I know." She wanted to tell him all the ways she knew—how she'd catch the way he looked at her, how he protected her from Garrett that day in the office, or worried about her when she managed a panic attack. It was in his gaze, his voice, his touch. In all the things she wanted more of.

She grabbed his shirt, a shirt she fully intended to have on her floor in the morning, and pulled him to within an inch of her face.

"You don't have to tell me. *Show* me."

Sunday, September 23

AUBRIE WOKE TO the smell and sounds of coffee brewing. The

morning sun shone through her window, indicating she had slept at least past seven. There was no knowing what time they had fallen asleep last night. The fireworks had long died down before their hunger for each other had.

Bran walked through the bedroom door in blue checkered boxers and no shirt. She couldn't imagine getting tired of seeing his muscular body. He wasn't thick like a bodybuilder, but lean and fit like a runner. The fact that she didn't know how he stayed in shape—did he hike more than she thought?—bothered her for only a second. She knew the parts of him that mattered.

"I'm not much of a breakfast maker." He handed her a mug.

"Thanks." Her voice sounded sleepy, even to her.

"Now breakfast *buying,* I'm all over that. Maybe we could go grab something?"

"Sure. Give me a few to wake up first?"

He nodded and slid into bed next to her. After a few sips, she set the mug down and found the nook where his chest met his shoulder to rest her head. Perfection.

She had wanted to open up yesterday, to tell him about her past. She knew he wanted to know, wanted to get closer to her. Understand her. And after last night, it seemed wrong to leave it for later.

"Bran? About the other day."

"What about the other day?" He set his mug aside and placed his newly-free arm over her in an embrace.

"With Ben and Annabel. I wanted to tell you sooner, but I didn't know how."

"It's okay. You don't have to tell me until you're ready."

She took comfort in it but also wanted to let it out at once. "I had many patients come through my department in Dallas. The good thing, if there is such a thing, about pediatric cancer is that most patients have good outcomes, especially caught early. Of course, not every patient does."

"That must be hard." He caressed her arm.

"My last patient, before I moved here… he wasn't technically my patient, but I pushed for a procedure." She left the comfort of his hold, sitting up and leaning against the headboard. "He was my sister's son. My nephew Reid." The tears were unstoppable, clouding her vision. "His prognosis wasn't great, but he could've had a few years… if I hadn't pushed my sister into the experimental treatment." All composure was lost, and she cried into her hand, afraid to show him, to show the world, her grief.

"Come here." Bran held her tight, letting her release a year's worth of pent up frustration, regret, guilt.

"I was there, outside his room, when he passed. Just this limp, lifeless boy, hooked up to tubes and machines. By then, we knew it was coming, but my sister…. She was at his bedside. I had never heard such a guttural cry in my life. I couldn't bring myself to go in."

"Annabel being carried in listless… that brought it all back?"

Aubrie nodded.

"I'm so sorry, Aubrie. I can't say I understand exactly what you went through. But as a doctor… you hear other people tell you it wasn't your fault, that you were doing what you thought best. I at least understand how none of that is comforting. Even if they are right."

She sighed, the tears managing to die down. "You're right. Had it been anyone else, anyone, I would say those same things to them. So, why can't my mind wrap around that logic when it's me? My sister tried to tell me as much, several times after. But I didn't want to hear it."

He squeezed her again, and they sat in silence for a moment. A chuckle ended the solitude.

"What?" She looked up, and he pinched the bridge of his nose.

"Nothing."

"No, tell me."

He chuckled again. "I was just thinking what a sorry lot of doctors we are. One of us can't take care of the elderly, the other kids."

Through the relief and pain, he could still make her laugh. "Maybe we can specialize in eighteen to sixty-year-olds."

He laughed harder. "Basically, we can handle the healthiest cohort of patients."

She broke into laughter. It felt good to have the truth out and be able to laugh in the same five minutes. Maybe meeting Bran was what she had needed. A new relationship. A doctor who knew where she was coming from, how she thought.

Bran's phone buzzed, and he looked at the caller ID.

"No, don't get it." She nuzzled her head to his chest.

"It's Edith."

Aubrie raised her head as Bran answered. His relaxed joyfulness quickly turned. He shot up in the bed.

"What do you mean? Did you call 911? We're coming." He hung up the phone and ran out of the bedroom.

She followed after him. "What is it?" The living room flashed with lights and shadows coming from below. She rushed to the windows and looked outside.

"It's Doc." Bran stared down at the ambulance, as if in disbelief. "He's unconscious."

TWENTY-TWO

"WE'RE HEADED THERE right now." Bran pressed the end call button on the touch screen, other hand on the steering wheel.

"Does he have a history of this?" Aubrie clutched her purse in the front passenger seat.

"Not that I know of." But Bran had been out of Maiden's Bay for years. It wasn't hard to believe he was kept out of the family loop when it came to just about anything. Like his dad and stepmom moving to Florida. "I wouldn't put it past him not to tell anyone. You know how doctors make the worst patients."

Aubrie nodded, and they rode in silence the rest of the way to White Bend. It didn't have quite the prestige as Seattle University Hospital, but Bran was thankful it was here. There was no telling how bad Doc Bernie's situation would be if he had to go all the way to Seattle.

The hospital was a beige, two-story, rectangular building. Bran swore The University of Washington's library was larger. He parked the car, and they entered through the emergency doors. Edith shot up out of her chair in the waiting room upon seeing them.

"Hey, Edith." Bran gave her a hug, something he hadn't ever done. She looked so worried and ran right up to him, it was the natural thing to do. "What happened? You were both in the office on a Sunday?"

"You know Doc. He had gotten behind on some paperwork at the office. Had a stack of papers a mile high. I offered to help him go through them, and he offered me overtime. Said that Sunday would be best since we wouldn't be open for patients except for emergencies."

"What happened then?" Aubrie asked. "Were you in the room when it happened? Or did you find him?"

"I heard a noise and ran to his office. I found him passed out on the floor. Nearly fell on top of his desk. I thought maybe he'd had a heart attack or stroke. But he was just out cold. By the time the paramedics arrived and I called you, he came to. I think he'll be okay." Edith touched his shoulder.

"Can we see him?" Aubrie asked.

"They won't let anyone see him yet. They assured me they'd come out once they had more information."

Bran hated the waiting game. He knew how parents, spouses, loved ones of patients fretted in the waiting room. How they watched the television screen like zombies, not processing anything because all they could think about was their loved one possibly dying.

He grabbed a cup of water from the water jug and sat down next to Aubrie. What if Doc Bernie didn't pull through? What would happen?

Bran paced the waiting area, feeling awful it took an emergency to knock some sense into him. How could he even have considered selling Doc's practice, and kept it a secret? The water suddenly didn't sit well in his stomach.

He rubbed his face in his hand. It all made sense what he had to do. In order for Doc and Aubrie to have what they wanted, for the town to have what it needed.

He had to walk away from it.

It was the right choice, one he should've made a long time ago, before things got complicated. Before he fell for Aubrie, before he grew fond of town. He had to tell Doc and Aubrie he was out of the running. The thought of Doc Bernie dying with the chance he'd leave the practice to Bran, when it should go to Aubrie, would eat away at him. More than it already had. Not just that. He could lose the family member who actually gave him a chance to prove himself. To believe in himself.

"Hey." Aubrie grabbed his hand, squeezing it lightly. "He's going to be okay. He's a strong man. Not just fit for his age, but he's got the will of a lion."

Bran faintly smiled. "You're right about that. If anyone could pull through, it's my grandfather." His attention veered to the new arrivals through the entrance doorway, surprised at the recognition. A grayer, aged version of Nathaniel faced him. "Dad?"

"Bran." Dad came over, Rita with her cropped dark curls and worry on her round face behind him. Dad grasped Bran in a hug.

Bran didn't know whether to pat his back, squeeze tighter, or ask what happened to his father.

Dad released him from the awkwardness. "What's going on?"

"We don't have any news yet. Just waiting."

"Rita and I worried about this sort of thing happening."

"You knew he was having issues?"

"No." He shook his head vigorously. "It's just that your grandfather is getting up there in age. With Rita and me moving to Florida, we worry there's no one looking out for him when he's up here. But knowing you'll be here, taking over the practice... I have to admit it's a bit of a relief."

Bran didn't think his heart could sink any further, but his father's words managed to push it deeper. Who knew Dad actually had genuine concern over Doc Bernie, let alone trusted Bran to look after him? And what did he mean when he's up here?

"Actually, it's good you're here, too. Not just for Doc Bernie's sake. There's something I need to tell everyone." Bran turned to Edith and Aubrie. "Dad, Rita, this is Aubrie Turnbridge. The doctor I've been working with at Doc's."

Dad firmly shook her hand. "Nice to meet you, Aubrie. I'd love to hear what it's been like working with this guy."

Aubrie smiled briefly.

"I'm sorry to cut this short, but there's something you all need to hear."

"What is it?"

A man in scrubs came through the double doors near the check-in desk. He lowered his mask and took off his cap. "Are you all here for Bernie Jackson?"

"Yes." Bran swallowed down the lump in his throat.

"He's doing okay. Looks like he fainted due to anemia. It's not an uncommon side effect of the rheumatoid arthritis medication. We're running a few more tests just to rule out anything else."

Bran had a thousand questions that refused to line up in his mouth.

"Can we see him?" Dad asked.

"We can send two back at a time. But he has asked specifically for Doctor Jackson and Doctor Turnbridge."

Bran looked to Dad, who nodded in agreement.

"I can take you two back, and when you're finished, rotate."

"Thank you, Doctor." Bran followed him with Aubrie at his side, going over the steps he'd have to take to concede. He'd have to close matters out with attorney Mitch Henderson, keep in contact with Doctor Fredericks in Seattle to make sure he survived probation. Then, maybe look for something else in Maiden's Bay. Maybe this hospital would want his expertise.

But the silver lining in all of this was thinking of a life with Aubrie. Giving their relationship all he had.

The doctor stopped at a doorway to a patient room. "I didn't mention before, but we nearly had to give him a sedative the more he came to. Of course, with the anemia, that wasn't advisable."

"What?" Aubrie eyed Bran. He thought the same thing. Did passing out freak Doc Bernie out?

"I just want you to be aware of his mental state." The doctor tapped the doorway, door ajar. "Doctor Jackson? The visitors you asked for." He nodded for them to walk in. Bran entered after Aubrie.

"Hey, Doc," she said in a sweet voice. "Had us in a good scare there."

"Tell me about it." He sighed and smiled, seemingly in good spirits given the circumstance.

Aubrie sat in the chair next to his bed, and Bran remained standing next to her.

"How are you feeling?" Bran asked.

"I've been better. Been worse."

"I don't think I want to hear about the worse bit." Aubrie tapped the back of Doc's hand, minding the wires from the IV. "Let's just agree that is behind us, and we'll go from there."

"I didn't know you had rheumatoid arthritis," Bran said.

"No one did but me and my medical team." Doc Bernie said it with an heir of obstinacy. "No one asked me why. Why retire now? I know plenty of doctors practicing in their seventies."

Aubrie took a deep breath. "Your hands." She clasped his hand tighter. "I had noticed a while back but didn't put it together."

Doc Bernie nodded. "With the stiffness, and mobility not what it used to be, I just knew it was time. Luckily, there are more medications out there than ten, twenty years ago. Unfortunately, this latest one doesn't seem to agree with me." He smiled with an air of sadness.

"I'm sorry, Doc," Bran said. About many things. He had noticed, thinking back, but he'd been so wrapped up in his own drama to be concerned about Doc's health. "I should've paid more attention."

Doc nodded. "Actually, could you help me out?"

"Sure." Bran stepped closer to the bed. "Do you need up?"

"Can you grab something out of my clothes. I think they're over there, in a bag."

Bran turned around and located a big plastic bag with Doc Bernie's items in it.

"There's an envelope in my jacket pocket."

"Okay." Bran fished through the clothes, locating the jacket and the envelope inside. He glanced at the return address, and the lump in his throat returned. Seattle University Hospital... Health Care Real Estate Group.

"Would you hand that to me?" Doc Bernie stared right into his eyes. The charade was over.

Doc knew.

Bran slowly handed it over to Doc.

"Edith was helping me go through paperwork earlier today, when I came across this. At first, I thought it was a shot in the dark, perhaps spam that all practices were getting."

"Doc—"

"But then I put it together. Of course. I should've known, but then again, I didn't think my own grandson would trick me into handing him the practice, only for him to sell it."

"What?" Aubrie turned to him. "What is he talking about?"

"Here," Doc said. "Read it for yourself." He handed Aubrie the letter. "Or did you want to tell her first, Bran?"

"Aubrie, I—"

Aubrie held up a finger to quiet him. She rose out of her chair, scanning the letter. "But this, this wasn't you, Bran, right? You didn't pitch them the practice." She read clear to the end, her breathing quickening. "You want to sell the practice to Seattle University Hospital? All this time, you...."

"I didn't know they'd send something out before—"

"Before *what*? Before Doc gave it all to you? You'd sell your family's practice? The one that provides care to so many people in town?"

"You said yourself how the area could use better access to medical care." It was not the answer he should've said. But it didn't register that way until hearing it.

"Oh, so, what? You were trying to trick me into agreeing with you? Bran, I meant it wouldn't hurt to have new satellite locations out where Grace Donchik lives. Don't twist my words around." She pointed at Bran, her anger in her shaky hands. "And even so, I would never agree with throwing away Doc's practice. Especially behind his back."

"Why, Bran?" Doc's voice broke, breaking Bran's heart. "What could they possibly give you to do such a thing?"

Bran looked down, shoes and floor tiles blurry.

"I know why." Aubrie nodded. "That's right. Makes sense now. I know exactly why."

"Aubrie—"

She turned back to Doc. "It's because he's on probation. And he's worried they won't reinstate him into the residency program. Serving your practice on a platter would make some board members reconsider." She turned back to Bran. "Am I missing anything out of that?"

Bran wanted to scream. To tell her he had been wrong from the start. That he knew better now, that the practice meant more to Maiden's Bay than it ever could to some other hospital. That she helped him see how self-absorbed, selfish, and hurtful his behavior was. That things were different now.

But all of that didn't matter. It didn't erase the fact that he came up with the plan in the first place. So, he didn't scream. "That's the gist of it."

Even though Aubrie had guessed it, the letdown in her eyes was unbearable. As if a part of her held out hope she was wrong.

"I don't know what to say." Doc Bernie took a long blink. "I have a grandson who would squander my legacy, the one thing I built over my life that means the most to me. The most outside of family." He eyed Bran again, a stare full of daggers and disappointment. "I guess it just hit me hard, reading those words, realizing their full meaning. I thought my heart hit the floor, but everything turned black." His eyes filled with tears, the heart monitor beeping faster.

Aubrie patted his shoulder. "Maybe we should go so you can rest."

"Why didn't you tell me about the probation, Bran?"

"I…." There was no legitimate excuse. It was purely to save his own ass. And in order to save it, he behaved like one. "Because I failed." He shrugged. "I didn't want anyone to know that the one person everyone expected to fail did."

"And you, Aubrie," Doc berated. "You knew about his probation and didn't say anything?"

"Aubrie is innocent in all this," Bran said.

Aubrie whipped around. "I don't need you to defend me." She turned to Doc, holding his hand. "I am so sorry. It was wrong of me not to say anything. I had hoped Bran was going to speak to you about it and encouraged him to. I didn't think it was my place to mention it, since we were both trying for the same thing. But I'm sorry."

Bran's blood boiled through his veins. He wanted to both beg for forgiveness and run out of here, out of town, as quickly as the gossip would travel. It wasn't supposed to go this way. But maybe that's what he deserved.

"I'm gonna go get Dad and Rita. They were only letting two at a time, and they're waiting out there." Bran headed through the door out into the hallway. He couldn't stand to look at Doc or Aubrie. And if he thought his relationship with Dad was rocky now, wait until he heard the truth.

He walked down the hallway to the waiting room.

"Bran!" Aubrie chased after him and caught up. "What are you going to do?"

"I'm getting Dad and—"

"No, Bran. I mean…." She clenched his arm, holding him in place, forcing him to look at her beautiful disdainful face. "What are you going to do?"

He took deep breaths before answering. "I'm going to leave, Aubrie."

"Then what? Huh?" She let go, folding her arms across her chest. "Hope Seattle takes you back? What about us, Bran? Are you going to leave us, too?"

It was the last thing he wanted. But he'd never make her understand. "It's for the best."

"So, that's it?" Her eyes welled with tears. "What about last night? I thought… I felt…."

This was worse than any torture he could ever imagine. "I told you, I don't deserve to be with you." He couldn't look her in the eyes. Not anymore.

"You know what? You're right."

She ran off past him to the waiting room and out the front door.

TWENTY-THREE

Thursday, September 27

THE PAST SEVERAL days slogged on. Aubrie went back and forth between staying until she found another job and getting the hell out of Maiden's Bay. She didn't know where exactly Bran was, but the most logical choice was his apartment in Seattle. Still, she hesitated every time she considered going to Campy's Bait and Bar, or out to pick up a coffee and pastry at Crescent Cafe, with the fear of running into him.

Was there anything left to say to him at this point? He knew what he had been doing the entire time. Knew that making Doc Bernie's practice affiliated with Seattle University Hospital would take local money without providing the local level of care. Patients would either have to travel farther for more serious ailments, or they'd opt to go to White Bend Hospital, which would mean they probably wouldn't continue going to the practice. Who knew what it meant for their insurance coverage?

She swore to stop thinking about it, but it kept nagging her. How could he have been so cold-hearted? Did the people of Maiden's Bay mean nothing to him? Did she mean nothing to him?

She closed her jacket tighter, the gray day adding to her melancholy. The cold breeze and dreariness felt more like what she pictured a winter day here, not one in September. She had braved the walk to the lighthouse, one of the last sites on her bucket list to see before leaving. Where to, that was the question. Doc Bernie had pleaded with her to stay two weeks, giving him time to find a replacement. And honestly, giving her time to figure out what the heck she was doing with her life.

She walked the curvature of Pearl Avenue, the lighthouse behind her and a cluster of houseboats floating on the water. Maybe that's what she needed to do. Get on a boat and float wherever the current took her. It was about as decisive as her current situation.

Her phone buzzed in her pocket. For a moment, she found herself hoping it was Bran, yet she had no desire to speak with him. Perhaps knowing he was thinking of her as much as she thought about him, despite her not wanting to, would give her a little hope in his humanity.

She checked the caller ID and sighed. "Hi, Mom."

"Finally! I've been trying to reach you since your father told me about what happened."

Aubrie's plan had worked, at least for a few days. Calling Dad to explain the situation at the practice was the right move. He'd tell Mom so at least she'd know the big picture, then Aubrie could decide when to pick up whenever Mom called. Whenever she was ready.

She still didn't feel ready for the barrage of questions, but it'd be rude of her to let it linger any longer.

"I know. I saw your missed calls. I just needed some time to process everything."

"What are you going to do? Are you still in Washington?"

"For the time being." Aubrie walked by Campy's, the porch as barren as the sunlight. "Doc Bernie asked me to stay to give him some *time to find someone else."*

"How long will that be?"

"I agreed to two weeks. It wouldn't be right to just drop him and the patients." Although that's what Bran did. Saying it out loud would only poke the inquisition bear.

"And then you'll come home?"

Aubrie stopped in front of Bea's Bouquets. A woman with sleek dark hair pulled back into a bun busied herself with taking out the sunflowers, making way for the next window display.

"I've applied to a few other places." Luckily, several of the positions she had eyed before spotting the Maiden's Bay opening were still open for applicants, though closing out soon. Hopefully, she'd get a call for an interview from one of them.

Mom's silence on the other end was enough for Aubrie to know how the woman felt. No sense in hiding the truth now.

"San Francisco. Pittsburgh. Boston."

"Dallas?"

Aubrie sighed, a staggered one in time with her quickening steps. "No, Mom."

"Aubrie, I know losing Reid—"

She stopped again, nearing the television and radio station on the southern end of Pearl Avenue. "This isn't about Reid. I mean, I've come to realize that I'm not entirely healed. That I need to actively take steps to move forward with it. I know speaking to a professional will help, and I fully intend on doing so. But this is not all about what happened there. It may have started out that way, and me running away from it, but not now. This is about me finding my purpose. Figuring out where I should be. And I wish you'd not just listen to me, but *hear* me. Really hear what I'm saying."

The silence lingered. Aubrie started to think the connection had been dropped, but Mom spoke up. *"I do hear you, honey. All I can go by is your word, and I do hope what you're saying is true. I hope you've processed what happened with Reid and have learned to move forward. As much as it hurts me that you won't be around, I really do hope you find what you're looking for."*

It was the first time Mom acknowledged her words over her circumstance for what they were. The truth.

Emotion swelled through her, the wind not helping with the tears forming in her eyes. "Thank you."

"You'll let me know when you hear back from those places you applied to?"

Aubrie looked up at the sky, two seabirds holding out their wings, letting the wind do the work. "Of course. Bye, Mom."

She hung up and plodded onward to the front door of KSMV, the local TV station for Maiden's Bay and most of the Crescent Coast. Meeting up with Josie had been in the back of Aubrie's mind for some time. But between Doc Bernie's practice, the date with Garrett, and time with Bran, she hadn't found a window of energy. She would've preferred to meet with Cynthia to have a third person to help with conversation, but she was out on *Harpeth Rose* with Ben Campbell. Which reminded her to check in with his wife Angela about their daughter while he was out.

A man at the front desk greeted her.

"Hi, I'm supposed to meet Josie?"

"Go ahead on back. They're done with the midday news."

"Thanks." Aubrie walked through the hallway. At the end of it lay a large room divided into sections, with a news desk in one area and a more laid-back couch arrangement next to it.

A hand tapped Aubrie's elbow.

"Hey, Aubrie." Josie's hair was perfectly still, the tight brunette curls sprayed frozen, most likely for the camera. Her makeup was thick but not cakey, perhaps the most flawless a newswoman could look given what she had to wear for the camera.

"Hi, Josie. Sorry if I'm late."

"You're fine. Come on back." Josie guided Aubrie to a side room of the hallway, a break room with a mini kitchen and table. "I got us salad and sandwiches delivered from Crescent Cafe, if that's okay."

"Yeah. Sounds great." Aubrie took off her blazer and hung it off the back of a chair before sitting.

"Thanks for coming out to the station. I know it's not an ideal luncheon place, but it's hard to get lunch in between the live broadcast and then editing, filming advertisements, all that stuff."

"No worries. I've never been to a television studio."

Josie divided the salad onto two plates. "You should come back some time to watch us shoot. I can get you a pass."

"That'd be cool."

"That is, if you're still around?"

Aubrie's shoulders slumped. "Okay, what exactly did you hear?"

"You know. I joke that our local broadcast is always late when it comes to Maiden's Bay." She winked and offered up the two sandwiches.

Aubrie opted for the turkey and swiss over the ham on rye.

"I didn't get the fine details, but I do know something happened with Doc Bernie? That maybe he had a change of heart about retiring?"

Aubrie considered whether or not to correct her. On the one hand, she wouldn't have to explain the drama with Bran. On the other, she didn't want the town putting that kind of pressure on Doc.

"He had a little emergency. That part's true. But it's a bit more complicated when it comes to me and Bran."

Josie nodded. "I figured as much. Well, Nick said something in passing about it. Oh, and Cynthia." Josie bit into her sandwich.

Aubrie got the feeling she knew more than what she was letting on. "What did they say?"

"They were talking about visiting the practice. I guess they had a day of physicals? Nick is a stickler for safety. I can't hate him for that. In fact, I love him for doing his due diligence as captain."

Aubrie picked at her salad, not really taking a bite.

"Anyway, they said they sensed something was up between you and young Doctor Jackson."

Aubrie bit her bottom lip. It's not like there were dozens of people she could talk to about this. If any drama had come up, she would've talked to Bran. But Bran was in the center of all of it. It was one of the reasons, beyond having promised her, that she called Josie to meet up.

"I'm sorry," Josie said. "I'm prying. We barely know each other."

Aubrie held up a hand. "No, it's okay. It's good to have a girlfriend to talk to. I'm only sorry I didn't call you sooner. Maybe I wouldn't be in this mess."

Josie pouted, a sincere emission of pity.

"I thought there was something between us. That I had misjudged him as a jerk, a player. He seemed to really care about the patients and about the town. Then, I learned his plan was to acquire the practice to sell to Seattle University Hospital."

"Is that a bad thing?"

Aubrie left her food untouched. "I know Doc Bernie's isn't the only medical practice in town. But it's the most trusted, and probably most valued. With such a change, in some ways healthcare would be less accessible. But it's not the idea of selling the practice. It's how he was sneaky about it. That he would do it behind Doc's back. And after all that, he's gone. Dropped everyone like we meant nothing."

"Are you certain that's why he left?"

It was a simple question. She hadn't considered that he left for any other reason than selfishness.

"I mean, why else? Doc Bernie found out, and it nearly killed him."

Josie laid down her fork and pushed the salad plate aside. "Maybe he was embarrassed. From what Nick has told me about him, he wasn't exactly the most reliable person when he was younger. Is it that hard to think he was different, that he was genuinely passionate about practicing medicine here, got caught up in whatever it is he got caught up in, and was embarrassed? To show his face with yet another failure at his hands?"

The thought sent pangs through Aubrie's stomach. Could she be wrong? Bran had mentioned failure when Doc shared the letter. Were her feelings for Bran interfering with objectively looking at the situation?

No. What he did to Doc Bernie was inexcusable, even if it was his idiotic way of preserving his career.

"Have you asked him how he could do it? How he felt about it, about you?"

"Yeah." She thought over the fight in the hospital, some words clear in her mind, others a blur. "Maybe not directly."

"He didn't say anything to you?"

She sat up firmer, certain words blazed into her brain. "He said he doesn't deserve me."

"Hm." Josie slid her sandwich in front of her but didn't unwrap the wrapper. "I don't know, Aubrie. I don't know him, nor you that well. I'd like to think the best in people. It's not just part of my job with my series I do here, but it's in my nature. And for someone to admit you deserve better, sounds to me like he does care for you."

Aubrie shook her head. "Knowing you've done wrong and changing to be better are two different things."

Josie shrugged. "Maybe he needed time away from you, from Doc, to be better."

Aubrie didn't know if she should take Josie's approach, or be upset Josie was taking his side of things.

"So, if Doc isn't going to stay on at the practice, after all, why are you leaving?"

She had floundered answering this question for herself over the past couple of days. She wanted to say because she wasn't the right fit. Because Doc would need someone with different expertise. Because the right thing to do for Doc was to give him space from her and Bran. But those were all excuses. Not the truth.

"I don't think I can be there, in that office, with constant reminders of Bran around me. And it's not just the office. It's Pearl Avenue, it's Campy's. It's Sentinel Hill and Park. It's all of Maiden's Bay." Her eyes welled up for the second time today. Damn Bran Jackson.

Josie reached out and touched Aubrie's hand.

"I'm sorry," Aubrie said. "This is our first lunch, and I'm dumping my baggage onto you." She wiped her eyes with the back of her free hand. "It's unfair to you. I waited too long to do this. You're a good listener, and I feel like you'd be such a good friend. Here I am, trying to leave when I'm not sure I want to."

Josie smiled. "Hon, we're not done with us. Not by any means. Whether you decide to stick it out in Maiden's Bay, or you go to Timbuktu. We're just beginning."

TWENTY-FOUR

BRAN KNELT IN the grass alongside Doc Bernie's home, plopping another flat stone in place. It had pained him to leave the hospital last week the way he did. But how could he face the man he had set out to take advantage of? Some of the only family who had been supportive of him? Yet it hurt more not knowing how Doc's recovery was going. And that he was the cause of Doc needing a recovery in the first place.

"Why don't you take a break?" Nathaniel held out an iced tea. The weather had turned early in the week, a cold front frosting the leaves overnight and sending a biting wind through in the afternoons. It didn't register a whole lot after Bran worked up a sweat making Doc's pathway safer.

"I want to get this finished."

Nathaniel crouched beside him. "How long are you going to punish yourself?"

"That depends." Bran sat up, staring at his younger, albeit wiser, brother. "How long are you going to be the perfect son?"

"Come on." He handed Bran the tea and stood, waiting for him to follow. If Bran had known Doc would have Dad over, and Nathaniel on his fall break, he might've stayed away longer.

Bran took his time after standing, sipping the tea and catching his breath.

"I'm not perfect, you know." Nathaniel crossed his arms.

"I know." It really was in jest. Nevermind the underlying truth to it.

"Sometimes I don't think you realize what it's like being me. Being the one who is the responsible one, that follows the rules, that falls in line with what the family wants."

"I didn't mean—"

Nathaniel held up a hand. "No. You never mean for anything. You get to do what you want, like you have ultimate freedom. While I was stuck at home, having to make up for it with good behavior. Every time you got yourself in trouble, I made extra sure I wouldn't cause more trouble for Dad."

Bran ran his hand through his hair. He hadn't thought about the pressure his actions put on Nathaniel. "You're right. I had no idea." He looked at his brother, the little boy he knew all grown up. "I'm sorry, Nathaniel. It seems everything I do ends up hurting the people I care about." He shook his head. "I don't mean that as an excuse, like I'm helpless. I'm going to do better. I will do better. I just hope, in time, you can forgive me."

Nathaniel shook his head. "Of course I forgive you." His lips turned up in a smirk. "It *does* help seeing you struggle with physical labor, though."

Bran smiled. "I'm not struggling."

"You're certainly not thriving."

They shared a laugh, and Nathaniel led him to the back deck, where Doc Bernie and Dad were lounging in chairs.

"How's it coming?" Dad asked.

"Getting there," Bran said.

"I noticed a few loose railings along the deck." Dad glared at him.

Bran sighed. "I'll be sure to fix those up, too."

"Don't you worry about those." Doc shooed his hand at Dad. "He's done enough already."

"I want to make sure when you're here, you're safe."

Bran set down his iced tea. "What do you mean by that? When he's here?"

Dad looked up at him with narrow eyes. "I mean when he's not with us in Florida."

"Doc's going to Florida?"

"We purposely got a place with a guest room and bath. That way, Doc can stay with us whenever he wants. Plus, you and Nathaniel can have somewhere to stay when you visit."

This whole time, Bran thought Dad had been selfish, missing out on Doc's party, buying a place in Florida on a whim. But it wasn't on a whim. He was doing it not only for him and Rita, but for Doc, and his children.

"That's… really great, Dad."

They remained frozen, stuck in a silence, neither one knowing where to go from here.

Doc stood. "Would you two mind giving me a minute with Bran?"

"No problem." Nathaniel leant out a hand for Dad. "Come and see Bran's progress on the pathway." He helped Dad up and guided him to the side of the house.

Bran waited until they were out of earshot and eyesight, anxious for the one-on-one time he'd intended in the first place. "How have you been?"

"As well as I could be, given the situation." Doc sat back in the lounge chair, covering himself in a blanket.

Bran tightened his coat, fingertips growing colder by the second with the stoppage of work.

"I have some more blankets inside if you want."

Bran shook his head. It felt right to be cold. He downright deserved to freeze after what he had done. Yet here Doc Bernie was, trying to help the man that was going to take it all from him.

He sat sideways on a lounge chair, facing Doc.

"Where have you been, Bran?" Doc sipped on his herbal tea, the white steam weakening the longer they sat outside.

"Here and there." He folded his hands, elbows on his knees. "When I left the other day, I got in my car, and I drove north. I kept driving north, as if to Seattle, but I didn't want to be there either. So, I stopped at a small town inland. I didn't know where else to go. I walked on the streets. I stopped for a coffee. Which led to a meal. Eventually, I got a place for the night. And extended it for a few more."

Doc paid attention but let Bran talk, not saying a word.

"In some ways, it was nice to be away from everything I knew. Everyone. To be by myself, in my thoughts." He looked directly at Doc Bernie. "Yet my thoughts also made it miserable. I was forced to face myself in that time."

"And?" Doc Bernie raised an eyebrow.

"It wasn't great." He let out a short chuckle, rubbing his hands on his jeans.

"Why did you come back, Bran? Why are you here at my house, fixing up some stone path I never use?"

"I know you're expecting me to joke about how a grandson wants to visit his grandfather." He nodded. "But no joke. I haven't been the best grandson to you. That's why I'm here. I want to say I'm sorry. Genuinely sorry." His voice cracked, the sound resonating. "I should've told you about the probation. I shouldn't have tried to undermine your plans for the practice. I knew you wouldn't be happy with me selling to Seattle University, but I pursued it, anyway. And that's why I deserve to be alone, facing my thoughts."

He swiveled slowly on the lounge chair, propping his feet up and leaning against the tilted back. The two of them sat there quietly, looking out onto the town below, the bay an open swath of gray.

"That's not true, Bran." Doc Bernie said the words calmly, a slowness to them. "Yes, you did do those things. If you didn't feel remorse, I'd say then perhaps you did deserve whatever life throws at you. But you're here. And it's not lost on me what coming back means to you. I know how you're seen by everyone, including me—I admit, I'm guilty of it—as the one who couldn't get his life straight. Couldn't stick with anything. Never took anything seriously. Would never grow up and—"

Bran put up a hand. "Okay, I get it."

They both had a brief laugh.

"But you've changed, Bran. I've seen it for myself. Coming back to town, facing your past. The way you handle patients. How you welcomed Aubrie, even if it was a rocky start."

"Rocky start?"

"Oh, I know how you two were bickering. You think just because I'm old that I can't hear or see things?"

Bran shook his head, amused. He had underestimated Doc Bernie, in just about every way. "Wait, how much of it was Edith telling you?"

"It doesn't matter how it reached me."

Bran chuckled.

"The bay has eyes and ears, you know."

"I know."

Doc Bernie examined him, staring him down. "The very fact that you returned, that you're on my deck, proves my point."

"But when I was confronted, I ran."

"You removed yourself from the situation to think it through. That's not always a bad thing. You're so easily convinced you're a bad person because of the negative things you may do. Why can't you let the good things change your mind?"

"I guess it's because the bad tends to mess everything up. I messed up things with you and the family. With my job. With Aubrie."

Doc Bernie set down his tea and sat upright. "Okay. You're here working things out with your family, right? And know that you didn't cause my fainting. You give yourself too much credit."

"What do you mean? The letter didn't—?"

"The letter *did* get my blood boiling, I won't deny that. But I've been having issues. Holding and grasping things, achy joints that occurred in the morning lasting throughout the day. It's frustrating, to put it mildly. We're trying to work out which medications work best. Obviously, not that last one."

"Why didn't you say anything before?"

"Are you seriously asking me why I didn't tell you something?"

"Point taken."

"It's the main reason why I felt it was best to retire. I didn't want something like this or worse to happen, when I was the sole person responsible for the patients."

"I'm not gonna lie. I wish I had known."

Doc Bernie scolded him with his eyes.

"I get it, though. I'm just glad you're okay. You are okay, right?"

"I'm fine."

Bran fixed his doubtful stare on Doc.

"I promise. We've seen how useful it is to keep secrets from one another, haven't we?"

He had a point, and Bran trusted him. One of the few people he'd trust with his life. "Agreed."

"Okay." Doc Bernie clapped. "That's one mess-up down. Now, what about the job? Have you heard anything?"

"No. Not yet."

"What if they take you back in Seattle? What then? Are you going to go back?"

Bran sat upright to match Doc's stance. "I don't know."

"Much easier for them to make the decision for you, right? Then, you don't have to think about it. They say no, you do something else. They say yes, you go back?"

Bran shrugged. "I don't know if that's what I want anymore."

Doc wagged a finger in the air. "See, that is where you're lying to yourself. Which brings us to the third mess-up you mentioned. Aubrie."

"I—" Hearing her name knotted up his stomach. "I don't even know where to begin."

"How about seeing her? Wouldn't that be a start?"

"I could explain all of it to her until my voice left me, but I don't think it would make anything better."

"So, don't explain things to her. I think she has a good idea of what happened and why. Better than I did at first."

It hurt to hear it, the reminder of his actions. But he had no right in complaining about the pain.

"What do I say, then? Besides sorry?"

"That's a start." Doc Bernie leaned back again in the chair, talking up to the sky over Maiden's Bay. "You tell her how you feel, Bran. That's the only way to give both of you some clarity. Some peace. And you'd better do it before she leaves."

Bran's eyes perked open. "Leaves? Where is she going?"

"She got offers out of Boston and Pittsburgh. Not sure if she's decided which one to take."

"She can't go. You can't let her walk out on the practice like that."

"Ah. Wrong again. She's a grown woman, Bran. She can decide for herself where she wants to be."

"I don't mean it like—I meant that she's great at the practice. That Maiden's Bay would be better served with her here."

"Wrong again." Doc Bernie waved his finger in the air again.

"What? How could you say that? I think you'd be hard pressed to find anyone that would fill her shoes. That would grow to love this community and put her heart and soul into helping people. All the people we care about, mind you."

"So, you *do* care about Maiden's Bay?"

"Of course I do." Saying it out loud brought a finality to it. That he truly did care for his hometown, that it mattered what happened to its people. That a piece of him will always belong to Maiden's Bay.

"Then, you'll know why I say that the practice shouldn't go to Aubrie. It should go to the both of you."

"What? Doc, no—"

"I know you, Bran. Right now, you're trying to enumerate in your head all of the reasons why you don't deserve to set foot in the practice. Believe me, I had those initial thoughts in the hospital. But when it comes down to it, the two of you, together, are an impressive team. Imagine how well people here will be served with both of you in it."

Doc was right. Bran clung to the feeling he didn't deserve anything from Doc, the practice, or Maiden's Bay.

"What I needed from you, you've given to me already. Today, right here. I needed to know how you truly felt about Maiden's Bay. Now that you've confirmed it, there's only one thing left for me to know."

The thought of working together with Aubrie was euphoric. But unattainable. "What is it?"

Doc Bernie stood, and Bran instinctively made a move to rise, ready to help him up. "I'm okay, sit down."

Doc sat next to Bran at the end of the lounge chair.

"Is wanting Aubrie to take over the practice the only reason you don't want her to go? Be honest with me."

Bran looked down at his knees, his boots, the wooden deck beneath them. Doc deserved the truth. Maybe it was time Bran faced it, too.

"I care about her."

"You *care* about her? Come on, Bran."

"All right. I love her." He threw his arms up in the air. "Okay? I love her and have loved her since I think the evening I spilled wine on her and she kicked me out of the apartment. Which is crazy because it hasn't even been that long. I don't know how love works. But I can't think of a time where she's been in my life and I didn't love her." His mouth rattled as his eyes watered, taking all his effort to stop it.

"Good." Doc Bernie patted Bran's knee. "That's why it has to go to the both of you."

"I don't understand."

"You'll take care of each other. You'll have each other's backs and devote yourselves to the practice because you're devoted to each other, on top of your professions."

"It's a nice thought, in theory. But she'd never go for it. Not after what I've done. And especially not with offers from other places." How could he even consider interfering with her decision? "I wouldn't blame her for taking one of those jobs."

"No, but you may be able to stop her."

Bran shook his head. "No. I don't want to be that guy. The one who makes her choose between a person and a job. At the very least, she deserves to not have that kind of pressure."

"But *you* know what she deserves?"

"I'm just saying, I—I don't know. I'm just trying to do the right thing here."

"I'll tell you what she deserves." Doc Bernie stood from the lounge chair, shuffling his feet and stopping directly in front of Bran. "She deserves to hear how you feel about her. Whether she accepts it or not, feels the same way or not, you can at least give her that."

Bran stewed over the words.

"I swear, if you don't, you will be the cause of my first heart attack."

"Okay, Gramps. Calm down." Bran stood and helped Doc Bernie back to his chair.

"I'll calm down when you agree to talk to her."

Bran covered Doc with the blanket.

"And if you ever call me Gramps again, I'll call Seattle University Hospital myself to prolong your probation."

Bran chuckled. "I won't call you Gramps again."

"And?"

Bran sighed. "And I'll talk to Aubrie."

TWENTY-FIVE

Thursday, October 3

PITTSBURGH OR BOSTON? Aubrie had weighed the pros and cons of each but looked over her notes yet again. Both were far from Maiden's Bay. *Pro.* Yet both had harsher winters than she'd ever experienced. *Con.* Pittsburgh had room for her to move up in the department. Boston was a higher position, but she'd be coming in as a newbie managing people she hadn't worked with before.

Still, neither screamed out to her as the right path. Was there even a right path? At this point, she was playing it by ear, "it" being her life the past year. Or perhaps all of her adult life. Even when she did have a plan, life found a way to disrupt it. Throwing a dart at a map would be about as useful in making a decision as purposefully making one.

She scoured the two job offer letters yet again, as if they held tiny clues pointing her in a direction. Notifying Doc Bernie had been difficult, but part of her hoped he would have insight on which to choose. He merely congratulated her on both, then updated her on the prospects of her replacement.

She set the letters down and stepped into the kitchen. As the coffee brewed, she leaned against the cabinet and tapped her fingers on the counter. She needed to get out of this place. It didn't feel right staying in Doc Bernie's family's apartment any longer. Each day, she worked less at the practice, until finally Doc said she didn't have to come in unless he called her. She felt useless, all the while taking up space, using the utilities. It was time to pack up and get out. Where to was the question.

Despite knowing better, she sipped the hot brew, only confirming it needed time to cool.

A knock sounded at the door.

She checked through the peephole. Bran.

Another decision to make—answer the door or not. She looked down at her clothes, regretting not changing out of the red flannel pajamas before having coffee. She cracked the door open, Bran opening his mouth.

"Hold on." She shut the door before he could speak and ran to the bedroom. She threw on jeans and a Dallas Cowboys hoodie, the star cracked and lettering faded from wear. Looking in the mirror, she redid her ponytail and straightened her bangs. Why she bothered with any of it, who knew? If anything, she should've made herself look worse. But then she remembered he had seen her at her worst, in bed in the morning, opening up about Reid. Crying. Yet it didn't scare him away then. The thought of it tore at her insides.

Not bothering with socks or shoes, she hurried to the door and stopped. It couldn't hurt making him wait a few more seconds. She took a deep breath and opened the door.

"Bran."

"Hi, Aubrie."

They stood in the doorway, staring yet not staring at each other.

"Can I… come in?"

I don't know, can you?

She swallowed her pettiness and opened the door wider.

Bran entered, staying close to the door. Close to the escape route.

He pointed at her shirt. "Cowboys fan. I had no idea you were into football."

"It's my brother's from a while back. I drove him and his friends to a concert, and I got his favorite hoodie."

"I see." Bran nodded, the silence uncomfortable.

Aubrie wanted to get it over with. "What are you doing here?"

"I called a few times yesterday, but…."

The phone calls didn't go unnoticed. Only unanswered. What was she going to say to him? Was there anything he could say to make her feel better about what happened to Doc and the practice? What happened to them?

"Well, you're here, so…." She folded her arms across her chest.

"Yeah. Um, I made a promise to Doc to come talk to you."

"Is that the only reason you came? Because of some promise to Doc?"

"No." He held up his hands. "Not at all. I mean, he *did* encourage me to put on my big boy pants and do it. But I wanted to talk to you. I just didn't know how, I guess."

Aubrie sighed. "Coffee?" It was more a way to busy herself than to be polite.

"Sure." Bran pointed to the sofa. "May I?"

"It's your family's, after all." She regretted the steeliness behind it. It made her sound ungrateful for the place, the opportunity, and that was far from the truth. She poured him a mug and handed it to him, opting to sit at one of the stools at the kitchen island.

"Are those your job offers?" He pointed at the desk.

"Reading through my mail?"

"No. Doc Bernie told me about them. I just assumed."

She nodded. "You assumed correctly."

Bran set down the mug. "Look. I don't know if he told you this, but Doc has this crazy notion that we should take over the practice. Together, I mean."

"I'm leaving, Bran."

"I told him he should give it to you. You'd be better for it. No, not better. *Best.* You're the best person for it."

Was this his way of making things better? "What, now that you've been caught, you're going to easily hand over the prize to me?"

"No." He rifled his hands through his hair and jumped up from the couch. He walked to the window overlooking Pearl Avenue. "I feel like everything is coming out all wrong."

"Then, make it come out right."

"You're right." He turned around, back to the window and pitiful face to her. "What I'm trying to say is, don't leave for the wrong reasons. Don't leave because of me. Because of *my* screw up." He held up a hand. "I don't mean that your decisions revolve around me. Please don't take it that way. You may have many reasons to take a job elsewhere and leave Maiden's Bay behind. I just don't want my behavior to be one of them. I'd hate to think that I not only screwed up with Doc, and us, but the whole town. Because they deserve someone like you taking care of them."

He said *us*. As in, there was an us to begin with.

His phone buzzed, and he clenched his hand over his pocket.

"Go ahead, take it," she said.

"No, this is more important."

"Bran, take it."

He froze for a few seconds, letting the ringtone carry on, then nodded and answered it, turning away from her again to the window.

What was she to say to all that? She tried to say he had nothing to do with her decision, but that was a downright lie. Of course his actions had been the catalyst for all of this.

She stared at the letters on the desk. The letters that still provided no answers. She took a swig of her coffee, cool enough to do so, and then gulped half the mug down. Part of her wished there was more than caffeine in it.

And for Doc Bernie to think they could work together? After all that happened? Sure, they eventually worked great together at the practice. But that was before she knew of the lies. How could she trust Bran again? That he wouldn't hold things back from her?

Doc Bernie was holding onto an idyllic dream. No, it was best to hire one of the candidates in his list of qualified applicants, and for her and Bran to move on. Separately. She shouldn't even entertain the thought of working together again with Bran. So, why did it persist in her head right now?

Bran hung up, placing the phone back in his pocket. "That was the hospital in Seattle." He didn't bother turning around, as if his words were for the town itself.

"What'd they say?" The eagerness was a little too evident in her voice. As a doctor, she didn't want to see a colleague wrongfully get kicked out of his career. Convincing herself that was the only reason was hard.

"They've come to a decision. My probation is over." He turned around and looked at her, the desperation in his eyes visible across the room. They hurt to look at.

The victory was bittersweet. He was no longer in trouble and could carry on with his career. That alone made her relieved for him. Yet, now knowing the verdict, his ruse was rendered unnecessary. He wouldn't have had to do any of it, coming to Maiden's Bay, vying for Doc's practice.

"I'm allowed to return."

The small spark of joy at hearing his pardon extinguished. The past week and a half, she wondered if he carried on in Seattle. Not knowing perhaps was better than knowing he'd be there for certain. That he was out of her life for good.

"About what I said." He took a step closer.

"What about it?" She stood from the stool, returning to the crossed arms stance. "No, you know what? It's just as well. I'm happy for you. Really. You go back to Seattle, and I'll be going to Pennsylvania or Boston, or wherever I end up. The truth is, neither of us deserves that practice."

He took another step. "You can't really mean that. For yourself, that is. You did nothing wrong."

"I lied to Doc Bernie, too."

"No. It was my lie."

"Not saying anything makes me just as guilty, doesn't it?"

"No, it doesn't." He rubbed his chin. "Aubrie, you did what you did to help me. If I hadn't been there, if it were only you, would you still be leaving right now? Or would you stay?"

"I can't think of it like that because you were there. You were a part of all of this." She hated how her voice weakened, how her eyes watered. They weren't supposed to do that. Not for Bran. She had given enough of her time for him. Her energy. Her trust.

"Please, just go." It took everything in her not to let the tears fall.

"Aubrie—"

"Bran. We're done here."

His mouth was open for more words, but he heeded hers. "All right." He walked past her to the front door, turning around before going. "I wish you the best, Aubrie. You deserve it."

She gave a nod, the tears betraying her, having to wipe them with the back of her hand. "Good luck to you in Seattle."

He paused, as if he meant to say something else. But then he turned back around and left.

TWENTY-SIX

Monday, October 7

"DOCTOR JACKSON?"

"Huh?"

A nurse he didn't recognize stood at the nursing station in the trauma center, hand stretched out.

"Oh, right." Bran handed over the patient charts. Four days back at Seattle University Hospital, and it still felt surreal. It was like walking through fog, knowing where things should be, how things were supposed to go, but not seeing things clearly. Something felt off.

"Are you okay?" Her worried look grounded him back to reality.

He took a long blink and shook his head. "I'm fine. Just trying to get back into the swing of things after being away."

She smiled. "I understand. Would coffee help? We've got the good stuff back here."

"That's okay. I'll get some from the break room. Ease into my caffeine coma."

Bran walked around the desk and down the hallway to the break room. The lights flickered on after opening the door, no one else inside. The coffee pot lay empty on the counter, so he rinsed it out and started a fresh batch. The maker whirred to life as he leaned against the counter, looking out into nothing.

Four days like this. Of being a zombie. Something had to give. He needed to get his butt in gear. Trauma surgery was not a specialty to practice on autopilot. Not to mention how he had to be doubly alert. This second chance was nothing to squander. He couldn't give anyone a reason to report him again, even if he had been found to not violate the rules to warrant further probation or a worse punishment. And the next time would be worse. Causing the expenditure of money and time was not a good look on any doctor regardless of innocence.

The brew died down to a trickle at the end of the cycle. He lifted the mug, blowing on the surface, when the break room door opened.

The blonde-haired, curvy nurse sparked recognition in Bran's mind fog.

"Doctor Jackson." She smiled, closing the door behind her.

"Sharon."

"I heard you were back. Figured we'd cross paths sooner or later."

If that were true, she wouldn't have texted him on his first day. She would've waited until they actually did cross paths.

Bran stared into his coffee. Sharon stood there as another reminder of his years of reckless behavior, him not caring how his actions affected others. Or how they affected him.

She walked over to him, pointing to the coffee pot.

He took a step to the side, giving her leeway as she poured. "I'm sorry, for not messaging you back the other day."

"No worries." She poured a sugar packet in her mug. "You and I were never ones to call or chat." She stopped her coffee prep and stared at him. "We've been casual. And mutually so. I just wanted to congratulate you on the dropping of probation. I know that was a big deal for you. And Doctor Hycliff had it coming."

"Do you think he was forced out?" Upon return, he'd heard Sebastian Hycliff had transferred to Minneapolis, or Milwaukee. Somewhere with an M that he associated with cold. It would've been much tougher to return with a chance of seeing Sebastian's face every shift. A reminder not only of the fact there were absolute jerks out there, but that Bran couldn't hold back his anger regardless of who had thrown the first punch or its justification.

Sharon shrugged. "From what I've heard, his career here wasn't going to be as easy as it had been."

"I guess family donations only go so far." Bran sipped his coffee.

"That's not right of me. I'm sorry. I shouldn't say things like that. Doctor Hycliff had talent."

"Yeah, but what he had in talent, he lacked in social graces." Sharon raised her eyebrows. "What happened to you?"

Bran swallowed hard, the coffee still hot enough to burn. "What do you mean?"

"You hated Doctor Hycliff. And now you're saying he's talented?"

"I didn't *hate* him."

Sharon threw her arm on her hip, glaring at him.

"Okay, let's just say I really disliked him."

They both chuckled, and Sharon touched him on the shoulder. Bran looked at her manicured nails, a deep purple this week. He stepped away, biting his lip.

"I'm sorry, Sharon. I know I promised you dinner before I left. I—"

"No, it's okay. It's a lot to process, coming back."

"No. I mean, yes, it is. But I should've never promised you that. And before, I really did see this as a casual thing, and I honestly didn't care how it made you feel. I was terrible for doing that and feeling that way. I'm so sorry."

"Oh." She gulped from her mug, Bran trying to read her eyes. "That's a lot of apologies in the last five minutes."

"I've made a lot of mistakes in how I treat people. I want to do the right thing from now on."

She reached for his hand and gave it a squeeze before letting go. "Can I ask you something?"

"Sure."

"What do you mean by 'before?' You mean before your trip?"

He sighed. It was crazy how he saw his life as before Aubrie, and now, after Aubrie. Whether she was still in his life or not. "I, uh... I met someone."

"She's here in Seattle?"

Bran shook his head. "No, back in my hometown." He chuckled. "Actually, I don't even know if she knows how I feel. I was going to tell her, but things didn't work out as planned."

"I see." She paused, and Bran let the silence go on. Her mouth broke into a smile. "I'm not sure I've ever seen you light up like that, talking about a woman."

Bran cleared his throat, thankful for the coffee mug to busy his hands in holding it. "I uh… yeah."

Sharon giggled. "I'm happy for you. Really. You have your job back, you've found someone you care about. Those are good things, Bran."

"Yeah." He nodded in agreement, except those weren't good things. They sounded good in theory. His job was back, and he should be happy about it. So, why did it feel mundane and awkward? And it was true he cared about Aubrie. But he didn't fulfill the promise he made to Doc Bernie in telling her his feelings. He had planned to that day in the apartment. Then, his phone rang, and she all but told him she was over "them." If there ever was a "them" to begin with.

"Look, I'd better get back, but it's good seeing you, Bran." She raised her mug in a brief toast.

"You, too, Sharon." Bran stewed a minute longer in the breakroom, drinking half of what was left in the mug, then proceeded to his follow-up down the hall.

"How are we doing, Mister Laramie?"

"I keep telling you, Doc, Martin."

"And I keep telling you, I'll call you Martin when you call me Bran." He smiled at the patient in the bed. Mr. Laramie came in with a collapsed lung from a chest injury, and Bran wanted to check his latest x-rays. He flipped through the chart, then logged into the computer and checked out the x-rays.

"The team already looked over those, Doc."

"Good. As they should have." He scanned the images once more and swiveled the chair around to the patient. "Just wanted to see with my own eyes, that's all."

"So, how many years until you're chief here?"

Bran chuckled as he stood. "One year at a time." He shook the man's hand.

"I hope I live to see it." Mr. Laramie's eyes watered up. "At least

I have a chance now, thanks to folks like you. I don't know what I would've done without coming here. Poor Nancy, thought she was going to have a heart attack after my fall. She refused to take me anywhere other than here. I just didn't think it was worth the drive, but I wasn't exactly in the state to argue." He gave a hearty chuckle. "Boy, was I wrong."

"Have you told your wife that?"

"I will." He nodded. "I will every day."

It was why Bran had become a doctor. To help people live longer, better lives. As he walked out of the patient room, the thought of Aubrie sprang back up. She, too, knew the feeling of having that desire, that passion, and the satisfaction of what it was like to actually do it. To help someone, and have them recognize you've done that.

She had wanted to do it in Maiden's Bay. *For* Maiden's Bay.

Although Bran was happy things worked out well for Mr. Laramie, there was something missing. The joy that would normally bring didn't hit him right. Maybe it was because Mr. Laramie already received the good prognosis from rounds this morning. Or because Bran just wasn't himself these past few days.

He looked back at the patient through the window in the door. It was only an hour's drive for Mr. Laramie to come into the hospital. But how naive to think only an hour. That was a lot for some people. For those like Grace Donchik, living out in the rural parts of Washington, with little access to experts needed.

And then it hit him.

The lingering feeling grew definition. What ailed him wasn't that it was a hard return, or that he might not be needed here. It was that his purpose here no longer gave him satisfaction. He needed a new purpose, one that used his skills, challenged him every day. That gave back to the people he loved and cared about.

He thought about Mrs. Donchik, Mr. Laramie, the fishing crews. Doc Bernie. But most of all, he thought about Aubrie Turnbridge.

The spark ignited a new excitement. An idea that would encompass everything he had learned the past month. Something Doc Bernie would have to be on board with. Heck, it would benefit the whole town. Was it something the hospital would even consider?

More importantly, would it be enough for Aubrie to stay where she truly belonged?

Bran shook his head from the thought. This was something he had to do for himself. And he was going to tell Aubrie how he felt, whether his idea kept her in Maiden's Bay or not.

TWENTY-SEVEN

Friday, October 11

AUBRIE ZIPPED UP the last of her bags and slid it off the bed. Only one garment remained in the apartment. The jacket Bran had worn over the flannel shirt the night of the fireworks still smelled like him, but Aubrie refused to wallow in it. She folded it neatly and left it on the bed. Whichever family member would come in here next could give it back to him.

She carried the bags to the door and took one last look out the windows at the incredible view of Maiden's Bay. She would certainly miss the place, the apartment right in the heart of downtown, Crescent Cafe, even Campy's Bar. Hard to believe she'd miss a bar, but she already did.

With her car parked out front on Pearl Avenue, she loaded up the luggage in the trunk. If it were up to her heart, she'd get in the driver's seat and take off. But as she stared at the facade of Doc Bernie's practice, she knew it wouldn't be right to not say her goodbyes in person.

The door opened, and out came Edith. "You're not going to leave us without saying goodbye, are you?"

Aubrie let out a slight chuckle. "Of course not."

Edith stepped off the curb and approached the car. "Are you all packed? Anything I can help with?"

"No, I'm good." Aubrie hated hearing her voice choking up.

Edith sighed. "For what it's worth, I'm really sorry to see you go. You fit right in with us, with the town, in such a short period of time. We feel like we're losing a part of it."

"*We?*"

Edith nodded. "Come and see."

"What do you mean?"

Edith held the door open for Aubrie. Instead of the sign-in log and Edith's trinkets, the front desk was covered in flowers, the geraniums, gardenias, roses, and chrysanthemums she'd seen often through the windows of Bea's Bouquets. Helium-filled balloons swayed in the air, held down by one of Edith's paperweights, with sayings *Best Wishes! and Good luck!* and *Thank you!*

"What is all this?"

Edith smiled wide. "This is all for you. I know it was a short amount of time, but I don't think you realize how many lives you've touched here." She plucked a card off one of the bouquets and handed it to Aubrie.

Aubrie read it aloud. "'Ian and I are so thankful for your due diligence. He's fully recovered from his tonsillectomy. Keeping our fingers crossed no more strep!'" She recalled the boy with strep at the start of her job here. The boy who compelled her to review all things ear, nose, and throat related. A catalyst for an argument with Bran. She nearly laughed out loud, recalling the argument led to them having dinner. The start of their... well, whatever it was, it was over now.

"Here's another." Edith gave her another card.

"'We wanted to give chocolates but didn't know if that was too unhealthy for a doctor. Hope your next catch is as great as Maiden's Bay. The crew of *Harpeth Rose.*'" The tears filled her eyes, and she didn't bother fighting them. "That was sure an interesting day. Can't say I've ever done so many physicals in a row."

"Well, you never know what you're going to get in this town." Edith smiled.

It broke the eroding dam for Aubrie.

"Oh, honey, I didn't mean to do that." She laid her hand on Aubrie's back.

"No, it's not your fault." Aubrie sniffled and wiped the tears off her cheeks, the cleared ones replaced by fresh streams.

"What is it, honey?" Her voice was soothing. "Do you not want to go? Is that it?"

"How can I give this all up? I've never seen anything like this." She dabbed her eyes once more. "I mean, what am I doing? I wanted to start new somewhere, leave my past behind. Be a part of something I could get behind, that gave me a renewed purpose. I found all of that here. And I'm throwing it away."

"Here, come sit." Edith guided her to the waiting room chair, grabbed a few tissues, then sat next to her. She handed her the tissues. "I thought you wanted that new job?"

"I didn't know what I wanted." Aubrie cleaned up her face and blew her nose. "I mean, it's not even a possibility now, is it? I wasn't forthcoming with Doc Bernie, and that wasn't right of me."

"You apologized, and he forgave you, didn't he?"

Aubrie nodded, though she hadn't known Edith knew of her apologizing to Doc. Maiden's Bay. It nearly made her laugh, bringing a second of cheer.

"It's not just Doc. I... I'm not sure I'd want to stay if it wasn't with Bran. I know it sounds silly, but he's part of the reason I enjoyed being here. We really were a team, as much as I didn't want to see it."

Edith rubbed her back. "It's not too late to change your mind. Would you stay if Bran returned to work here?"

"It's not even worth thinking about." She chuckled. "Even though I've thought about it nearly nonstop. He's back in Seattle. That's where he belongs, in Trauma. I've come to terms with that. Or so I thought." She took a deep breath. She had denied herself thinking he'd return in order to move on. There was no sense in hoping for something that wouldn't happen. "I thought if I focused on the next thing for me, that it would be easier to deal with all of this."

Aubrie caught sight of Doc Bernie outside making his way toward the office. She sat up straighter and squished the tissue in her hand. It didn't serve anyone well for him to see her like this.

Doc opened the front door and stepped in. "Good morning, Aubrie! I didn't know if we'd see you this morning." He grinned, then scanned the assortment of balloons and flowers on the desk. "Well, what's going on here?"

Edith stood. "Those are for Aubrie, from past patients."

"How nice."

Edith approached him. "I think it's time you had a chat with Aubrie. She was just saying how she's conflicted, in leaving."

"Is that right?" He looked at Aubrie, who bit her lip. Was it out of shame? Embarrassment? She didn't have the energy left to be upset Edith had said anything.

Doc Bernie's attention swung back to Edith. "Are you sure?"

"I think it's best to tell her."

Aubrie perked up. "Tell me what?"

Doc Bernie and Edith stared at each other for a long moment. After an eternity, Doc nodded.

Aubrie stood. "What's going on?"

"It's about Bran," Doc said. "And the practice."

"What about Bran and the practice?" No reasonable idea melded Bran and Doc's practice together at this point. Aubrie's heart thumped and blood warmed.

"How about we go back to my office and chat?" Doc nodded toward the hallway.

Aubrie's feet were fixed, a leaden weight of anxiety. She wanted to demand answers, sick of the kept secrets between the people in this office. Doc Bernie not telling her about leaving the practice until she arrived, nor about her competition or his rheumatoid arthritis. Bran omitting his probation on top of his wretched plan to turn over the practice. Her holding on to Bran's secrets. There were too many, and the thought of another made her blood boil.

Doc must've sensed her mixed emotions. "Please, Aubrie. If you even have an inkling of a desire to stay, you need to hear this." He held out his hand, offering up his office.

Aubrie exhaled slowly and moved her heavy feet to Doc Bernie's office. She took the seat in front of his desk, while he walked around to his seat.

"I contemplated telling you this. I want you to know it was because I didn't want to interfere with your decision in leaving. I wanted that to be independent of whatever happened here. Not because I didn't want you to know."

Aubrie nodded but kept silent.

"I've come to a decision about the practice. Bran has been working out the logistics on his side of things, while I've been working with an attorney in town."

She nearly shot out of her chair. "Are you saying Bran is taking over the practice? After what he did to you?"

Doc Bernie held up a hand. "I know you were hurt by Bran. That doesn't escape me. In fact, he hurt several people by what he did. But he is *not* a bad person. I'm not just saying that because he's my grandson, either. I'm saying that because it's true. And in trying to make things right with me, the practice, the town, I think he's come up with an excellent idea."

How Aubrie would love to say she didn't want to hear it, but nothing could be further from the truth. "Go ahead."

"Bran is finalizing details with Seattle University Hospital to set up this practice with an amazing opportunity. I would help him in the transition of taking over, and Seattle would provide their expertise—cardiology, pulmonology, nutrition, and health—in a unique way. Members of their teams would visit the practice once a month on scheduled days to provide their care, in which patients across Maiden's Bay and the area could see these specialists without having to travel far. Follow-ups could be done through telehealth in between in-person visits. It's the best of both worlds and will really be a game changer for specialty care in the area."

Aubrie thought it over, looking for flaws. "And insurance—"

Doc held up a hand. "We are working things through with the hospital and insurance providers. Bran is also looking into a funding program for the underserved in order to cover care for those in need."

Aubrie bit her lip again. "Why are you telling me this now? When you didn't want to before?"

Doc Bernie sighed. "Because when Edith tells me you're conflicted in leaving, she's really telling me that you're looking for a way to stay. And I tend to believe Edith's gut."

"I don't understand. I mean, it sounds almost too good to be true. It would be a great opportunity for the community to get specialized care, for sure if the financial aspect is worked out." It was brilliant. Almost so obvious, she was upset they hadn't thought of it earlier. There it was again. They. "But you said you're handing it over to Bran. What does that have to do with me?"

"Would you consider staying now, knowing this information?"

Aubrie curled back into her seat. She was leaving today. *Today!* How could Doc Bernie throw this on her *now?*

Then again, how could he not?

It was Doc's style, throwing curveballs at the most inconvenient time. He wouldn't be Doc Bernie if he didn't throw it out.

"I'd love to stay." The waterworks built up again. Damn the tears. "I'm not so sure Bran would want that."

Doc Bernie nodded. "You're willing to leave us, drive thousands of miles east, with that uncertainty?"

The knot grew in the pit of her stomach. She knew what she had to do if she wanted to stay. And of course she wanted to stay. She wanted it all. To stay, work at the practice, work with Bran. Be with Bran.

"Not exactly."

Doc Bernie tipped his head in confusion. "Does that mean you're going to stay?"

"It means that I do have a drive to make." She stood and walked to the office doorway. "To Seattle."

TWENTY-EIGHT

"SPEECH!" STAN, THE triage nurse, shouted.

Bran took in the crowd in the break room—a moment when fourteen of the finest doctors, nurses, and staff took the time to see him off. He took one last bite of his slice of red velvet cake, a cake in the shape of a cartoonish patient in a hospital gown. The red interior added to the macabre humor.

He took a sip of water and set down his cake plate. "I'm very touched you guys put this together. Really, it's great to see the team I've been working with these past years. You are truly amazing, and as much as you know I'm not one for sappiness, I will miss you all."

There were a few awws and giggles from the party-goers.

"But, remember, I'm not completely gone. I will see some of you"—he pointed to two of the cardiology physicians—"in Maiden's Bay when you visit. I really think it's a great opportunity for that community, and thank you all for being so receptive to the idea. You will be changing lives. I know it can be tough sometimes to remember why we get into this profession to begin with, but that was it for me. To make a difference. And that's what we'll continue to do. Thank you."

They clapped, and he walked through the room, partaking in the handshakes and shoulder pats.

As the celebration died down, an administrator walked into the break room. "They told me I'd find you here."

Bran shook his hand. "Help yourself to some cake."

"Don't mind if I do. First, though, I came to give you these." The man opened the folder, stacked papers with yellow and orange sticky tabs. "Doctor Jackson—Senior—will need to sign the yellow, you the orange. You can run it by your legal team, of course, but it has what we've agreed upon."

Bran accepted the document. "Great. I've said it before, but let everyone know how thankful I am, how thankful we *all* are, in Maiden's Bay, for this opportunity."

"I will." The man clapped his hands, reminiscent of Doc Bernie's habit. "Now, where's that cake?"

Bran pointed it out to him, then walked out of the break room and down the hallway to the nurse's station. He stopped short of the desk, the sight in front of him a shock.

"Aubrie. What…?"

"Bran." She seemed out of breath, her bangs slightly disheveled and ponytail loose. In other words, gorgeous. She could've shown up in a frock, and his knees would go weak.

"Everything okay? Doc Bernie?"

She stopped him with a hand in the air. "He's fine. No, I, uh… came here to see you."

Could she have changed her mind about staying? Or did she have a choice few last words before heading east? "Okay. How about we…?"

She nodded and followed him to the makeshift supply room, the same one in which she patched Bran up after the scuffle with Sebastian Hycliff. Bran licked his lip, as if being in the room brought back the achiness.

He shut the door most of the way, the gray-blue tinge of the room gloomy like the Seattle sky. He stood across from her, the silence eating away at his guilt. Although she had come to see him, he had unspoken words to get out. A promise he had made to Doc Bernie.

"I'm glad you're here."

"It's not something I planned when I woke up this morning, that's for sure."

They exchanged nervous chuckles.

Bran swallowed the fear and went for it. "Look, before you say what you came here to say, there's something I need to tell you. I actually *did* plan on telling you when I came by the apartment that day. But it didn't turn out how I had envisioned."

She nodded. "Okay."

He stepped toward her. "Aubrie, I love you. I thought it was crazy to think that after knowing you for such a short time, but then I thought it was crazy they were hard to say. I hardly ever say them—in fact, I've never said them to anyone I've been with since my high school sweetheart."

"The one who left you for a fisherman?"

"What?" The dawning realization clicked. "Yes." Maybe that's why he'd been a jerk so long. He was jaded when it came to love. Mom had left him. His first girlfriend had left him. Since then, he left everybody else before they could leave him.

What a fool I am.

"I'm sorry I didn't say it sooner. Part of it was fear, I admit. Another part didn't want you to think it was my Hail Mary to keep you around. It's not. I genuinely want you to know. What you do with it is up to you."

Aubrie's lips quivered, eyes watering. "Doc Bernie told me about your plan."

She wasn't going to say anything about what he just said? Her bypassing it hurt, but he shouldn't have any expectations on her reaction. She came to visit him for a reason, and love probably had nothing to do with it. He got out his truth, and now he could carry on knowing he shared it with her.

"When did he tell you?" He didn't know what to ask, but wanted her to know he listened to every word. Every syllable.

"This morning. Right as I was saying my goodbyes at the practice."

"I see." But he didn't see. Why was she here? To critique his plan? Was she mad Doc Bernie agreed to it after what Bran had done? Could she not see he tried to make it right?

"I think it's wonderful."

The compliment froze his breathing for a second before he let out a long sigh. "So, you're okay with it? Even after—"

"Yes, even after what you had planned on doing. After the lying, deceiving, sneakiness. Because this is the right thing to do." She broke a smile. "I can't believe neither one of us thought of it before."

"Well, it's good to hear you support it. As much as I didn't do it just to ease the pain I caused, it makes me feel a little better that I'm on the right track. For the people of Maiden's Bay."

She nodded slowly.

"Aubrie, I don't know if it's in the cards for me, for your forgiveness. I'm okay with that. If it takes time. I'm doing this to put actions behind my words. Anyone can say they're sorry. But not everyone has the opportunity to show it."

Aubrie wiped a tear falling down her cheek.

"I'm sorry, I didn't mean to—"

"Just stop."

Bran held back more words. Was she mad? Sad? He didn't know what to do, except let it unfold.

"I've already forgiven you, you idiot." More tears were wiped. "This whole time I've been thinking what would've happened if you hadn't come to Maiden's Bay with your awful plan. And it keeps leading me to one conclusion."

He wanted to ask but kept quiet.

"If you hadn't thought Doc Bernie's was a way out of your troubles, you wouldn't have returned to Maiden's Bay in the first place. Most likely, we would've never met, let alone work together and get to know each other. It's almost as if you had to have done this terrible thing in order to make this beautiful thing."

Bran's heart raced at the words. He stepped closer, touching her hands, holding them in his. "What are you saying? Are you saying what I think you're saying?"

She let out a cry. "You big dummy. I love you, too."

Bran smiled. He touched her chin and tilted her head up, looking at those brown eyes. "I am a dummy. But I promise you, this dummy will never hurt you again."

Her hands moved to his cheeks, cupping his face. He leaned in, greeting her soft lips, tears streaking down her face, the streaks salty. He didn't care. He kissed her cheeks as if he could heal any hurt she felt. She could cry poison, and he'd taste it.

He'd take any piece of her, but she was giving him everything. His heart threatened to burst.

He backed away, a thought freezing him. "Wait, does this mean you *are* staying? What about your new job? And Doc Bernie's search?"

She placed a finger on his lips. "Funny thing. Doc said he didn't call any applicants yet. That he was waiting for me to actually leave before doing it."

"For a man his age, he's awfully conniving, isn't he?"

"Where else do you think you got it from?"

He chuckled. "Good point."

"As for my job, all it takes is a phone call. They had their share of candidates to choose from. But…."

"But what?"

"I haven't called because I wasn't sure if you'd agree, with your new plan and all, to having me as a coworker?"

He wrapped his arms around her, pulling her in close. She let out a quick yelp of excitement. Here she was, the love of his life, right here in his arms. He vowed to himself to never let a night go by without saying *I love you.* And now she wanted to be around him all day. Him, Bran. The man who couldn't commit, the man who lived the casual bachelor lifestyle. The man who had changed, to better himself, because of this woman who walked into his life.

"I wouldn't have it any other way."

EPILOGUE

One Month Later

"WHO'S NEXT, EDITH?" Aubrie bumped into Edith in the patient hallway on her way to the front desk.

"The Rowland boy. His mother says he has symptoms of colic, poor thing."

Bran stepped out of Doc Bernie's office—well, *their* office. "You want me to take him?" His eyes read sympathy. He understood why she'd be hesitant, and she loved him for it. But she was ready.

"No, I got this one."

"Are you sure?"

Aubrie laid her hand on his shoulder. "I'm sure."

"Okay." Bran stole a kiss from her, taking the chart from Edith's hand and using it as a shield to hide their affection.

"You're not fooling anyone, you know." Doc Bernie appeared out of the office, a box full of books in his hands.

Bran's forehead touched hers for a brief second before he backed away. "Maybe we just want privacy, Doc Bernie. It's not every day you get to work with your girlfriend."

"Except in this case, it is." Aubrie laughed.

"Okay, you two. Bran, help an old man out, will ya?" Doc Bernie handed the box to Bran, who *oomphed* at the weight of it.

"I don't think you need my help. Besides, what the heck do you have in here, cement?"

"I've got plenty more things to move out."

Bran moved to help Doc, then stopped. "Hey, don't forget—"

"I know, dinner at your dad's tonight."

"Nathaniel texted, said he's coming in with Gwen, so we don't want to be late."

"Already bought the wine." Aubrie kissed his forehead before moving on to the front office. It had been a whirlwind few weeks. She'd unpacked her bags and bought a few more items for the apartment, and Bran moved his things in with them. The fact they were together was enough for Mom to disregard Aubrie's location and new occupation. Mom even planned a trip to visit at Thanksgiving, much to the chagrin of her brother and sister.

Though the helium had leaked out of the balloons, and the cards lay stacked in a shoebox in her closet, she'd never forget how this community welcomed her with open arms. She had found more than what she hoped in coming here. As she looked at the mother clutching the wiggly baby, she was ready.

Ready for the fresh start. Ready to give back.

Ready for whatever came her way.

Mary Shotwell is the author of small-town love stories with happily-ever-afters for all seasons. Her debut romance novel *Christmas Catch* (Carina Press, 2018) was a Golden Leaf Finalist and earned a starred review from *Library Journal*. She loves incorporating her science and nature background into her fiction. When adulting, she's a wife to husband Matt and mother to three children. She currently resides in Tennessee.